FRIENEMIES

JANIE DE COSTER

STREET Essence

Published by:
G Street Chronicles
P.O. Box 1822
Jonesboro, GA 30237-1822
www.gstreetchronicles.com
fans@gstreetchronicles.com

Cover design:
Hot Book Covers, www.hotbookcovers.com

ISBN 13: 978-1-9405740-7-3
ISBN 10: 1940574072
LCCN: 2013955278

Dedication:

I dedicate this book to my grandchildren Shania, Jerod, Toure's Ethan, Jullian, Jaylen, Madison and Briana. May you all know the love of God. and in the words of Proverbs 18:16 A man's gift maketh room for him and bringeth him before great men.

Acknowledgements:

I give honor to my Lord and Savior Jesus Christ. If it wasn't for him I wouldn't be where I am today. To my family. I love you guys and thanks for your never ending support as I journey down this road. I would like to also give thanks to George Sherman Hudson and Shawna A my publishers. I appreciate all the time spent on my projects. I am looking forward to many novels to come with Gstreet Chronicles. I also like to thank the designer for the covers of my novels. You've done an amazing job. And last but certainly not least, readers and fans, you are the reason I spin stories for your enjoyment. As I tell my stories I always strive to not only entertain but educate and I do it all with a christian backdrop which I hope will touch someone in a special way. God bless you all and happy reading!

Janie De Coster

Faithful are the wounds of a friend.
Proverbs 27:6

A friend loveth at all times.
Proverbs 17:17

Greater love has no one than this,
than to lay down one's life for his friends.
John 15:13

INTRODUCTION

Some of you may not be familiar with the word, "Frienemies" even though it's been tossed around quite frequently these days. Frienemies have taken center stage on talk shows, reality television, movies and other forms of entertainment. Frienemies may not be a term found in Webster's Dictionary, but the relationship it describes has been around almost as long as another word we use to describe how we feel about one another; *Love.* Love is the most important and powerful word in the universe. Love can heal as well as wound.

Creatively speaking, love is at the basis of what really defines frienemies. At some point in our lives, we have all developed a close bond of friendship with someone that we cared about deeply and respected. Some of those relationships have even moved forward to a point where we have shared our deepest, darkest secrets with someone that we feel is special in our lives. This friend always had our back, no matter what.

As the relationship matured, that *friend* became a confidante—someone to share our happiest times and who provided a shoulder to lean on when our lives became more difficult. Having faith and trust in that person became second nature as the years progressed. But what happens to that special bond if, one day, the loyal and trusting friend began to show subtle signs of jealousy? What if that friend embarks upon a journey to undermine and sabotage the relationship you've grown to love and cherish throughout the years?

You may ask why a friend would do such an inconceivable thing. Well, the simplest answer is the human heart. The heart is a tricky thing, and so are the emotions that it pushes through the blood. It is so easy to feel the pangs of jealousy, envy, hurt, and even possessiveness when it comes to someone we love. You might be in a positive stage in your life, while your closest friend feels as though their life is falling apart or it's not as glamorous or meaningful as your life seems through their eyes. Or possibly, someone new has captivated your time, leaving your friend feeling alone or on the verge of being replaced.

To go even deeper, your spouse and close relatives can also be labeled as frienemies. No way, you might say; but, yes, it can happen. When one person is climbing the corporate ladder of success and the other is stagnant in their career, this may leave the latter feeling unappreciated or unfulfilled. And with relatives, there is always someone in every family that envies a favorite cousin or other family member that has done better than they have. The feelings of resentment may sometime surface unexpectedly; and suddenly, a friend becomes an enemy. How would you handle such a frienemy? More importantly, how far would you go to salvage the precious and binding relationship once a real friend becomes a rival? Enjoy this story of friends who must look into their hearts to find the answers to these questions.

NATASHA

Natasha slipped out of her black pumps, reached under her black-and-gray pencil skirt, and gently rolled down her charcoal-colored panty hose, throwing them on top of the bed. Next to taking off a pinching bra, ripping off control-top panty hose was definitely second in line to providing instant relief at the end of a long day.

Natasha plopped down on her cozy bed and took in a long, deep breath. She looked over at the clock on her nightstand; it read 6:30 PM. It had been another long day at the office, and there were no signs of her workload getting any lighter; at least not until Mr. Emerson could find a replacement after firing David over a month ago. In fact, there were two positions that needed to be filled right away, but Mr. Emerson was taking his sweet little time, as usual.

Natasha reached for the remote to her flat screen TV which was positioned on her bedroom wall and pressed the power button. *CNN News* came into view as she stretched across the full length of the bed. The flat screen was a reminder of the luxuries her two-timing ex-boyfriend had left behind. She couldn't believe she had wasted almost three years of her life with him. Darin had appeared to be the perfect man. He had wined and dined her, showed her off to family and friends, and even bought her a pre-engagement ring that should have rung wedding bells in her head. What twenty-seven-year-old man would give a twenty-five-year- old woman a pre-engagement ring? And what twenty-five- year-old woman would be stupid enough to take it? Give her a round of applause, because when Darin slipped the small diamond on her finger, Natasha was in seventh heaven. She was so happy that she had finally found a man who was willing to commit. But what she had actually discovered was a man who didn't have an inkling about what the word even meant.

After listening to several news documentaries, Natasha stood up, finished undressing, and walked into the bathroom. She slid the glass shower door open and stepped in. Turning the faucet on full speed, Natasha closed her eyes and enjoyed the warm, vibrating pressure of the water on her back. The image of her ex, Darin Slater, filtered through her mind. She questioned the relationship's end and wondered why things had fallen apart. Darin had been everything she wanted in a man. "Handsome" didn't do enough justice in describing his chiseled features. And even more importantly, the man had brains. He was an ambitious and driven visionary. He was definitely going places. You see, Darin was the CEO of a prestigious marketing firm, Barton Enterprises; and after five years of climbing the corporate ladder, Darin had finally arrived. And once he did, Natasha had thought they were destined for a glorious life together.

In the beginning, they spent so much time together. They enjoyed everything Atlanta had to offer: fine restaurants and candlelit dinners, and front row seats at theaters musicals and plays. They even danced the night away at the hottest clubs in the city. About a year into the relationship, things began to change. It was subtle things at first, such as missing dinners and staying out a little later than usual. Then it graduated to heated arguments over trivial things. It all came to a head one day when Natasha was unpacking his suitcase. Darin had just returned from a business trip to California. The phone rang while he was in the shower. As soon as Natasha picked it up, a baritone voice belonging to Darin's boss, Mr. Edwards, came through.

He was inquiring about a file Darin might have mistakenly picked up and taken along with him on the trip. She relayed the information to Darin, and he asked her to check his briefcase while he finished in the shower. Sure enough, the file Mr. Edwards was referring to was right there, along with some bright red panties—panties that did not belong to Natasha. Needless to say, the relationship ended. Darin moved out and her life fell apart.

Natasha shut off the water and stepped out of the shower. She reached for the thick, blue towel hanging from the brass hook over the bathroom door while making her way back into the master bedroom. After slipping on her fuzzy, tiger-print slippers, she went into the kitchen and opened the stainless steel refrigerator door. She frowned as she peeked inside. It was practically bare. She had forgotten to go grocery shopping. Letting out a whiff of air, Natasha closed the door and leaned against it as she contemplated her next move.

The ringing phone jolted her out of her thoughts. She leaned on the marble countertop where the phone sat as she answered it.

"Hello."

"Hello, Me-Me," Sloan replied, using his nickname for her. "What's cooking?"

"Funny you should ask that, Sloan, from what I can see in my refrigerator, not a thing. I've been so busy, I forgot to go shopping." She chuckled as she propped her elbows on the countertop.

"Well, I guess I have to come to your rescue and take you out for a good meal." Sloan laughed. "See you in thirty," he said as he hung up.

Natasha smiled as she placed the phone back into its cradle. *Thank God for best friends,* she thought to herself. Most women had a girl for a best friend, but Sloan Stevens had been her best friend for almost fifteen years and counting. They had shared everything from bumps and bruises, to playful kisses. Now, as adults, their relationship was still the same, except for the kissing part. That had ended way back in school.

As they grew and formed other relationships, they still remained very close. Sloan was there for her when she broke up with her very first boyfriend in seventh grade and many boyfriends thereafter. His shoulder was still there for her to cry on. She was the one who told him who he should and should not hook up with. Family and friends often wondered why the two of them had never gotten together as a couple. Sloan was as fine as they came. He was over six feet tall with smooth, caramel-colored skin and light-brown eyes. His head was adorned with fine, dark-brown curls, and he had a small dimple in his chin. She had never told anyone, but she had always imagined being Sloan's girlfriend. Sometimes she would even pretend that she was. Once, she even worked up enough nerve to tell him playfully that she wanted to be his girlfriend, but he just shrugged it off and said that she would always be his "girlfriend until the end"—a mantra they always sang together when they were growing up. And with a playful hug and a kiss on the cheek, he would be on his way to call some girl he had met at the mall.

A memory of one of Sloan's latest conquests crossed Natasha's mind while she dressed. Monica Jenkins was her name. She was a tall, slim, wanna-be model. Natasha hated the way she drooled over Sloan whenever they were in her presence. Tonguing him down and wrapping those long arms of hers around him as if he were her prized possession. It was enough to make Natasha gag. Sometimes she wondered if it was really a twinge of jealousy that smoldered within her whenever Sloan was with another woman; or was the thought of him being happy with another woman just a concept that she wouldn't let herself entertain. She was determined not to let her mind wander any further than that.

SLOAN

Sloan couldn't believe Monica had stood him up again. *What's wrong with her?* he wondered. He had several other women just waiting in the wings for a night out with him, but he had decided a few months ago that he was finished with all of that. He wanted only one woman now, and he thought Monica Jenkins was the one. They had been dating for more than a year, and things had been going pretty well, or so he thought. Monica was the only woman he had dated for any length of time. Most of his relationships ended before ninety days were up. There were just too many beautiful women out there, and it was very hard for him to settle for just one—that is, until Monica came along. It wasn't that he was a womanizer—not at all. He wanted to find that special woman that would sweep him off his feet. But, as his luck would have it, he ended up with women who wanted to sweep through his bank account instead. So he had decided to play the game. As soon as they showed their gold-digging ways, he dropped them and moved on to the next. But Monica was so different. She never asked him for anything. Instead, she wined and dined him and treated him like a king. He felt as if she really cared for him, not his bank account. And, of course, he did the same, as well.

He was so happy that he had finally found a woman he felt was similar to his best friend, Natasha. Now, there was a woman with a loving heart, beauty, and brains. If he had ever found a woman like her, he would have married her yesterday. Looking at himself in his bathroom mirror, he had to admit he was a good-looking fella. He kept himself well groomed. Women practically fell at his feet. He could hardly keep up with the phone numbers that he collected on nights out at the clubs. He picked up the cologne bottle and splashed on small amount of P. Diddy's newest fragrance.

He walked out of the master bath and headed into the living room. As he grabbed his keys off the coffee table, his eyes landed on the small, leather, black book resting near the leopard-print lamp on the end table. He usually didn't leave it lying around like that. *How careless of me,* he thought as he picked it up. He returned to his bedroom and shoved the black book into the pocket of one of his many Armani suit jackets in the closet. He paused for a moment as he thought about retrieving the book and calling one of the phone numbers. He had listed them in alphabetical order and placed stars by the names of the women who were especially good in bed. Exhaling, he stepped out of the closet and closed the door. What he needed tonight, he decided, was a friend, not a booty call.

NATASHA

Sloan rang the doorbell of the Victorian-style home. His concealed vision was to have a home like this one day, with a beautiful wife inside, waiting to greet him. But, for now, he had to accept what he did have, which was a lovely best friend, who opened the stained-glass door with a gorgeous smile. Natasha looked stunning. She wore a white sheath summer dress that accentuated her curves. The dress's low-cut neckline showed just enough of her breasts to give her a sexy, yet classy look.

"Well, hey you," Natasha said, smiling as she waved him inside. Sloan let out a low whistle.

"You're looking too fine tonight, Natasha. Are you sure you don't have a date waiting for you someplace?" Sloan said, giving her a once-over.

Natasha continued to grin. Sloan always gave her compliments, and it made her feel very beautiful inside.

"Stop it, silly," Natasha chuckled. "You're my date; remember?" she said, giving him a light tap on the shoulder. "And, to tell you the truth, Sloan, if you hadn't called and asked me to join you for a meal, I would be right here at home, munching on a bologna sandwich. I would prefer that than to endure another gruesome date with some brother who was counting down the minutes to get into my panties." Natasha smirked with a roll of her head.

She and Sloan were comfortable talking to each other that way. After all, he was her best friend and they shared everything. Sloan dropped down onto the sofa and scooped up a handful of chocolate kisses from the candy bowl she kept on the glass coffee table.

"Sloan, please take it easy on the candy. You're going to ruin your appetite," Natasha chastised.

With a chuckle, Sloan replied, "Yes, Mother."

As she walked past him to retrieve her purse, she said, "Oh, I just got off the phone with Travis."

Sloan leaned forward in the seat. "Well, how's that baby brother of yours doing?"

"Mmmm, he would be doing great if he could keep a job," Natasha said with a measure of disappointment in her voice.

Her brother, Travis, had held several jobs during the past year and had just been fired from the latest one. He had three baby mommas whom he played tag with, and he was back at home with their mother, who still believed there was hope for the man.

"He's back at Momma's," Natasha sighed as she folded her arms across her chest. "Ladesha put him out again," she said in a flat tone of voice.

"How many times has it been?" Sloan inquired.

"At least three," Natasha confirmed. "He's trifling, Sloan. Travis has got good brains, but he just doesn't know how to use them." Natasha reflected on the numerous arguments between her and her brother concerning his lack of responsibility.

Sloan let out a brief sigh. "Check this out, Natasha. The dude just had some bad breaks. He was a father at sixteen, you know. Then, again at seventeen, and now, he has a six-month-old with Ladesha. That's a lot for a young man to handle."

"And it's all the more reason for him to keep it in his pants and grow the heck up," Natasha huffed without sympathy.

"Do you want me to have a man-to-man with him?" Sloan asked as he stood. Natasha gazed up at the over-six-feet-tall, fine, hunk of a man standing before her and smiled.

"If only he had half the brains you do."

Sloan gave Natasha a surreal look.

"Now, don't go making me out to be some kind of monarch. I've made plenty mistakes along the way, especially with women," Sloan retorted as Monica Jenkins crossed his mind.

"Yeah, well, I will second that emotion." Natasha grinned as she touched his smooth, caramel skin. She loved the way it felt to her touch. Her best friend always wore expensive cologne—the kind that drew you in as it tantalized your senses. *Mmmm,* she thought to herself, *if I were his girl, I would be all over him by now*. Just the thought of being in Sloan's arms made her warm all over. Coming out of her fantasy, she said, "I know you didn't get all spiffy just for me, Sloan Stevens." A small smile crept across her face.

"Truthfully, I thought I had a date with Monica, but…she stood me up, again." Sloan stammered as he met Natasha's gaze. "Why are you looking at me like that?"

Natasha was still reeling from her fantasy. She quickly dropped her stare. Her heart began to flutter. She wondered if Sloan could see her true feelings. *Surely not,* she thought. She was good at hiding her feelings. Lord knows, she'd had years of practice.

"It's nothing," she said as she reached for her purse, "So, we're outta here." Sloan grinned as they both walked out the door.

As Sloan pulled into traffic, Natasha gave him a quick glance. "So, the diva stood you up, huh?" Natasha asked as she turned on the radio. Her favorite station was already playing. She bobbed her head to Mary J. Blige's, "I Am." She sang a couple of verses, and then she uttered in Sloan's direction, "Maybe this is payback for being such a playa. They always say what goes around comes back around."

"Ah, come on, Natasha, you're acting as if I'm some kind of womanizer," Sloan sputtered with a shake of his head.

"My thoughts exactly," Natasha crooned as she tapped her fingers to the beat of the music.

"Well, maybe I was; but not anymore. I'm changing my ways. I'm getting tired of these games, Natasha, and hopping from one woman's bed to another. It is getting really old," Sloan said with frustration. After a moment's pause, he said, "And I thought Monica was the one…but…" he let out a low breath. Turning his head briefly to Natasha, he said, "The last thing I want to do is talk about Monica, I just want to have a good time tonight. Can we please just do that?"

Natasha nodded her head as a slow smile touched her lips. Sloan seemed to be finally seeing the light. She couldn't have been happier, but it wasn't at Sloan's expense. She knew how it felt to be disappointed in someone you love.

"I know what you mean, Sloan. I thought I had finally found my true love, but I guess it just wasn't in the cards. I don't know if I told you this before, but I really appreciate you being there for me when Darin walked out." Natasha let out a low breath. "And thank you for accompanying me to the doctor's office after I found out he was cheating on me. Thank God he didn't leave me with some dreaded disease," Natasha spouted, recalling the humiliating memories of sitting on the cold, leather examining table that fateful morning. Oh, how she hated Darin for putting her through such a devastating ordeal. Natasha shifted in her seat. Sloan saw her discomfort and reached for her hand.

"You know I'll always be there for you, Natasha. That's what friends are for," Sloan smiled as his eyes peered her way.

Natasha turned down the music and fixed her eyes on Sloan. "I know you said that you don't want to talk about it, but can I say just one thing?"

Sloan knew Natasha like he knew the back of his hand. She wouldn't let anything go until she was good and ready. He exhaled. "I'm listening."

"So, are you thinking about ending things with Monica? I mean, there could be a reasonable explanation as to why she stood you up."

Sloan didn't want to tell Natasha that this wasn't the first or second time that Monica was a no show. It was the third time, and that didn't include unreturned phone calls. He was beginning to suspect that he was the one being cheated on. Like Natasha had stated, what goes around comes back around.

"Yeah, I am thinking about it, and to tell you the truth, I've been thinking about it for a long time now. I want it all, Natasha. A successful career, the big house on the hill, and a loving family. But how can I have that if I can't trust my woman and she can't trust me?"

"Mmmm, that's really deep, Sloan."

"Well, that's how I feel," Sloan said as they pulled up to the restaurant. Natasha raised her eyebrows and parted her lips. "Sloan, are we dining here?"

"Yes, we are. I've made reservations and I'm not canceling them."

Natasha took in the beautiful design of The Vistro. Elegant Hawaiian trees lined the walkway, giving it an exotic look. It was one of the most expensive restaurants in the city.

"Wow, you were going to put out a pretty penny for Miss Thang. Well, all I can say is her loss, my gain." Natasha chuckled as Sloan opened the passenger door for her.

"Let's go, Me-Me," Sloan said while extending his hand. Natasha gladly accepted it, because being with Sloan felt really good tonight.

Sloan and Natasha enjoyed the restaurant without a care in the world.

The food was delicious; they shared a meal of calabash shrimp, rice pilaf, and Greek salad. They were having such a good time as a couple as they sipped their chocolate mocha lattes after the meal. The night had been so perfect that neither of them was ready for the evening to end.

"Are you feeling a movie?" Sloan asked as they walked over to his SUV.

"Why not? I have no one waiting for me at home," Natasha said solemnly.

Sloan stopped abruptly. He turned Natasha's body around to face him. Looking whimsically into Natasha's eyes, he uttered, "Look at the both of us. Aren't we such pitiful souls? Here we are, young, sexy, and articulate, but yet we have no one to call our own." Sloan feigned acting in a Shakespearean play.

Natasha let out a belly laugh. Sloan was always comical. Giving him a playful punch in the side, Natasha said, "Well, I guess it's just you and me, kid."

Sloan grabbed her hand and pulled her into him, kissing her gently on the forehead. "Let's check out a funny movie. I think we both can use a good laugh."

G STREET CHRONICLES
A LITERARY POWERHOUSE
WWW.GSTREETCHRONICLES.COM

SLOAN

Monday mornings were always hectic at Emerson & Stuckey; a fast-paced marketing firm that took in millions of dollars for successful advertising. Sloan had been at the company for almost six years now, and he had climbed that corporate ladder, as they say. He was the firm's top-notch marketing director and was handsomely compensated for the job that he did.

As Sloan sat behind his dark mahogany desk with his head buried in an upcoming contract, a soft knock came at his office door. Peering up, he looked into the eyes of his pudgy-faced boss, Mr. Emerson. The man reminded him of the actor Tom Bosley. For the most part, Mr. Emerson was a nice and fair man, but everyone knew not to get on his bad side. Mr. Emerson had an ugly streak that a few of his employees had experienced. And, just like a mother who shoves bitter medicine down her child's throat, so was the aftermath of Mr. Emerson's temper. Mr. Emerson wasn't alone when he entered Sloan's office. Two people accompanied him. Clearing his throat, Mr. Emerson gave Sloan a gaunt stare. Sloan immediately came from around his desk as Mr. Emerson popped into the office.

"Uh, sorry, Mr. Emerson, please excuse my manners. I was bringing the Morris account up to date. I have an appointment with him later today," Sloan responded as his eyes raked over the beautiful female who joined Mr. Emerson on his trip to Sloan's office. The woman standing before him looked like an Asian doll. She was an older woman, but she had a figure that would make any man stop and take notice. Her dark, almond-shaped eyes stared back at him. She gave him a slight smile with her full, strawberry- colored lips.

"Mr. Stevens," Mr. Emerson said as he turned to face the tall woman, "This is Miss Essence Kirkland." He gestured toward the man who had also accompanied him, "And this is Mr. Derrick Perkins."

Sloan extended his hand to Miss Kirkland and then to Mr. Perkins;

each gave him a firm handshake. While looking at the gentleman, Sloan thought he could pass for a Denzel Washington stand-in. Sloan couldn't help but notice how impeccably dressed Mr. Perkins was. His navy, double-breasted Kenneth Cole suit gave him a domineering look. In the pit of his stomach, Sloan felt a little threatened. Mr. Emerson's gravelly voice pulled Sloan from his inner thoughts.

"Miss Kirkland will be taking over the position that became available in the accounting department, and Mr. Perkins will be in your department, Sloan. He will start training today. You will be his trainer, and I expect for you to do a good job of showing him the ropes," Mr. Emerson said gruffly.

"Consider it done, Mr. Emerson," Sloan said while . Emerson shooting a firm look in his boss's direction. Sloan looked at Miss Kirkland and then back to Mr. Perkins.

"Welcome aboard, and I hope you two will be happy here," Sloan said as he began the Emerson & Stuckey new-employee speech.

Mr. Emerson smiled and exited the office. He knew they would be in good hands with one of his best employees.

NATASHA

Natasha's favorite gospel music filled her ears via her earphones as she worked. Yolanda Adams was her idol, and she had collected all of her songs. She hummed to the tune as she sat in front of her computer and typed away at the keys. Out of the corner of her eye, she caught a glimpse of Sloan and two new employees as they walked down the long hallway, stopping a time or two as Sloan introduced them to coworkers. Natasha quickly pulled the plugs out of her ears and stared in their direction. Her eyes were immediately drawn to the tall, dark, and lovely Adonis that pranced beside Sloan.

The woman on the other side of Sloan was attractive as well. She was older; Natasha thought she was maybe in her early forties. But she was very pretty, and her silky black hair was pulled back in a bun.

Lisa Ray tapped Natasha on the shoulder, which almost caused her to jump out of her seat. "Chill, girl, it's just me," she whispered as they both stared down the hall. "Mmmm, girl, isn't he fine? If I wasn't in a committed relationship, I would jump on that with both feet," Lisa Ray chuckled.

"You are so bad," Natasha said as she snickered while they both continued to stare. The group had arrived at the elevator, and Sloan was pressing the button. He was taking them upstairs to meet the bigwigs. Natasha took in the man's handsome features, and she couldn't help but drool.

"A man as fine as that has to be married, with a string of kids," she declared.

"Natasha, cut it out! You don't know that for a fact. Think positive. That could be your future husband, girl." Lisa Ray said with a wink of her eye.

"Ummm, yeah right," Natasha said with a smirk. "Well, if he's not married and doesn't have any kids, I bet he has a thousand women he's bedding," Natasha said while letting out a low breath.

"Oh, girl, everybody is not like Darin. If you keep comparing every new man to your ex, you will never find anybody."

The elevator opened and the three went inside. As the doors closed, Natasha exhaled and said, "Girl, the show is over, and I'm going back to work."

"I know you will be grilling Sloan on the newcomers, so fill me in later," Lisa Ray said, turning on her heels.

The ladies returned to their computers. Natasha put the earphones back in her ears, but now she had more than work on her mind. The man's handsome face played sultry rhythms in her brain, allowing her to daydream.

SLOAN & NATASHA

Sloan was seated across from Natasha at the corner deli. Charley's was only a few blocks away from Emerson & Stuckey, and its popularity drew a lot of the firm's employees there for lunch. Natasha took a bite of her sandwich as she listened to Sloan rant about his now-ex, Monica. His suspicions had been right on the money; Miss Thang was cheating, alright. She was cheating with her boss, Jack Strickland, who was almost twice her age. Sloan had busted them when he'd stopped by her apartment unexpectedly. Jack was just coming out of the shower when Sloan walked in. Sloan hadn't bothered to knock, because she had given him an extra key. Monica's face nearly hit the floor at the sight of him walking in the door unannounced.

Natasha thought ending that relationship was the best thing that could have happened to Sloan, because she had felt all along that Monica Jenkins wasn't the right woman for him. In fact, Natasha couldn't pick out even one of Sloan's conquests that she considered perfect enough for him. Maybe she was biased because she thought Sloan deserved someone who knew him well, someone who could bring out the best in him—someone like *her.*

Coming out of her trance, Natasha said, "Count your blessings, Sloan. Just like me, you found out what she was really about before you got too deeply involved."

Sloan took a swig of his Coke and leaned back in his seat. With conviction in his voice, Sloan said, "From this moment on, Natasha, I'm hanging up my playa's shoes. I'm remaining celibate until I find the right woman." Natasha gave him a sidelong glance.

"Yeah, right," Natasha said, taking another bite of her sandwich. "So, tell me about the new couple I saw you with this morning."

Sloan finished off his sandwich and wiped the corner of his mouth with the checkered napkin.

"Mmmm, let's see," he began. "Essence Kirkland hails from Austin, Texas, and she will be working in the accounting department. And Derrick Perkins, who is also from Texas—Dallas, that is—and he will be the thorn in my side from here on out. I'm supposed to train him," Sloan mumbled.

"Oh, so he will take Dave's place," Natasha retorted with a smile.

"Exactly, and I hate it. I think I work better and faster by myself," Sloan said as he finished his glass of Coke.

"Nobody is as good as you, Sloan Stevens, so don't sweat the small stuff." Natasha's eyes twinkled as she stared at her friend.

"Show you right!" Sloan said, smiling as she stroked his male ego. As long as he and Natasha were friends, she had always known how to make him feel like he could do anything and be anything. She was definitely the wind beneath his wings.

"Now, tell me the dirt on the two," she said perkily, snapping him back to the present. Natasha kept her smile as she inched closer to him.

Sloan let out a small chuckle at her tactics. "Natasha, I don't have their personal files in my back pocket, you know."

Natasha's expression hardened as she puckered her lips. She stuck her finger in her glass of ice water and flicked it at Sloan.

"Me-Me, cut it out," Sloan said, frowning with his hands raised.

"Oh, come on, Sloan, I know you got more than what you're telling me."

"Alright, I will tell you what little I do know," he said as he leaned forward.

"Essence was born and raised in South Carolina. After college, she said she needed a change of scenery, so she moved to Austin, Texas. She has no husband or kiddies."

He paused as he watched Natasha absorb that little piece of information.

"And…" Natasha said with a raised brow.

"Oh, you're waiting on what you and every woman at the office wants to know—the scoop on the brother, huh?" Sloan smiled smugly.

"Go on, Sloan, and stop holding me in suspense."

"Okay, don't get your panties in a bunch," he spouted as he leaned back in his chair. "Derrick Perkins is originally from Dallas, Texas. He's an ex-football player. He was hurt during the highlight of his career and his contract wasn't renewed. So he went into marketing and applied for the position here in Atlanta, and here he is. He's also not married and no kiddies." Sloan's tone changed to a lower octave. "But he thinks he's smart as hell and God's gift to women."

"Oh, do I detect a little animosity or maybe even jealousy?" Natasha teased as she gently pinched his cheek.

"Let's just say that I know his game. He is not husband material, so don't go looking in that direction," Sloan warned.

Natasha dropped her hand. "And how would you know that, Sloan Stevens? Did he actually confide that piece of prudent information to you?" Natasha said defensively.

Sloan saw the smoldering look Natasha was giving him. It was amazing how she could see all the faults in the women he had dated, but when the mirror was reversed, she couldn't see her own nose on her face.

"Just take my word for it, okay? I know game when I see it, and the brother is full of games," Sloan warned.

"And what about sister gal, is she full of game, as well?" Natasha said in a cool tone.

"You see…I can see your claws coming out already. What is it with you, Me-Me?" Sloan asked, getting a little irritated.

Natasha gave him a blank stare. Sloan could bring out the best—and the worst—in her, at times. Now, her jealous streak was starting to show.

"Oh nothing, Sloan, I'm just looking out for a brother," she said with a wave of her hand. "Look, I have an idea," she added quickly. "Let's invite the couple out to dinner or maybe have a pool party." Natasha's eyes sparkled as if she were a child in an ice cream store. "I think I like the latter idea even better," she crooned. "It's been a long time since I've done any entertaining, Sloan, and I really want to do something special, and plus, that way, we both can get to know them better." Natasha finished with a smile.

"Whatever," Sloan replied, standing up. "We both better get back to work, or the newcomers may have our jobs," he said as he placed a tip for the waitress on the table.

"Will you give them the invite?" Natasha asked as she gazed into his hazel eyes. Sloan knew Natasha was on a roll, and once she got started on something, there was no stopping her.

"Yes, Natasha, and when will this event take place?" Sloan said, allowing her to get in front of him.

"Let's do it this weekend."

Sloan's face crumpled into a frown as he stopped abruptly. "I don't know about that, Me-Me. That's kind of fast," Sloan spurted with a tilted head.

Natasha turned to face him. "Sloan, I can pull it off, trust me," she said as they walked back to work.

ESSENCE

Peering into the handsome face of Sloan Stevens, Essence knew that working at Emerson & Stuckey wouldn't be bad at all. With the exceptional pay and healthy benefit package, Sloan Stevens would just be an added bonus to an already sweet deal. Taking in his chiseled features, she loved the way his long lashes framed the lids of his eyes. The slight mustache that outlined his full lips gave him a male, fashion model look. She realized she was a few years older than him, but age had never stopped her before, and it certainly wasn't going to stop her now. Nothing got in the way of what she wanted once her mind was set. Plus, she loved to dabble in the playpen. Younger men had more energy and a sense of adventure that most men her age were lacking. Another advantage that captured her fancy was how opened-minded younger men could be. They gave her the freedom she needed to explore. But, deep down inside, she really wanted to settle down one day. Maybe Sloan could help her out on all that she mused as he continued to discuss the training manual with her.

Essence tried her best to keep her mind on work, especially since this was her very first day, but she just couldn't help herself. Taking in Sloan's musky fragrance sent warm tingles down her spine. The scent spelled sexy. Sitting in such close proximity to him was making it harder and harder for her to concentrate on work. As he bent his tall frame over her shoulder, Essence could feel the warmth of his breath close to her ear. She could have easily looked up and tasted his sweet lips. Just the thought of that made her tingle within.

"Do you have any questions, Miss Kirkland?" Sloan asked, breaking into her reverie. Essence peered into his hazel eyes, giving him an intriguing smile.

With a sexy twang, she uttered, "I have just one question, Mr. Stevens. Are you married, engaged, or free to pursue?"

Her question caught Sloan strictly by surprise. Clearing his throat,

Sloan gave her a quick smile.

"I see you don't waste any time, Miss Kirkland."

"Life is too short to waste even a minute of it; and please call me Essence," she purred.

Sloan took in the woman's succulent beauty. He knew she had him by a few years, but age, by no means, took anything away from her sexuality. In fact, it added. Her dark, Asian eyes captivated him so. It was like being pulled into a mysterious place.

With a small grin, Sloan answered, "Essence, I'm not married or engaged, and yes I am free to pursue."

Essence picked up the gold pen Sloan had just placed on her desk. She scribbled some numbers onto a yellow sticky note. She tore a single sheet from the pad and handed it to him.

Staring into her eyes, Sloan muttered, "You've just made my day a little easier."

"And how is that?" Essence asked, her neatly-trimmed eyebrows lifting with curiosity. Sloan had a wide grin on his face as he held the yellow paper in his hand.

"My best friend and I are having a pool party this weekend at her place, and since you're new in town, I would like to invite you. That is, if you don't have any other plans." Sloan was hoping like crazy that she would accept his offer. He wanted to be near her. Her beauty was intoxicating, and it was making him sweat.

Essence smiled widely. She stood up and gave Sloan an intense, yet sexy stare.

"A pool party," she said excitedly, "Well, I guess that means some serious shopping for me."

Sloan's eyebrow rose. "Shopping?" he asked inquisitively.

"Yes, shopping. I have to find the perfect swimsuit… just for you," Essence said in a flirtatious tone of voice.

Her long, slim fingers brushed his cheek. Sloan found himself growing a little hot under the collar as he thought about her curvaceous body in a swimsuit. Fireworks were brewing between them. Essence's eyes traveled to the office door, where Natasha was standing with a blank stare on her face. She was holding a manila folder in her hand.

"Excuse me," Natasha said smugly as she walked through the door.

"I hope I'm not interrupting anything," she stated as she stared at both of them.

"Why, of course not," Sloan uttered as he stepped away from Essence and regained his business composure as his friend stepped farther into the office.

"I was just telling Miss Kirkland here about the pool party. She accepted our invitation," Sloan said quickly, his eyes twinkling with delight.

"Oh, so this is the best friend you were speaking of," Essence responded, giving Natasha an amused stare. Sloan smiled broadly as he touched Natasha's arm.

"Yes, this is my best friend of what…fifteen years or more," Sloan said, catching Natasha's cool demeanor.

"Something like that," Natasha mumbled as she returned Essence's gaze. "Well, this is, as I said, my best friend, Natasha Jacobs. And Natasha, this is Miss Essence Kirkland."

"It's my pleasure," Essence uttered as she extended her hand, which Natasha shook effortlessly.

"A childhood friend, huh? That's very interesting," Essence said as she continued to stare into Natasha's eyes. "I can't begin to think where my childhood friends are right about now. I can't say if I even remember half of them," Essence mumbled with a smile.

Natasha took in Essence's lovely features. She seemed nice enough, but there was something about this woman that didn't quite sit well with her. But who was she to judge? She knew nothing of her—yet.

"So, you are coming to the pool party. I'm sure you will have a good time," Natasha said, giving Essence a generous smile.

"If Mr. Stevens has anything to do with it, I'm sure I will," she said, giving Sloan an alluring look.

"Um, what time will the party start?" Essence asked cheerfully.

"Um, let's say about one-ish," Natasha responded, mimicking Essence's uncanny behavior.

"Natasha, I will need directions to your home. Unfortunately, I don't know my way around as well as I would like," Essence said in an innocent tone.

Before Natasha could respond, Sloan piped in. "How about me picking I pick you up, I mean, if that's okay with you?" Sloan secretly held his breath.

Essence smiled coyly as she responded, "Why, Mr. Stevens, that would be just wonderful."

Natasha gave Sloan a look that said, "I don't believe this chick." Sloan had spoken to her about game, and this chick was certainly playing hers. The way she was looking at Sloan reminded Natasha of a fly buzzing around a picnic table full of food.

"Here, this is yours," Natasha said, giving Sloan the folder. "It's the Morris account," she said tightly.

"Oh great, this is just what I've been waiting for," Sloan said, accepting the folder and walking over to his desk. He couldn't believe how smoothly his day was going. He now had a hot date, and the account he was waiting on all morning was in his hand. Everything was just perfect.

Natasha made her exit quickly. It was time to get back to business. Sloan was on Essence's agenda, and Essence was on Natasha's agenda. A business plan was in the making. At the end of the day, Natasha quickly closed her briefcase, which was stuffed with paperwork she was taking home. She was hoping that things would slow down after getting caught up with her current accounts now that they had two new people on board. A masculine scent teased her nostrils and made her look up. Sloan was standing before her, wearing that sexy smile of his.

"I see you're almost outta here," he said, glancing down at her. Natasha gave him a *what-if-I-am* stare.

"And I see you're not through with chasing the cat." Natasha grimaced, letting her eyes fall away from his stare.

"Whoa!" Sloan said, placing his black leather briefcase atop her desk. "I don't know what you're talking about."

"Save it, Sloan Stevens," Natasha said as her voice raised an octave. "One minute you're telling me you are tired of playing the game," she said, emphasizing "the game" with her fingers. "And the next thing I know, you practically got your tongue down a woman's throat that you just met."

"I think you misunderstood what you saw," Sloan said in his defense.

Natasha squinted and let out a low breath. "Don't use your tired little lines on me, okay. I'm not one of your mindless bimbos," she uttered as she picked up her now heavy briefcase. "I know what I saw, and I know what I heard." Natasha mimicked Essence's tone of voice along with her movements. "I must go shopping for a swimsuit, just for you. Please, give me a break!" Natasha huffed as she sauntered around Sloan. She headed down the long, freshly-waxed corridor with Sloan close on her heels.

"That's not how it was, Me-Me," Sloan muttered.

"Yeah, right," Natasha said, rolling her eyes. "Did you get a chance to show her the accounting books, or were you too busy getting between her pages?" Natasha said with a twinge of sarcasm.

Sloan stopped abruptly, breaking Natasha's stride, as well. "You know something, Me-Me, I don't care what you think you saw. And you're absolutely right. You're not one of my bimbos, and therefore I don't owe you a damn explanation about anything; and frankly it's none of your business if I do like her. It's all my decision, just like it's my life!" Sloan blared, leaving her standing in the hall with her mouth ajar.

NATASHA

Natasha slammed the sunburst door of her home so hard that she thought she had shattered the stained glass. That was how angry she felt inside. Throughout the years, she and Sloan had shared many disagreements, but there was something different about this one. The lining of their friendship was changing, and it shook her very soul. After slinging her gray Chanel bag onto the plush royal-blue sofa, she headed for the fridge. It was another hot day in August, and Natasha's linen, peach-colored suit clung to her like silk gloves. *Thank God for air conditioning*, she mused as she entered her kitchen. "Dog days" the older people called it. She wasn't sure how the dogs felt about it, but she couldn't wait for winter, which was her favorite time of year. As she reached inside the fridge for a can of Pepsi, her phone rang. *It had better not be Sloan,* she thought, *because if it is, boy do I have an earful for him.* She snatched up the receiver and huffed a hello.

"Natasha, is that you? What on earth is wrong, baby?" Florene asked.

"Oh, hi, Mom, I'm sorry about that. I thought you were Sloan," she said after taking a big sip of her pop.

"How are you doing, baby?"

"Mom, I'm just fine."

"Fine, but pissed! I know that temper of yours, Natasha. So, what has you all fired up this time? Don't tell me that you and that boss of yours banged heads again?"

Natasha exhaled as she climbed onto the barstool and propped her elbow on the marble countertop. "No, Mom, Mr. Emerson has been staying out of my way since I told him what he could do with that worn-out toupee of his." Natasha chuckled. It was funny, out of all the employees at Emerson & Stuckey, she was the only one who had stood up to Mr. Emerson and still received a paycheck. But she was fairly warned that another incident would put her out the door.

"Thank God Sloan was there as a buffer between the two of you," Florene relented.

"Mom, please don't mention Sloan's name again, because I don't want to hear it."

Florene took in a deep breath of air. "Oh, child, what has he done this time to rattle your cage?"

"Ughh, I could just strangle him, Mom," Natasha blurted out.

Florene giggled on the other end of the line. "You act as if you're married to the man, Natasha. Remember he's only your best friend, not *your* man," Florene chastised.

Natasha gulped down the rest of her soda and tried to calm her anger. Her mother's observation was correct. Why was she behaving like this? How silly of her. Florene's voice jolted her back to reality.

"What has Sloan done this time?"

"Oh, nothing really, Mom, just being the typical male when they see fresh meat," Natasha admitted slowly.

"Natasha, how long have I been telling you that your feelings for that man run deeper than you care to admit, but for some unearthly reason, you refuse to see it. Wake up, girl!"

"Mom, please, Sloan is like a brother to me. I…love him like a brother and that's it," Natasha said, trying to convince herself as well.

Florene sucked her teeth. "You don't get bent out of shape the way you do when your brother is falling for someone, now do you?" Florene questioned.

Natasha shifted her weight on the barstool. "Mom, I'm not getting bent out of shape, alright. I just don't want Sloan to make the same mistake I did. I fell for someone that I thought would have been my husband by now, but you see how all of that turned out."

"Yeah, baby, and I'm sorry you had to experience such heartbreak. But everything happens for a reason, and maybe he just wasn't the one. It's possible that you may have the right one under your nose and just don't know it yet," Florene said cautiously.

"Okay, Mom, I see where this conversation is going, and I'm getting off the phone now."

"Mmmm, can't stand hearing the truth, huh," Florene quipped into the telephone.

"Bye, Mom. I'll call you later," Natasha said while hanging up. Natasha hated ending her call so briefly, but sometimes Florene made her think too deeply about things, and today was one of those times.

SLOAN & DERRICK

It had been an excruciating day at the office for Sloan; and now, thank God, the day had finally come to a close. He wished Mr. Emerson would have given him fair warning about the new hires instead of just throwing them at him. But who was he kidding? When did Mr. Emerson give anybody a heads up about anything, unless it directly affected him and his deep pockets? Sloan walked out into the parking lot and headed for his SUV. He had just purchased this baby, and he was proud of it. His honeys couldn't get enough of styling and profiling in his 2009 pearl-white Navigator. He rescinded his statement—his ex-honeys, that is. He was serious about settling down with just one woman. As he strutted to the SUV, he noticed the new hire, Derrick Perkins, a few feet away. The dude was standing near a black-on-black 2008 Infinity. The ride was sleek and smooth with silver trimmings. From the moment they were introduced, Sloan knew Derrick had style about him, and from the way he dressed, Sloan couldn't imagine Derrick driving anything but class.

"Hey, man!" Sloan yelled out, getting Derrick's attention. Derrick turned and looked in Sloan's direction. Sloan walked toward him, and the gap between them closed. "Nice ride, man," he said as his eyes traveled over the vehicle. Derrick gave him a gratified smile.

"Thanks. I just got her a couple of months ago," Derrick said.

"I bet the honeys drool every time they see you behind the wheel."

Derrick's smile grew wider. "Just say I have quite an audience."

"Isn't it something how most women judge a man by what he drives?" Sloan asked.

"Well, they used to say that clothes made the man, but in these days and times, I think what we drive has more of an advantage. I've been swatting ladies like flies since I been here in Atlanta, but I'm not complaining," Derrick said with a grin. Both men chuckled.

"I know exactly what ya mean," Sloan acknowledged as he nodded his head. "Hey, dude, I've been meaning to get with you earlier, but I didn't get around to it."

Derrick's eyes widened as Sloan piqued his interested. "So, what's up? I hope I didn't do something detrimental on my first day," Derrick said jokingly.

"Oh, naw, man, it's nothing like that," Sloan said, giving Derrick an amicable look. "My best friend, Natasha Jacobs, and I are having a pool party this weekend, and we wanted to invite you. I've already spoken to Essence Kirkland, and she has accepted," Sloan said quickly.

A fine line formed across Derrick's forehead. "Oh, she did?" he said amused.

"Do you two know each other?" Sloan quizzed.

Derrick shook his head. "Oh, not at all…I just met her today," he stumbled.

Sloan gave him an uneasy stare. "Ah, well…I thought because you both came from Texas…I just…forget it man," Sloan said, waving his hand. "So, are you down?"

"Sure, why not. I haven't been to a pool party since my college years." Derrick grinned.

"I'll hit you up with the directions and time tomorrow," Sloan said as he turned to walk back toward his SUV.

"Um, Sloan," Derrick called out. Sloan stopped, turning to face Derrick. "You said your best friend was Natasha Jacobs. Did I meet her today? I've met so many people, I don't know," Derrick said with a dip of his shoulder. "The name just sounds familiar." Derrick grinned.

"Mmmm, I don't think so. She's in the advertising department, but I'll be sure to introduce you two tomorrow."

"Alright then, tomorrow it is," Derrick muttered as he headed back to his car. Both men jumped into their vehicles and sped away.

SLOAN

Driving down I-85, Sloan retrieved his Kenneth Cole shades and placed them on his face. The afternoon sunlight beamed brightly. He selected his favorite Lenny Kravitz CD from his collection and placed it into his CD player. Lenny's smooth sound filled the air and soothed away the day's stress. As he drove, his mind drifted to thoughts of Natasha. He loved her like his very own sister, but sometimes her attitude really got next to him. He wondered why she broke on him the way she did. What had he done to her? The questions kept coming to his mind, but the answers failed to show. Natasha was a complicated woman, but she was his friend and had been since third grade. He knew her almost as well as he knew himself; and by now, he should have been used to her personal quirks. *But, still, she didn't have to break like that,* he thought as he turned his SUV into his driveway.

After walking up the steps to his door, he noticed a yellow card stuck in the door casing. He pulled it from the door and began to read the message that was scribbled on the back of it. It was a message from one of his recent honeys. Bonnie Fairchild was the bomb. If being fine was a crime, she would have been locked up for life. Sloan's face broke into a smile. She wanted to know if they could chill tonight. Sloan stuck the card into the pocket of his Kenneth Cole trousers while reaching for his house key. He slid the key into the keyhole and entered his home. The smile lingered on his face as his mind reverted back to the hot times he and Bonnie had shared. Even though they hadn't seen each other in months, they still remained friends and occasional lovers. He had dipped into her bed a few times when he was between relationships.

Bonnie was a good woman, but she was also needy. She wanted him in her presence like the air she breathed. That would be fine if he really had true feelings for her, but, in all actuality, she was just a booty call. And as demeaning as it sounded, it was the truth. Placing his briefcase by the door,

Sloan made his way into the kitchen. At the touch of the stereo button, the sound of music filled the empty spaces of his home. For a bachelor, his place was beautifully decorated. The living room was done in black and white. Expensive furniture was scattered about, and African paintings adorned the soft-white walls. Sloan opened the door of his stainless steel refrigerator and grabbed a can of ginger ale. He popped the top and took a long swig.

As he returned to the living room, his mind flowed to thoughts of his homeboy, Ricky Davenport. They had been friends for almost seven years now. Sloan used to date one of Ricky's cousins, and that was how he and Ricky had met. The relationship with Ricky's cousin, Diane, had ended, but Sloan and Ricky had remained close friends. Now, years later, Diane was married, with two kids, and even though their relationship was a bust, they still remained civil toward each other. Because of his friendship with Ricky, Sloan was always invited to their family get-togethers. Sloan finished his can of pop in deep thought; he could hear Ricky's grilling, *Hey, man, I can't believe a grown-ass man downing ginger ale instead of a beer? What planet are you from, dude?* If Ricky only knew what Sloan had gone through with his alcoholic father, he would know the answer to that question. But that was a part of his life that Sloan kept virtually to himself.

The cliché expression, "drinks like a fish" was an understatement when it came to Sloan's father. The man drank from sunup to sundown, but he wasn't the kind of drunk that fell over his feet and made a fool of himself. Under normal circumstances, you wouldn't have known his father was drinking just by looking at him. He kept a reserved persona, but the alcohol changed him. It made him mean and hateful. He seldom smiled, and when he did, it was at his family's expense. Sloan, his mother, and his sister tap danced around him because no one knew when he would explode. He had vivid memories of one beautiful Sunday afternoon when things turned particularly ugly.

The family had just returned from church, and his mother had prepared her famous Sunday dinner of pot roast, garlic potatoes, and buttered corn. She even made a cinnamon-crust apple pie. Sloan's mouth watered just thinking about his mother's cooking. Everything was going just great in his twelve-year-old mind. His baby sister, Jeanette, who was six years old at the time, was playing quietly in the living room with her dolls. Sloan was strumming his guitar, a present given to him by his favorite uncle, Leroy, who was his father's brother. Sloan's dad had a jealous streak when it came to Leroy, because he was very successful. He was involved in real estate and owned several properties. Leroy drove a black Cadillac—like the ones in the old pimp movies. He'd had it custom designed, and even had his initials engraved in the creamy-white leather seats. His dad always copped an attitude when Leroy came by. For the life of him, Sloan couldn't figure out why. His dad was doing quite well for himself as the manager at an A&W restaurant, and Sloan's mother was a school teacher. So, they weren't standing in line at the local food bank.

That afternoon, the atmosphere was mellow as he plucked the strings of his guitar. He hummed a few notes from a church song that had touched his heart. His mother heard him and joined in. His mother, Peggy, had a beautiful voice. It was common knowledge that she had wanted to be a singer in her earlier years, but, as the story goes, she got pregnant with Sloan and married his dad. So, now his mom only sang in the choir. She was the lead singer of the Mount Mariah Adult Choir.

They were deep into the song when his dad walked in. He had the most disturbing look on his face –you would have thought they were doing something utterly wrong from his sour expression.

"Didn't we just leave church?" his powerful voice boomed. "I don't want to hear another song from those hypocrite choir members of yours, Peggy!" he yelled with a scowl.

In unison, they stopped singing and stared at each other. They both knew what was coming if they didn't oblige.

"Go get ready for dinner, Sloan," his mother whispered as she headed back into the kitchen.

Just like Sloan thought, not only did dinner smell delectable, but it tasted delicious, as well. He was into his second helping when his father smacked his hand away from his plate.

"Boy, you eat as if this is your last meal!" his dad snapped.

"It's…good…Daddy," Sloan mumbled as he lowered his head and stared down into his plate.

"I don't know why your mother cooked this pot roast," his daddy uttered as deep lines formed on his forehead. "Did I not tell you, Peggy, that I wanted fried chicken today?" he growled as his eyes blazed in her direction. "But, Eugene, we had fried chicken on Friday." Peggy spoke as if she were talking to one of her third graders. Her voice was soft and soothing.

"I don't give a damn if we had it Thursday, Friday, and Saturday. Peggy, when I tell you I want chicken, I want chicken," he huffed as his big, dark fist hit the table.

Sloan swore he saw the plate raise a couple of inches from the table. He looked over at his sister, Jeanette, and saw the fear in her eyes. He wondered what would come next. Would his father grab his mother, pull her by the hair, and scream obscenities at her as if she were some lowlife in the street? It wouldn't have been the first, second, or third time. Sloan took a deep breath; he was hoping to suck up the courage he needed to come to his mother's rescue.

"Dad, maybe Mom can fry chicken…tomorrow? Will you, Mom? I…would love to have some more chicken tomorrow," Sloan uttered in a small voice.

Peggy met his gaze. She knew what her young son was trying to do—attempting to calm the storm before it even began. She felt so guilty for having her children exposed to such terror from their father.

"Yes, son, I will. I will fry chicken tomorrow," Peggy complied as she tore her eyes away from him and placed them on the rigid face of her husband. His dad lowered his head and resumed eating his meal. They all let out a low breath of relief. The storm didn't come that day.

As he got older, the mental abuse slowed because of Uncle Leroy. Uncle Leroy had become Sloan's sounding board. He told him everything. One day, short of Sloan's high school graduation, his father up and left. Sloan was relieved, yet saddened. He wondered how a father could do such a thing to his one and only son. During the graduation ceremony, he looked out into the audience and found his mother's smiling face, which was not only filled with happiness, but also held a glow of peace. She looked as if an anchor had been taken from her shoulders, and for that, he was overjoyed. He found out months later that there had been an altercation between his Uncle Leroy and his father that had led to his father leaving. Sloan found out that Uncle Leroy had dated his mother long before his father was in the picture. Leroy had left for the Army, and by the time he returned, his brother was married to Sloan's mother. Sloan's father felt as if his mother never had gotten over Leroy, which was the cause of his drinking and erratic behavior. And, ironically, it was true. A year after his parents' divorce, Sloan's mom married Uncle Leroy. At first, it was very odd. But as he matured, Sloan grew to understand it well. He came to realize that love conquers all, and he had seen it firsthand.

Sloan prepared himself for a shower. He removed his business attire, stepped into the shower, and turned on the water. He was contemplating giving Bonnie a call, for old time's sake. As he lathered his body, he heard the ringing of his landline through his sliding shower door. Sloan stood still as the gushing water ran smoothly down his chiseled body. He figured whoever was calling would leave a message if it was important. After his shower, Sloan slipped on his Ecko shorts and walked over to check his answering machine. He clicked the red button and began to listen to his numerous messages. There was Candy, a girl he'd met at Pluto's several weeks ago. She was followed by Melissa, Terri, Mandy, Ricky, and his mother, Peggy. And the last one, which had come while he was in the shower, was Natasha.

He mumbled under his breath. *Is she calling to beg forgiveness? That would be the womanly thing to do,* his ego stroked. *Well, I'm not about to call her back. Not yet, anyway.* He strutted back into the kitchen, looked inside the fridge, and pulled out a TV dinner. He ate a lot of microwaveable dinners. After popping it into the microwave oven, he went back into the living room, retrieved his briefcase from the foyer, and placed it on the coffee table. As he went through the files, he noticed the sticky note Essence had scribbled her phone number on. Sloan stopped and mused over the note. He had dated older women before, but the age gap had never been as wide as the one between him and Essence. He was definitely attracted to her, though. Essence was beautiful and charming, and she had a body that could stop traffic. He had never backed down from any woman who showed interest in him. He contemplated to himself, *So, what's the problem? Why should I stop now?*

Thinking back to his college days, Sloan recalled his roommate's mother. A slow grin came across his face. Now, that was an educational course he would never forget. His roommate, Camden Davis, was a total nerd, and Mrs. Davis had come to visit him a few times. The man never participated in any activity that had the word fun in it. Camden might have been a bookworm, but his mother was very outgoing. A recent divorcée with an only child, Mrs. Davis was ready for action. At first, he had been nervous when Mrs. Davis came onto him. But at nineteen, his hormones were raging and Mrs. Davis was fueling the fire. She wanted action, and action is what they had whenever Camden wasn't around. To this day, the man still didn't know Sloan had boned his mother.

Sloan picked up his phone and dialed Essence's digits. She answered on the second ring.

"Hello," her smooth voice chimed into the phone.

"Hello, Miss Kirkland. I hope I'm not disturbing you," Sloan said, letting his voice dip into a sexy tone.

"Mmmm, is this who I think it is?" Essence flirted.

"Well, if it's not, I'm sure I can be whoever you want me to be," Sloan responded. Sloan heard the soft chuckle she made.

"I hope you don't think I'm being too forward, but would you like to have dinner with me sometime?" Sloan asked. Another soft chuckle came through the phone's earpiece.

"Why, sure, Mr. Stevens, I would love to have dinner with you, but can I make one suggestion?"

"You have my undivided attention," Sloan said as he smiled.

"Can I make dinner for you? I love to cook," she admitted.

"That sounds like a wonderful idea to me. You pick the night, and I'll be there."

"Well, there is no time like the present, now is there?" Essence crooned.

"You seem to know exactly what you want and when you want it," Sloan danced.

"Mr. Stevens, I don't know the kind of women you've dated in the past, but I assure you that I'm very different from any of them. I don't play games."

ESSENCE & SLOAN

"Thank you for rescuing me from another night of loneliness," Essence crooned as she handed Sloan a glass of red wine.

Sloan was seated comfortably on the plush, almond-colored sofa in Essence's lovely townhouse. His eyes took in the soft features of her beautiful face. Her slanted, dark eyes reminded him of his mother's doll collection. Peggy was a fanatic when it came to dolls, and she had a broad range of dolls whose faces represented every nationality. Essence looked as picture-perfect as the Asian doll that sat in his mother's glass curio cabinet. As Sloan inhaled her lovely fragrance, they chitchatted nonstop about politics and current events. Her intellect astounded him. He couldn't begin to compare her to the women he had dated before, because if he did, she would bring them all to shame. Sloan felt very relaxed as he stretched out his long legs. Glancing down, he noticed she had placed her small hand on his knee. Essence found his eyes and smiled at her gesture.

Sloan enjoyed the meal Essence had prepared for him. The filet mignon and wild rice was delicious, and so were her juicy red lips as he kissed her goodnight at the front door. Sloan knew he could have bedded her if he'd wanted. Essence was making it as easy as the apple pie she'd served him for dessert. And boy, did he crave her, but there was something deep within that held him back. Maybe the love game had finally ceased. It didn't give him the kind of thrill he once knew. He wanted more than a woman's body in bed now. He wanted her mind, soul, and heart.

NATASHA

Natasha sat out on the deck of her beautiful home. It was a lovely day, and she was enjoying the sun as she planned her pool party. She scribbled a few more names on her Betty Boop notepad. She propped her legs up on the white wicker ottoman. Her phone was tucked in the crook of her neck as she talked to her cousin Gretta.

"I sure hope you are inviting some handsome hunks and not immature, ugly punks," Gretta chimed.

Natasha let out a belly laugh. "Don't blame me if you can't find a man."

"That's just it, Natasha. I don't want just a man," Gretta wailed. "I want someone who can blanket my life with warmth and security. I want a husband," Gretta pouted.

"Mmmm, sounds like you need to contact one of those dating services," Natasha said absentmindedly as she penned another name into her notepad.

"Have you ever done that?" Gretta almost whispered.

"Done what?"

"You know, contacted one of those dating agencies," Gretta said quickly.

Natasha removed her golden-tan legs from the ottoman and sat up straight. "Honestly?"

"Yes, honestly, Natasha," Gretta responded.

Natasha let out a low breath. "Well, after Darin and I broke up, I considered it. But, you know, I never got around to it. My workload picked up at the office, and what spare time I had, I spent it with Sloan." Natasha sighed.

"You know, Natasha, sometimes I can't tell if you and Sloan are just friends or really a couple. The way you two behave is mind boggling. If you asked me, I think something nasty is going on between you two."

"Well, you know what, Gretta? No one asked you," Natasha huffed as she stood up from the lounge chair.

"Alright, Natasha, don't go ballistic on me for stating my observation."

"Gretta, I'm so sick of people assuming something is going on between me and Sloan. For heaven's sake, I've known the guy since we were kids. And you know that? He is like a brother to me."

"Yeah, a fine-ass brother." Gretta giggled.

Natasha closed her eyes in frustration. She wondered why her family couldn't just mind their own business. Gretta's voice broke into her thoughts.

"Hey, Natasha, let me ask you a question." Before Natasha could protest, Gretta began. "Have you ever thought about sleeping with him?" Gretta asked cautiously, as if someone was watching her.

If Gretta only knew how many times she'd dreamt of sleeping with Sloan, she would've thought Natasha was a sex addict. And lately, things had been getting even worse. Those friendly hugs and kisses she and Sloan had shared weren't so sisterly anymore. Not for her, at least. His smell, the softness of his lips, and the firmness of his body haunted her daily; making her drip with desire in her fantasies.

"Will you just stop it?" Natasha barked into the phone.

"That's not an answer, Natasha," Gretta retorted.

"Look, I'm not going to entertain you in your foolishness." Natasha wanted to change the subject and do it fast. "Don't forget your bathing suit; and Gretta…keep it tasteful, please. It's a pool party, not a nude party. I'll talk to you later." And with that, she hung up the phone.

Natasha stared down into her pool. The sparkling water seemed to soothe the restless spirit within her. She stood ever so still as her mind lingered in the dreamy, blue water. It was almost six o'clock in the evening, and she hadn't heard a peep from Sloan, which was unusual. Sloan was her wakeup call in the morning and the call that tucked her in at night. It had been that way even when she and Darin were together. It had bothered the hell out of him at first, having another man calling his woman so frequently. But he quickly began to see that their relationship was completely harmless, at least from her perspective, and he stopped nagging her about it.

As she followed the stone walkway to the back door of her home, she wondered where Sloan could be and if he was still angry with her. She knew she had over stepped her boundaries with him, but she just couldn't help herself. Thinking back to that day in Sloan's office made her lips curl. Essence Kirkland was looking at Sloan as if he were eye candy. She wasn't blind to the fact that women Essence's age dated younger men all the time.

Like Vivica A. Fox and Terry McMillan, just to name a few. And she didn't have a problem with it—until now, when it involved her precious Sloan.

NATASHA & SLOAN

The best friends managed to tap dance around each other for the remainder of the week. Now, here it was Friday, and the pool party was tomorrow. Natasha wondered how in the world they were going to pull it off without speaking to each other. Talk about some stupid crap; this was one for the Guinness Book of World Silliness. As Natasha strutted down the hall, she glanced at her gold designer watch. It was almost lunchtime and she contemplated what she wanted to eat. Her appetite hadn't been up to par lately. It was awfully funny, but true. Whenever she and Sloan bickered, it seemed as if the world was falling apart. *That's just crazy*, she mused with a shake of her head. She turned the corner of the hall and ran smack-dab into six feet of Hershey-colored Derrick Perkins. Her nostrils sucked in his manly fragrance as she struggled to steady herself.

"Uh…Please excuse me. I should have been paying attention," she stammered.

"No damage here," Derrick said in his baritone voice. A small smile crossed Natasha's face. "Do you mind if I ask where you were going in such a hurry?" Derrick asked, peering into her hazel eyes.

Clearing her throat, she uttered, "Well, I was on my way to lunch." Natasha took a step back while inhaling Derrick's sexiness, which made her a little dizzy. It had been a long time since a man had had that kind of effect on her. Derrick looked quickly at his Rolex.

"It certainly is that time." With a playful grin, he asked, "Are you dining alone?"

Natasha's eyelids fluttered. "I am."

"Well, I'll be happy to join you Miss…"

"Natasha Jacobs, and please, just call me Natasha."

"Alright, Natasha. Do you have a particular place in mind?"

Natasha's mind rushed for an answer. *Where can I dine with this fine man? It has to be someplace nice.* "How about the Olive Garden?" she blurted out.

"Sounds good to me," Derrick said, flashing a sexy smile as they headed out the exit door.

Sloan stood beside the water cooler, paper cup in hand. He crushed the empty cup and threw it in the trash. He'd heard their conversation and wasn't happy about it. Natasha and Derrick were so engrossed in each other, they hadn't even noticed he was only a feet away.

He watched the happy couple as they whizzed by, and he decided to follow them. From the office window, Sloan kept them in his view as they crossed the parking lot. A twinge of jealousy tugged at his heart, but was quickly replaced with anger because he had been on his way to Natasha's desk to ask her to lunch. A few minutes earlier, and it would have been his ride she was getting into. They hadn't spoken in days, and he was ready to end the feud between them. He didn't know why, but he felt the urge to follow them—and he did. Sloan walked briskly to his SUV and hopped in. Seated in the restaurant, Natasha noticed the many stares from other young female patrons nearby. They looked at Derrick like kids in a candy store. Natasha picked up the menu and scanned the items. Suddenly, her appetite returned with a passion.

"Order whatever you like, beautiful, the meal is on me," Derrick's uttered in a sexy voice.

After their orders were placed, Natasha and Derrick engaged in deep conversation. Derrick filled her in on his heyday as a highly-sought-after football player. After three years, his career had come to an unexpected end. A knee injury may have ended his football career, but he never stopped believing in himself. He went on to get his MBA degree.

As Natasha sipped her iced tea, he told her about his two older brothers. One was an accountant, and the other was an assistant principal at a junior high school. His parents were also well educated. His father owned his own construction business, and his mother ran a beauty school. Natasha was impressed with Mr. Perkins's background. Derrick had a pleasant personality and she found herself laughing an awful lot. He had a way of making her feel right at home, and his affectionate laugh warmed her heart. For the very first time that day, Natasha had forgotten all about her feud with Sloan.

"So, Natasha, are you busy tomorrow?" Derrick's copper-colored eyes seemed to peer deep into her soul as he waited for her response. Natasha found herself quivering under his spell.

"Um...tomorrow...I, uh, I mean." Natasha lightly hit the top of her head with her palm. "I don't know where my mind went to," she said, slightly embarrassed. "Yes, I am busy. We are having a pool party tomorrow. Sloan didn't invite you?" Natasha asked with a puzzled look.

Derrick's eyebrows rose. "Are you the best friend he was telling me about?" Derrick said with a smile. Natasha nodded.

Natasha's smile held firm. "I can only imagine how it feels to be new in town with no close friends."

"Well, that is very nice of you both. I most definitely will be there, and I am honored to be a friend of yours."

Derrick placed his large hand over Natasha's small one. A spark of fire ran through Natasha's body. She found this man so captivating, and she wanted to know more. What had started out as a simple lunch turned out to be a beautiful meal.

Unbeknownst to the couple, Sloan was seated a few tables away. He was boiling in his seat like a pot of clams. He watched the smooth moves Derrick laid on Natasha. Touching hands was his opener, but Sloan knew there was more to come.

What kind of fool does he think Natasha is? Sloan wondered angrily. She wasn't going to be just another notch on Derrick's belt if he had anything to do with it. Sloan was very aware of the itinerary of guys like Derrick Perkins. After all, he used to be one of them. He thought about his little black book and how he had women categorized like the letters of the alphabet. He even placed gold stars by the names of the ones who were the best in bed, like a kindergarten teacher handing out grades. Yes, he was one who played the game and did it well. Sloan's eyes narrowed as he watched the couple leave their table. Derrick's hand was positioned in the small of Natasha's back as they left the restaurant. Sloan let out an uneven breath as he held his menu in front of his face. He needed to have a serious talk with his best friend, and this day couldn't end soon enough.

ESSENCE

Essence lit a scented candle and allowed the fragrance of vanilla bean and jasmine flowers to fill the air. Soft, mellow music played in the background. She sauntered through her elegant and spacious living room, making her way to her master bedroom. She had already indulged in a luxurious bubble bath. Her skin felt like smooth satin through the sheer-pink loungewear that adorned her delicate frame. Essence wrapped her arms around her body and closed her eyes. She couldn't wait for Sloan to feel this body of hers. She was sure that once he did, he wouldn't be able to let it go. It had been a long time since she'd felt so much passion for a man. Sloan was the youngest man she had ever fallen for, and his age didn't bother her one bit. Sloan may have been younger, but he was very intellectual. He possessed all the qualities she wanted in a man, and his finesse was measureless. Men were an emotional high for Essence. They were like a drug she craved. But what carried her to newfound heights was taking them away from the women in their lives. She loved the moment when she prevailed over the younger woman whose man had fallen prey to her beauty. This made her feel as though she'd exacted revenge upon all the men that had ever left their women for a young powder-puff chick. *Talk about reverse psychology.*

Essence sat down at her Shepherd vanity table and peered in the mirror. She admired her natural, wholesome beauty. At forty-five, her face was flawless. There wasn't a wrinkle in sight, and thanks to her Botox treatments, there never would be. A pleasant smile formed on her lips. Getting attention from younger men had never been a problem for her. With her outward beauty and sophisticated style, younger men practically fell at her feet. Her mind reflected back to Brandon, a man from her past, who appeared before her like a haunting dream. Their relationship had ended a few months before. Thinking back, she remembered how she had taken him away from his young wife. *What a pathetic little thing she was,*

Essence thought as a giggle escaped her lips. That wife thought her young beauty and hour-glass figure were enough to keep him. When Essence cast her intoxicating spell, no man could resist her. Brandon fell into her web and practically crawled out of his bedroom window in the wee hours of the morning just to be with her. She kept him under her spell until she'd had enough of him. Letting out a sigh, Essence picked up a bottle of Queen Perfume by Queen Latifah and sprayed it gently behind each ear.

I am a queen, she thought as she fluttered her long dark lashes. Memories of Brandon still lingered in the back of her mind. After he'd left his wife and married her, they were happy for a while. He had given her everything she wanted, but then he began to smother her with his love. He was possessive, insecure, and demanding of her attention. Maybe it was his inexperience. After all, she was ten years older than him. In any case, it became boring for her and she wanted out. She needed something new to rock her world. She felt as if she had conquered him and now it was time to move on.

After two weeks of planning, her clothes were packed, movers were hired, and her plane ticket was stashed in her purse. She left Brandon with nothing more than a golden teddy bear holding a Hallmark greeting card displaying a broken heart. The teddy bear sat on the king-size bed which she had decided to let him keep. It was the least she could do; there were so many hot memories of the sweet love they had made in that bed.

Essence glanced up at her bedroom clock. Sloan would be arriving within the hour. She leapt up and went back into the kitchen. She opened the stainless steel door of her oven and checked on the casserole she was preparing. It was almost ready. *Just like my smooth, satin skin,* she thought as she imagined Sloan's full lips ravishing her body.

NATASHA

"Okay, okay, I'm coming already!" Natasha yelled as she made her way to her front door. Her wet hair was wrapped in a pink turban. She had just finished rinsing the conditioner out of it when her doorbell chimed.

"This better be good," she uttered as she placed one of her eyes over the peephole. She recognized the chest of curly hairs. It was all she could see of the tall frame of her best friend, Sloan. She flung the door open and stood in a stance with her hands placed on her hips and her lips held tightly.

Natasha sputtered, "Why in the heck are you ringing my doorbell like you're the police?"

Sloan didn't bother to respond; instead he brushed past her and headed into the living room. Throwing up her arms, she followed him with a scowl.

"Answer me, Sloan. What's going on?" she asked as they faced each other.

As Sloan stared into her hazel eyes, he promised himself he was going to remain cool. Two hot-headed people couldn't put out a fire if they wanted to, so he had chosen to remain cool once he arrived at her place.

"I should be asking you that very same question," Sloan responded in an even tone.

Natasha stared at him with a blank expression. With a frown, she said, "I don't have an inkling of what you're talking about."

Sloan shook his head. "Oh, yes, I think you do," he said taking a seat on her plush sofa.

Natasha followed suit. "Sloan, have you lost a piece of your mind on your way over here? And I don't appreciate you ringing my bell like that," she said with pursed lips.

"Natasha, will you just forget about that dumb doorbell and tell me what the hell were you thinking?"

Natasha's eyes widened at Sloan's outburst. He was clearly upset with her, and she didn't even know why. What had she done to upset him so? Staring back at him, she opened her mouth to speak, but was interrupted by another outburst.

"Derrick Perkins is not the kind of man you should be hanging around," he practically shouted.

Natasha's face was a question mark. "Now, wait a minute. I thought we both agreed to get to know him and Miss Kirkland. They're the reason we're having this pool party, remember. And you haven't done a cotton-picking thing to help me," she spat as she folded her arms. "Wonder why on earth that is, Sloan?" Natasha's face held a skeptical look as she waited for Sloan to respond. He attempted to speak, but Natasha held out her hands. "Don't even try to get out of this one, buddy. I know you've been spending most of your free time with Essence, and yet you have the audacity to come up in here and school me on Derrick. Oh, no," Natasha spouted with a roll of her head. "You need to check yourself before you wreck yourself, my friend."

Sloan reached out and grabbed her hand. His touch sent warm sparks through her body. "Natasha, you got to listen to me. Derrick is not the one for you. He's a playa and I don't want you to end up being played."

"Takes one to know one, doesn't it?" Natasha said, snatching her hand out of his. Sloan grimaced at her statement.

"Please, Me-Me. I'm telling you what I know. The man is bad news when it comes to relationships." Sloan's voice softened as his eyes stared into hers.

Natasha couldn't stand his stare anymore. She diverted her eyes.

"Where is all this coming from, Sloan?" Natasha shrugged her shoulders. "I've only seen the man a handful of times at the office."

Sloan cupped her chin. "Natasha, I saw you with him today…at Olive Garden."

Natasha's eyebrows lifted, and she stood up angrily.

"You were spying on me? How dare you, Sloan? You had no right!"

"I have every right. You are my best friend, and I'm not going to let you get hurt again," he said as he stood as well.

"I'm a big girl, Sloan. I can take care of myself," Natasha insisted. "And since you are all up in my Kool-Aid, what is the story on you and Mrs. Robinson?"

Sloan dropped his head. He knew where this was going.

Natasha placed her hands back on her hips. "Oh, I see now," she said shaking her head, "It's cool for you to jump her old bones, but you want me to sit on the sidelines and watch you have your fun."

"It's not like that, Natasha."

"Oh…so you're not sleeping with her. Is that really what you want me to believe?" Natasha challenged.

"Yes, because it is the truth. Me-Me, I'm tired of the game, bedding woman after woman." Sloan shook his head. "It's getting old and I want something deeper. I need something more meaningful. I told you all this before, and I'm sticking to it."

Sloan grabbed Natasha by her arms and sat her back down on the couch. He sat next to her and looked into her hazel eyes.

"Let's call it a truce, Me-Me. I don't like it when we fight this way. I miss you, girl."

He gave her his heart-stopping smile, and she couldn't help but reciprocate. At this moment, her heart was tugging at her to tell him how she truly felt about him. Oh, how she wanted to taste those sweet lips of his and tell him her true feelings, but her head wouldn't let her. Sloan was her childhood friend, her make-believe brother, and her play cousin. There were so many titles, and none included the word, lover. Before she knew what was happening, Sloan pulled her into his arms. He took her moment of silence as a peace treaty. Natasha held onto him. It felt so good to be in his arms, even if it was just as a friend. Sloan let her go while his face held a brilliant smile.

"I'm glad we had this talk, Me-Me. I feel so much better now. And you're wrong about the party. I have done my share. I've invited a slew of guys and girls already. I hired a slamming DJ, and I will be here an hour before the party starts," he said as he headed for the door. "Later," he yelled over his shoulder.

Sloan had to leave because Essence was expecting him; but he wasn't about to tell Natasha that. He was sure she was going to take his advice about Derrick Perkins and stay away from him, and that was all that mattered right now.

Natasha heard her front door close. She curled her legs underneath her and allowed a silent tear to slide slowly down her golden cheek. Her mother and Gretta had been right all along. Those private feelings for Sloan Stevens were as deep as the ocean, and she would never tell them to anyone—ever.

ESSENCE

At seven o'clock, Essence's doorbell chimed. Her dinner date had arrived. The long, flowing aqua-colored skirt danced around her ankles as she made her way to the door. Sloan stood on the other side, looking scrumptious in his tan polo shirt. It had a few buttons undone, exposing a mass of curly hair that she couldn't wait to run her fingers through.

"Come on in, sweetie," she cooed as she stepped aside.

"Something sure smells good," Sloan commented as he made his way into the living room.

Essence tilted her head and chuckled, "I'm sure you will enjoy every morsel, if you know what I mean."

Sloan took in the seductive gaze Essence gave him. He cleared his throat, bending his tall frame as Essence ushered him to have a seat. He sank into the plush, crème-colored Italian sofa.

"I'll be right back. Just make yourself at home," she uttered as she strutted out of the room.

Sloan took in the sight of the huge living room. He admired the pieces of art that adorned the ecru walls. There were also black porcelain figurines posing in different positions placed all over the room. One photo in particular caught his eye. Sloan eased his way over to a photo of a black couple with brown skin. *That's strange,* Sloan thought as he stared at the picture. The couple could have been him and Essence. Their features were so similar. They were naked, in a sexual embrace; engraved in the frame was the title, "The Nakedness of Love."

"So, you like?" Essence said, startling him.

Sloan turned to face her. She handed him a glass of white wine. Taking it, he uttered, "Yes, very much so."

Essence smiled. Waving her hand around, she said, "Well, as you can see, I'm a collector. Whenever I travel abroad, I always carry an empty suitcase for the pieces I'm sure I will find." She escorted him back to the sofa. "So, how was your day?" Essence asked, setting her glass on a wooden coaster on the glass coffee table.

"Well, truthfully, kind of hectic. I'm working hard on landing a contract I've been after for a few weeks now. S & J is a prominent business, and having them on board would be a great advantage for Emerson & Stuckey; and a great bonus coming my way, if I may add." Sloan chuckled lightly.

Essence smiled as she leaned back into the sofa. "I stopped by your office today at lunch time, but you had already left, and in quite a hurry according to your secretary. She said she saw you leaving the building. Was everything okay?"

Sloan's mind traveled back to seeing Natasha and Derrick and following them out of the building. "Uh um…yes, I was in a hurry. I was on my way to meet with Mr. Jordon from S & J. Lunch was the only available time he had," Sloan lied. He wanted to move away from the topic. Touching Essence's hand, he asked, "Are we still on for tomorrow? I remembered you said something about purchasing a bathing suit."

Essence's eyes lit up. "Yes, we most certainly are, and I did purchase that suit," she uttered with a sexy smile. "I can't wait for you to see me in it. Maybe I can give you a private showing after dinner."

Sloan swore the temperature in the room rose a few degrees. He was amazed at the woman who sat before him. She was meticulous about making smooth moves—and he'd thought he held the title of the ultimate playa.

Sloan devoured the meal before him. Essence was almost as good a cook as Natasha, and Natasha could burn. After all, she'd learned from the best; Mama Florene could rattle some pots like an expert. Sloan remembered so many lazy Sunday dinners at Mama Florene's. He had spent so much time at their home that he was like a piece of furniture. Mama Florene welcomed him into her home the first day he and Natasha had become friends.

When he'd met Natasha, he and his sister were the new kids in the neighborhood. Their parents had just moved from Memphis after his father landed a higher-paying job with a hefty bonus. Sloan loved the tree-lined streets and manicured lawns of the modest homes. It was a far cry from the three-bedroom apartment back in Memphis, where the only place he and his sister could play outside was the park about six blocks away, and his mother would never allow them to go there by themselves. There were too many bullies in the neighborhood. They were known to make playtime anything but playful. But in their new neighborhood of upper-class people, they could practically run free without fear.

Sloan's parents had bought him a new blue bike a few weeks after moving, and he loved riding it. Actually, the bike was responsible for how he and Natasha had met. Sloan had just circled the neighborhood for the second time when he noticed a red-haired, freckle-faced girl on her red bike. She was humming along when her bike suddenly hit a bump in the road, and down she went. Sloan remembered jumping off his bike and running toward the fallen little girl.

"Are you okay?" he asked. His tall, lanky frame loomed over her like a tall oak tree. Sloan held out his hand and helped her up. Natasha's hazel eyes filled with tears as she looked down at her skinned knee. Sloan looked at the bloody, scraped knee as she sobbed.

"Where do you live?" he asked.

Between sobs, she uttered, "Down the street." Her brown pigtails hung loosely from her head as she pointed.

"Come on, I'll get your bike and take you home."

"What about your bike?" she asked, looking over at the curb where Sloan had hopped off it.

"Oh, it will be okay. It won't take me long to get back to it." Sloan was secretly hoping no one would bother it. He could envision his father's infuriated expression, and he could feel the backside-burning beating he would surely have to endure if anything happened to the bike. But it didn't matter to him right now.

The freckle-faced girl smiled at him, and even though one of her front teeth was missing, Sloan thought she was very pretty. When they arrived at her home, Sloan was amazed at how the wrap-around porch gave it an old-fashioned appearance. As they trotted up the walkway, the girl's mother came sailing out. She barely noticed Sloan as he held her bike. The red-headed girl explained to her mother what had happened. With a smile on her face, she finally recognized the lanky kid that had come to her daughter's rescue. He was invited in for milk and cookies. It was then that he learned the little, red-headed girl's name was Natasha Jacobs. The rest, as they say, is history. He and Natasha spent most of their time together as they grew up. They shared life's ups and downs as they entered adulthood. They were best friends, and until this day, nothing had threatened to change that.

"Sloan, where did you go?" Essence asked with an impatient stare.

Sloan blinked. "Sorry, what were you saying now?"

Essence pursed her lips. "Evidently, it wasn't important enough for you to continue listening."

"Essence, I apologize again," Sloan said sincerely. "My mind just drifted back into the windows of time. But I remember, now. We were talking about one of your old friends whom you lost contact with, and it made me think of my childhood friend and how we had met."

Essence's eyes darkened. "That wouldn't happen to be Miss Jacobs, now would it?"

A weird smile formed across Sloan's lips. You would have thought the man had a million dollars stashed away from the expression on his face. "It certainly was," Sloan acquiesced.

"Well, as I was saying," Essence continued with a little irritation in her voice. Essence folded her hands as she spoke. "My friend and I eventually became lovers."

Sloan's eyebrows lifted. He had not been aware that she was talking about a male friend. Essence noticed the surprised look on his face. She definitely had his attention now. "It was awesome in the beginning." Her face was beaming at the memory. And just as quickly as it brightened, it dimmed. With a tight look, Essence uttered, "But it soon fizzled."

"Oh," Sloan responded, taking another sip of his wine.

"Yes, those kinds of relationships never work out, you know. Friends that become lovers cross a line, which leads to disaster," Essence said solemnly.

Suddenly, Sloan's mood began to change. He thought this subject needed to be dropped in a hurry. Sloan was about to steer the conversation in a different direction when Essence interjected.

"So, have you and Natasha ever been lovers?" Sloan nearly tipped over his glass of wine as he

reached for it. He steadied the glass and met Essence's inquiring stare. Sleeping with Natasha had not only crossed his mind on several occasions, but he couldn't count the times he'd dreamt about it as well. Natasha was a beautiful woman inside and out, and he would have to be blind and crazy not to see that. But she was not only a friend, she was his best friend, and he would never let those feelings rise to the surface. The feelings that told him he loved her more than a friend and perhaps even a—

"What's wrong, sugar? Did the cat steal your tongue?" Essence chuckled lightly. She enjoyed seeing Sloan sweat.

"No…your question just threw me, that's all," he lamented. Clearing his throat, he said, "I've…never thought of Natasha in that kind of light. We've been like family for so many years. I couldn't imagine us…doing something harried."

Sloan took the glass of wine and finished its contents with one sip. His nerves were now frazzled. Essence's eyes never left his face. *How easily men can lie*, she thought. But it didn't matter. Sloan would be all hers.

"Let's change the subject, okay." Sloan returned the intense stare she was giving him.

"Well, if talking about you and your best friend being lovers makes you so uncomfortable, I guess it would be best to change the subject," she said to pacify him.

"Wait a minute. Why do you think talking about Natasha and me sleeping together makes me uncomfortable?" Sloan spoke with more control than he felt.

"Looking at your demeanor tells it all, sugar," Essence responded as she folded her arms. "If you could see the expression on your face…it's as if I caught you two in bed together."

"Now, that's ridiculous." Sloan grimaced. He felt a twinge of anger rising within him. How did she even go there? She knew nothing about his and Natasha's lives. Sloan fought to hold his composure. "Essence, I want to change the subject because I don't like where this conversation is heading. Natasha is my best friend, and I have the utmost respect for her." Sloan's voice became stern. "I don't like anyone thinking sleazy thoughts about our relationship, do you feel me?"

Essence knew she had stepped on his sore spot. She had to bring back the pleasantness he'd had when he had first walked in the door if she expected to have him in her bed that night. She stood and draped her arms around his broad shoulders as he remained in his chair. She placed a kiss on the tip of his earlobe, followed by tender kisses on his neck and cheek.

She began to massage his shoulders; she hoped her gestures would relieve the stress she had caused.

"I feel you, sugar, and I would like to feel even more of you. Follow me upstairs," she purred.

Sloan felt the tension being drained from his body. His manhood was ready for action as Essence's soft kisses continued. But he was determined to do things differently this time. He slowly pushed her away and stood. Peering down into her pretty face, he uttered, "As tempting as it sounds, I must decline." Sloan grabbed his linen jacket from the cherry wingback chair. Essence followed him with a blank look on her face. He saw the disappointment in her eyes. "I think I better get going." He turned away from her.

That's right, the playa of the year turned down what he knew would have been the hottest booty call he'd had in a very long time. He remembered what his Uncle Leroy had told him years ago: *a man's substance is his word.* And he was adamant about sticking to his, even if it meant a lot of cold showers.

DERRICK

Placing his black swim shorts into his designer duffle bag, Derrick chuckled to himself. Never in a million years would Derrick Perkins, a man whose social events had led him to dining with the upper-crust members of society, ever have imagined being invited to a pool party. His itinerary usually consisted of elegant balls and black-tie events. A pool party had never been on his list of exciting things to do, but something intriguing piqued his interest, and her name was Natasha Jacobs.

The woman had left a lasting impression, giving him a desire to get to know her more intimately. He found her to be unlike any woman he had met before. There was something special about her. He could feel it. Derrick considered himself an expert on women. He'd had his share; he'd even married one he cared to forget. After that experience, he kept his heart at a distance. Choosing to play the field had kept him sane; or maybe it was a drug that numbed him. Whatever it was, it kept his life interesting. Speaking of his free spirit, one of his playmates was calling. He pulled his cell from its holder and answered.

"Hello, Connie, baby. What's up?"

"Hey, Derrick, what happened to you yesterday? I thought we were supposed to be spending the day together?"

"Connie, baby, I got busy."

"Too busy for me?" she crooned.

"Now, baby, you know me better than that. But dude has to make his money, or else he wouldn't be able to take his baby out." Derrick chuckled. He didn't get a response. "Connie, you know I never stopped *thinking* about you, girl." His voice was smooth and seductive, just like his women loved it.

"Well, how about putting some of that *thinking* in action and bring that chocolate body of yours over here," Connie retorted. Derrick peered at his Rolex.

"Mmmm, can't do it right now, babe. I got a meeting in a half an hour."

He heard sucking of teeth on the other end of the phone line. "Here we go again," Connie remarked.

Derrick popped a mint into his mouth. "Look, baby, I will make this up to you. Tell you what…I will try to end this meeting as soon as possible and maybe we can have a late dinner and a sex-filled night, if you know what I mean," he said in a lower octave.

"You mean it, Derrick?"

Derrick rolled his head impatiently. He wanted to get this chick off the phone, so he could be on his merry way. "Yes, babe, I mean it. So, I'll hit you later."

Derrick heard Connie's soft giggles. He knew she was pleased. "Well, alright, Derrick. I'll be waiting," she said before hanging up.

Another satisfied customer, he thought as he pushed the end button on his cell phone and picked up his car keys. "Pool Party, here I come" he popped as he headed out the door.

NATASHA

It was Saturday and Natasha woke to a room drenched with sunlight. The sound of birds chirping filled the air. This was nature's way of telling her it was going to be a beautiful day; at least that's what she hoped. Her nerves were a little frazzled as she swung her legs off the bed, stretching long and hard. Her sleep hadn't been the best due to dreams of all that could go wrong today. She still had not received a call from Sloan. She took off her nighty and headed to the bathroom. Just as she stepped out of the shower and wrapped the candy-striped bath towel around her wet body, her phone rang. Expecting it to be her best friend, she uttered in a tight voice as she picked up the phone, "Sloan, what happened to you last night?"

"Sorry, but I'm not Sloan," Gretta quipped.

Natasha could have kicked herself for not looking at the caller ID before answering. Now she would have to deal with Gretta's interrogation.

"What happened between you two? And don't you dare say it's nothing. I heard the irritation in your voice when you answered the phone."

Natasha flopped down on her bed and exhaled. She was caught like a deer in headlights.

"Okay, Gretta, but really it's nothing," she said with a shake of her head. "Sloan and I had a small disagreement about something, and he was supposed to give me a call last night. I guess…something must have come up. But it's no big deal," Natasha said lightly. She hoped Gretta would just let it go. *How ironic*, Natasha thought to herself, *If only I could do the same.* There was silence on the other end of the phone. She wasn't so sure Gretta was buying her explanation.

Finally, Gretta exclaimed, "If you say so, cousin."

"Well, what do you want, Gretta? It's mighty early in the morning for you to be calling."

"Naw, I was just checking on you, cousin. I wanted to see if you had everything under control for the party. It's been quite a while since you done any entertaining?" Gretta pointed out.

"Yeah, girl, you're right about that," Natasha said as she curled her legs up under her. "Darin was always the one to throw the elaborate parties."

"Yeah, and the man had such a flair for entertaining. People chatted for days about the good times they had at the parties you all threw. Too bad Darin's extra activities got out of hand, if you know what I mean," Gretta said, chuckling.

"You know, you're not helping me here." Natasha sighed as she placed her hand atop her forehead.

"Sorry, cousin. I know you going to have the same success with your party. You said yourself that Sloan got the best DJ in the city, so that's half of it right there. And I'll be over in an hour to help you with the food. So, you see, we got it all together, cousin. Don't worry about a thing," Gretta chirped happily. "Thanks, Gretta," Natasha said with a slight smile. "Wait a minute, now. I hope you remembered to invite some unattached, good-looking dudes."

Natasha's smile grew wide. Gretta was all into the finest of the barrel. Too bad she seemed to always come up with the bottom of it.

"Gretta, there will be enough dudes for you to mingle with, alright."

"See you soon," Gretta said, hanging up.

Natasha selected a black-and-white bikini set. Holding it up, she scrutinized the outfit. She must admit that she had the body for it. But did she have the self-esteem to wear it? Since her split from Darin, she found herself second- guessing the simplest things. The man had left her feeling as if she didn't measure up anymore.

Natasha turned to her bedroom window. There was a red bird chirping in the birdhouse in her backyard. Darin had bought the birdhouse a week after they moved into this extravagant home. Everywhere she looked, her view was tainted with memories of him. Why did he cheat? Didn't she give him enough attention? Enough love? Was it her fault? *No,* she concluded, *I'm not going to accept the blame.* Taking another look at the bikini, she decided she was going to wear it, after all. Thinking of Derrick, she smiled. It was time for her to start living again.

POOL PARTY

The party was on. The DJ, Froggy Style, was mixing his tunes. He had a variety of selections from the oldies to present-day jams. Natasha's guests had arrived, and it looked as if everyone was having a good time. Her eyes traveled over to her cousin, Gretta. She was a petite woman with a full figure. Her copper-brown skin glowed in the sunlight and her red, white, and blue bikini was drawing a lot of attention from the single men that floated around. And from listening to her cousin's giggling sounds as she enjoyed the conversation of one of the male guests, Natasha knew she was having a good time, as well.

She turned to see Derrick Perkins heading her way. Her heart skipped a thundering beat as she took in his solid six-pack, firm thighs, and dazzling white smile. The man could have replaced Michael Jordan in the Hanes underwear commercials. Out of the corner of her eye, she saw Sloan. He stepped out of the pool and walked over to the DJ. His muscular frame caught the attention of a group of women sitting by the pool. Natasha didn't recognize any of the women, but she felt the same admiration for him as he walked by as they did. She looked back and forth between the two men. Two handsome men, two sexy bodies…and she was attracted to them both.

"Stop this madness," she muttered under her breath.

"Stop what?" Lisa Ray asked as she and Derrick approached Natasha at almost the same time. Lisa Ray was holding a bottle of Gray Goose vodka.

"Nice party." Derrick smiled as his gaze traveled between the two women.

"Thanks, Derrick, and I'm glad you could make it," Natasha addressed him first, and then she turned her attention to her friend. "I uh…was just giving myself a small pat on the back. I can't believe the turnout," Natasha said as she scanned the growing crowd. "Excuse my manners."

Natasha smiled as Lisa Ray gave her a gentle nudge in her side. Lisa Ray felt invisible standing between Natasha and Derrick.

"Derrick, this is my friend and coworker, Lisa Ray Downs. You may have seen her at Emerson & Stuckey." Derrick peered into Lisa Ray's eyes and smiled. "Yes, I certainly have. I never forget a beautiful face," he flirted.

Natasha felt a twinge of jealousy, which she knew had no bearings. She had no claims on this man. Only a lunch date had transpired between them.

"So, Derrick, are you enjoying yourself?" Lisa Ray asked, basking in his attention.

Derrick turned his gaze to Natasha. "I must tell you, Natasha, I was a little hesitant to attend a pool party. I haven't been to one of these things since my college days," he relinquished.

Natasha picked up on the insinuation in his voice and, needless to say, it irritated her. *Who does this man think he is…President Obama?* Natasha wondered, *Does he think he is too good to socialize with me and my friends?* Her mind shouted as her mouth spoke, "Oh really?" Natasha mused.

Derrick also noticed the coolness in Natasha's voice. "Oh no, please don't misunderstand," he said smoothly. "The party is cool…It's just that the events I have attended have been a bit more sophisticated in nature. You know, black-tie events," he said with a fortified smile.

Natasha raised one brow. *How arrogant of him,* she mused.

"But this is good, really. Would you like to join me for a swim?" Derrick asked, taking in Natasha's gorgeous figure. Lisa Ray gave Natasha a *you-better-go-before-I-do* look.

"Maybe later," Natasha muttered with a turn of her shoulder.

Derrick's ego was a little bruised. He wasn't used to women turning him down. "Well, what about you, Lisa?"

Lisa Ray looked at Natasha like a child waiting for permission. "Go on, enjoy yourself," Natasha said with a fake smile pasted on her face.

Natasha watched as Derrick showed off in the pool. You would have thought he was trying out for the Olympics from the way he swam with such swanlike grace. The laughter coming from the couple was making Natasha ill as she watched Lisa Ray and Derrick playing with each other in the water. He had such an enormous ego. If he didn't want to come to her pool party, he sure as hell didn't have to, but his actions suggested he was enjoying himself and the attention. Natasha walked away, past a group of male guests. She recognized one from the office, and the other two must have been Sloan's buddies. The tall, slender one, with a short-cropped haircut, gave Natasha an appealing smile. She waved politely as she strutted her stuff.

"Nice bathing suit!" he yelled out, which made her blush with confidence. She was glad she'd made the choice to wear the two piece after all.

Natasha scanned the patio area; the pool was in the middle of the backyard and had a large gazebo with tree lights all around it. Memories of the moonlit nights she and Darin had shared came flooding back to the forefront of her mind. She took a deep breath and shook her head as if to shake the memories away. She refused to let them spoil her perfect day. As she continued toward the gazebo, she saw Sloan and Ricky with their backs turned; oblivious to her presence. She listened quietly as they rambled away.

"Yeah, man, I mean everything was set. Candlelit dinner, soft music playing, and an open invitation to her bed loomed before me like a carrot in front of a rabbit." With a swaggering look, Sloan uttered, "Or should I say, that sexy body of hers was just calling me as R. Kelly sang." Both men broke out into thunderous laughter.

Stopping to catch his breath, Ricky asked, "Now, tell me, man, did you hit it? And if you did, what's her rating?"

Sloan tilted his head and smile widely. "You think I'm really going to tell you all that?"

"Come on, man, you know I ain't ever hit it with an older woman before. Tell me, is the meat as tender?" Ricky hedged.

Natasha gasped as she placed her hand over her mouth. She knew who they were referring to. *And to think, Sloan almost swore to me that he wasn't sleeping with the cougar,* she thought. "Men," she uttered bitterly to herself.

Were women really just pieces of meat for them to obtain and devour like wild animals? She wondered how she ever could have thought that Sloan would be any different from the rest. Yes, he was her best friend, but he was also still a man. She had heard enough. She turned quickly on her heels and ran smack-dab into the hanging plant on the side of her deck. The plant came down with a thud, attracting the men's attention.

"Natasha, where are you going?" Sloan asked as she turned to face them. "Come on back and join us. We're just shooting the breeze, as they said back in the day."

Natasha scanned their boyish faces. She wondered how they could be so insensitive when it came to women. "I think I'll pass," she uttered in a cold tone.

Sloan stretched out his hand. "So, what's up? Do you need me for something?" Sloan asked, noticing her chilly demeanor.

Natasha pivoted a little closer, giving him a smug look. "No, not really, but your date might be wondering where you are. I saw her at the pool a few minutes ago, she looked like a little lost puppy." Natasha stared at Sloan with a mischievous grin. "Maybe she's out of her territory, you know… being with the younger crowd and all." Natasha raised her eyebrows with each word; she knew she was getting under Sloan's skin.

Sloan jumped off the gazebo deck and headed in her direction. Closing the distance between them, he asked, "What's the deal, Me-Me? And why are you taking cracks at Essence? She's not the only older person here."

Natasha tilted her head and looked over to the pool area. "Oh, are you referring to the bartender over there? Yes, I think they are around the same age," she chuckled sarcastically.

"Well, since you're in the joking mood…where is Mr. Game Machine? Don't tell me he's found some new players already."

Natasha shot him a dirty look and started to walk briskly away. Sloan caught her by the arm and spun her around. If folks didn't know better, because of their actions, people would have thought there was a fight brewing between a husband and wife.

"Me-Me, let's not do this here. Anyway, I thought everything was straight between us. What's with the attitude?" Sloan asked as he peered into her eyes searching for answers to her erratic behavior.

Natasha was hesitant to answer. She could feel the burn of Ricky's stare on them. At the same time, another couple was heading toward the gazebo. She concluded that making a scene would not be wise. Natasha gave Sloan one of her prettiest smiles, dropping the attitude that swelled inside of her. "I'm sorry, Sloan. I guess I'm just overreacting. You know, this is the first party I've had in a long time. My nerves are a little frazzled. I was up half the night worrying how this thing would turn out," Natasha rambled.

"The party is a success, Me-Me," Sloan said, taking in the full view of her body. And what a body it was. *She could easily be one of those models on the cover of Sports Illustrated*, he thought to himself.

Natasha picked up on the vibes between them right away, because as Sloan surveyed her from head to toe, she was staring at his bare six-pack and muscular physique. They hadn't seen each other with this limited amount of clothing on in quite some time, and they both couldn't help but stare.

Sloan quickly diverted his eyes away from Natasha's firm chest, which seemed to be beckoning his attention.

"Um…well, I better get back to my guests," Natasha stammered as she walked away.

"Sure," Sloan uttered. He walked back to where Ricky was standing and let out a low breath. "That girl can be mind boggling at times," he chuckled.

"That girl got the hots for you, man," Ricky quipped with wide eyes.

Sloan waved his hand. "Get out of here with that, man. You know me and Natasha go way back. She's my best friend, dude."

"Uh huh, and I'm your long lost son, right?" Ricky responded.

"Man, you don't know what you talking about," Sloan muttered as they headed back to the party.

"I might not know what I'm talking about, but I sure know what I see; and that home girl right there is feeling you." Ricky laughed.

The temperature around the pool began to drop, giving way to the setting of the sun. A cool breeze kissed Natasha's cheeks as she sat upon the lounge chair, sipping her drink. But her feelings were heating up as her eyes stayed glued to Essence and Sloan while they danced to the slow jam of Brian McKnight. The woman was grinding into Sloan like she hadn't been laid in years. A slight chuckle escaped from her throat. *Maybe Miss Cougar hasn't felt a pipe in years,* Natasha thought as she felt a slight tap on her shoulder. Turning, she looked into the handsome face of Derrick.

"May I have this dance, or will you diss me again?" Derrick asked in a deep, sexy tone.

After taking a quick look over at the couple in heat, Natasha said, "Why not?"

If Sloan was having such a good time, why shouldn't she? Derrick took

Natasha in his arms, and they swayed to the mellow sounds of jazz music that the DJ was playing. She had to admit, being in Derrick's arms felt really good. She rested her head in the crook of his shoulder, allowing herself to relax. Derrick was feeling her as well. Natasha's body was soft and smooth like a newborn baby. They fit together like a hand in a glove as he held her close. There were several other couples also swaying to the music, but Derrick felt as if he and Natasha were in a world of their very own.

Sloan had to admit that Essence was a remarkable woman and a persistent one at that. She had been chasing him around all day, and he should have been flattered by her attention. After all, Essence was absolutely stunning in her two-piece, navy blue, polka dot swimsuit. Her beautiful coffee-colored body was in perfect shape to dare such a risk and pull it off with ease. But somehow, being out with friends his own age, especially women friends, gave him an uneasy feeling as if he was a gigolo of sorts. No, it wasn't that way at all. Maybe it was the remark Natasha had made earlier about Essence being out of her territory that was rattling around in his mind.

Sloan came out of his trance when he felt Essence's hands cupping his buttocks, giving them a gentle squeeze. The woman was sizzling like eggs on a grill. Temptation was slowly getting the best of him. How much more could a red-blooded man take? If he didn't do something now, he and Essence would be turning the party into a freak show. He stopped dancing abruptly, catching Essence off guard.

"What's wrong, sugar?" she asked with a puzzled look.

"I…uh, need a drink," Sloan murmured as he headed for the bar.

He ordered a drink and gulped the shot down as fast as the bartender could pour it. Essence was right on his heels and slid into the vacant barstool beside him. She nodded to the bartender to pour her a drink as well. They each sat in silence for a moment. Essence pulled a strand of her hair away from her face before taking a sip of the margarita that the bartender placed in front of her.

"Sloan, can I ask you a simple question?" she asked. "And I expect a simple answer."

Sloan felt himself grow a little tense, from the tone of her voice, he knew the question had everything to do with him.

She leaned closer to him and asked in a soft tone of voice, "Are you afraid of me?"

Sloan let out a thunderous laugh. Now, that was a question for the books.

"Am I afraid of you?" Sloan repeated with an unbelievable look. "You got to be kidding me," he said, gulping down the rest of his drink. Essence let out a whiff of air.

"Well, why is it that every time I try to make a move on you, you damn near hightail it the other way? Aren't you attracted to me?" she asked with a slight frown.

Sloan felt like such an idiot. The attraction was like a neon sign, and the old Sloan would have been rocking her world by now. But the new Sloan wanted more than just sex. As he peered into her eyes, he felt an overwhelming need to come clean with her. He reached over and took her hand. His voice became serious as he began to explain.

"I guess it's time for me to tell you the truth," he said.

Essence inhaled as she braced herself from some unsettling revelation. "Please don't tell me you're gay," she uttered quickly.

Sloan tilted his head back and let out another thunderous laugh. "Woman, you are cracking me up," he bellowed. Essence didn't share in his humor. Her face was serious. Sloan stared solemnly at her. "You can relax, Essence. I am not gay. I'm strictly into females."

Essence let out a puff of air. She felt as if someone had lifted a hundred pounds off her shoulders. "Well, what is it then?" she prodded.

Now, Sloan gave her a serious stare. Leaning forward on the barstool, he said, "Essence, I want more than a sexual partner in my life. I've come to a point in my life where I've had my share of those and I need more than just that. What I am looking for at this point and time is someone that can share more with me than my bed." Sloan shifted in his seat. His serious expression remained. "Essence, I want a solid relationship." He let out a brief chuckle. "Heck, someday I want a wife and couple of mini-me's running around. You get what I'm saying?"

Essence was getting it and loving every minute of it. She leaned into him and placed a sultry kiss on his full lips. Her move took Sloan completely by surprise. Pulling away, she asked, "What if I told you I am willing to give you all of those things and more?" Essence's voice was dipped in seductiveness.

Their eyes held. Sloan couldn't believe what he was actually hearing or feeling. At this moment, he felt as if they had made a solid connection. It no longer mattered to him how old Essence was. What mattered was her heart, and it was in the right place—the place he was searching so hard to find. This time, he was the one who kissed her, and it lingered for several moments. Pulling apart, they both giggled like teenagers on their very first date. Essence was totally engrossed in what had just occurred. Sloan Stevens was now under her spell.

"So, does this mean I'm your woman now?" she asked with a bright smile.

"I guess it does," Sloan answered slowly as thoughts of Natasha crossed his mind.

GRETTA

The evening shade had fallen, and bright stars lined the sky. The party was getting even better. There were couples dancing, laughing, and hanging out at the bar. *Natasha should be proud of her accomplishments,* Gretta mused to herself. The lights around the pool shined vibrantly; casting a romantic spell as she sat on the lounge chair, holding her strawberry daiquiri. If only she had a man to share this wonderful feeling; she sighed. Gretta thought about her two-timing boyfriend, Jermaine, and what he had put her through. Thank God she wasn't head over heels in love with him anymore. But, to ice her own cake, she had cheated on him as well. And as a testament to her shameful ways, it was with Jermaine's cousin. She had known for a while that Jermaine was stepping out on her, and so, swearing to never be hurt again, she developed a thick skin; so to speak. It was a dog-eat-dog world in her book—every woman for herself. That was her motto in the world of dating. From her experience, everybody played everybody.

As she placed her empty glass on the patio table, she noticed Derrick with her cousin Natasha. They were dancing like delicate leaves carried by the wind. Gretta watched as Derrick held Natasha ever so gently. Gretta swore it was like a scene from a prom, only the guest weren't wearing anything that resembled a tux or a gown. At that moment, she envied her cousin. Natasha always had a knack for attracting men who were successful –not to mention as drop-dead gorgeous as they come –unlike her, who always seem to end up with nothing but scrubs.

Gretta imagined being in Derrick's arms again, soaking up his masculine scent. Just a few minutes ago, he'd held her the way he was holding Natasha now. She'd even tasted his inviting lips for a moment. It was all done in fun after a little too much to drink. After the swim with Lisa

Ray, Derrick had made his way over to Gretta. Conversation flowed like a river between them, and eventually they ended up in the pool. She'd had so much fun with Derrick as they playfully swam together. Later, he'd dried her off with a long, plush towel. She knew he was checking out her curves and she was flattered by him doing so. When their eyes met, he pulled her into him, giving her the most tantalizing kiss she had ever experienced. He asked if they could hook up later, and of course, her answer was yes. He took her number and disappeared into the crowd. And now, here he was, swaying to the beat of the music with Natasha.

The music ended and the couple broke apart. Gretta saw Natasha whisper something to Derrick before heading in her direction. Natasha peered down at her when she approached Gretta's chair.

"Hey, Gretta, are you having a good time? You're looking kinda bored sitting here by yourself," she said while observing her demeanor.

"No, cousin, you got it all wrong," Gretta said with a smile. "I'm having the best time ever," she crooned as her eyes caught the glare of Derrick's and he gave her a distant smile. Natasha's head turned in the direction of Gretta's stare. She also caught Derrick's returned glance. He waved at them both as he stood by the bar.

"Looks like someone is waiting for you," Gretta said, trying to keep her voice even. She didn't want Natasha to notice anything strange. Natasha smiled as she gave Derrick a quick wave.

"You know, Derrick seems to be a nice guy after all," Natasha retorted, looking down at Gretta.

"After all? What does that mean?" Gretta asked, giving Natasha a questioning gaze.

"Well, earlier Derrick kind of got on my bad side, so to speak," Natasha said with a dismissive look. "He acted as if he was too good for my little ol' pool party. But he apologized by saying that I must have misunderstood him. He wasn't making fun of me or my party; it was just that it has been a long time since he had attended a 'pool party' and he had forgotten how much fun they could be. And well…" Natasha looked over at him once again. "Let's just say we are on the same page now." She smiled as her eyes found Derrick's again. Gretta forced a smile of her own as she saw the exchange between the couple. "So, tell me, have you met any unattached males?" Natasha asked with a sly look.

"Mmmm…I met a couple. One I am very interested in," Gretta said with a smirk of her own.

"Oh, that's great, Gretta!" Natasha bellowed as her eyes grew wider.

"Where is he?" she scanned the vicinity of the pool. Gretta knew she had to come up with something quick.

"Um…he…just left. But he gave me his number," she stammered. She had to think of a quick lie. Natasha could be very intimidating at times.

"Oh. Well, what's his name? I probably know him anyway," Natasha responded.

"Cousin, don't you have a man over there to entertain? Let me handle my affairs." Gretta perked up as she stood up from her seat. "I'm going to refresh my drink," she said, holding up her empty glass.

"Check you later, cousin." Natasha watched as Gretta strolled over to the wet bar. She had noticed the brief glance between her and Derrick and she wondered what was up with her cousin's attitude. The Lord only knows with Gretta, because it was always all about the drama with her. Natasha didn't know which one was worse when it came to their turbulent love lives, Gretta or her brother.

Natasha scanned the crowd, noticing how much it had grown. She knew it had doubled since earlier in the day. It never ceased to amaze her that whenever you invite a certain number of folks to a gathering, others always have a way of sneaking in. And with the added mouths, she wondered how the food was holding up. She decided to go into the kitchen to check with the caterers. She weaved through the crowd; just before she reached the back door to her home, she saw Sloan's friend Ricky standing by the DJ, Froggy Style. *Where on earth did he come up with such a name?* she thought as she let out a small giggle. Froggy Style was chewing down on a big plate of hot wings. She knew he had worked up quite an appetite. He was doing such a wonderful job with the music, she decided to thank him. While approaching them, she uttered her thanks to Froggy and then turned to Ricky. "Have you seen Sloan lately?"

Ricky gave her a nervous look. "Mmmm, can't say I have. Is there anything I can do for you?" he asked, checking out Natasha's sexy body. He knew she was of single status now, and he wanted to see if she was taking applications. Natasha took in his wide smile. Ricky was attractive enough, but he certainly wasn't her speed.

"Uh…I noticed more people have arrived, and I don't want to run out of food or drinks. I thought maybe Sloan could run to the store for me."

A wide grin graced Ricky's face. "I got you, babe," he said, flashing a

Colgate smile. Natasha gave him a solemn look. His smile dimmed. "Uh, I'm sorry, I mean…Natasha," Ricky corrected himself. He knew Natasha was a tough cookie, and evidently she wasn't crumbling his way.

"Well, let me make a list," she told him as he followed her into the kitchen. He tried his best to keep his eyes off her round booty as it swayed from side to side. After a second, he gave up. Booty watching was like second nature to him. Natasha reached into one of the cherry-stained cabinets and retrieved a glass jar filled with money. She opened the jar and pulled out a couple of bills. Ricky watched in awe, and then he let out a soft chuckle. "I never knew anyone did that these days. I mean, with bank cards and ATM's on every corner."

Natasha chuckled as well and gave him a small smile. "When I was a little girl, my Grandma Lillie always kept a jar with money stashed in her kitchen. She said her money was always at hand just like her pots and pans." Natasha couldn't help but grin at the memory of her grandmother's humor. She took a pad out of the drawer and proceeded to scribble several items onto the paper. Then, she handed the sheet to Ricky.

"Thanks," she muttered as she handed him the paper. He took the list and headed out the door.

After freshening up, Natasha made her way back to the party. Scanning the pool area again, her eyes fell upon *them*. They were seated at the picnic table adjacent to the pool. Her best friend and Essence sat with lips locked together as if they were glued into place.

"Liar," she hissed as steam seemed to flare from her nostrils. Before she realized what she was doing, she found her legs carrying her in their direction. Standing before the couple, she said in a perturbed tone, "Sloan, I need to talk to you right now."

Sloan was quite familiar with the look on Natasha's face. And he knew if he didn't comply, an unwanted scene would surely follow. As he began to stand, Essence reached over and pushed him back down onto the wooden bench.

"Excuse me, Natasha, but Sloan and I were having a private conversation, and I think you are being very rude to interrupt us with your attitude," Essence said.

Natasha's perfectly-arched eyebrows lifted. Did *she* really think she was putting her in her place? Well, she would just see about that.

With a roll of her eyes, Natasha said, "Well, you can just excuse yourself, Essence. Sloan is my best friend, and I don't need your permission to talk to him."

Sloan started to rise again, and again, Essence pushed him back down. He felt like a little boy caught between two feuding mothers.

"He may be your best friend, but he is my man now, and you're going to show me some R-E-S-P-E-C-T," Essence sniped as she spelled out the word.

Sloan saw the fire blazing in Natasha's eyes, and he knew something—or someone—was about to burn; and to add fuel to the upcoming blaze, a small crowd was forming. Sloan knew he had to quash this scene before the fire escalated any farther.

"Ladies, ladies, we are not on a school yard, and we certainly aren't children. Now, Natasha, I know you don't want a scene at your party, so let's behave like adults." Sloan thought he sounded just like his mother scolding her third-grade class. He stood again, quickly this time, and his eyes darted swiftly between the women.

"Essence, give me and Natasha a couple of minutes, please."

Essence held a cold stare as her eyes focused on the butterscotch-colored woman who was giving her a smile of satisfaction.

"I'll be right back," Sloan uttered as he quickly grabbed Natasha by the arm. They walked a few feet away before they started talking.

Natasha jerked herself from Sloan's grip and hissed, "What the hell is wrong with you, Sloan? You said that you two were just friends, and now I caught you with your tongue down her throat." Natasha searched Sloan's face for answers. Sloan fell silent as they faced each other. "So, I was right all along. It was only a matter of time before you made a hit. I guess you got tired of the young babes, so you're trying your luck at the mommy figures."

Sloan threw up his hands in frustration. "Natasha, I don't understand where this is coming from. I mean I've dated girls before and you never come off to me this way. What is it about Essence that trips you out so much?"

Natasha ignored his question. Instead, she uttered, "You lied to me, Sloan. How could you just openly lie to me?"

A line formed across his forehead as he gave her a blank stare. "Lied?

Lied about what?"

"You said you were through with hopping from one woman's bed to another, but it seems as if you're back to your old tricks again."

Sloan let out a long whiff of air. Shaking his head, he said, "Look, Me-Me, I'm not married, alright. I can see who I want and when I want. What I don't understand is why does it matter so much to you, anyway?"

Tears threatened Natasha's eyes, and she didn't know whether they were coming from anger, sadness, or just plain jealousy.

Before she could respond, Sloan said, "You need to stop this thing that you're doing, Me-Me. You're driving me crazy."

Natasha folded her arms across her heaving chest. So many emotions consumed her, and she was struggling to hold it all together. "Just tell me, is it true, Sloan?" she mumbled as a single tear escaped down her cheek.

Sloan stared into her misty eyes. He reached out to touch her, but she took a step back. Sloan's arm fell to his side. "Is what true, Me-Me?"

"Are you her man, now?"

Sloan let out a low breath. This was not how he wanted things to be. Lowering his head, he uttered, "Yeah." Natasha began walking back toward the party. "Natasha, please wait!" he called out.

She turned and said, "Go back to your woman, Sloan." And with that, she trotted away. Sloan stood in a daze. Ricky's words were making more sense to him now than ever before.

GRETTA AND DERRICK

Gretta sat at the edge of the pool, her feet dangling in the water. The crowd was beginning to thin out and she realized the party would soon be over. The DJ had changed the music to a soft, mellow jazz. Gretta slowly lowered her body into the pool. She was getting ready to take one last swim before she headed home.

"Mind if I join you?" a deep voice asked from above. She smiled back into Derrick's handsome face.

"Sure," she uttered as her eyes flickered around for Natasha. "If you're looking for Natasha, I haven't the faintest idea where she is," Derrick said, getting into the pool.

Gretta looked at him and then closed her eyes as she leaned against the cool wall. She was enjoying the mellow music as the water swayed around her body. "This is so peaceful," she said softly. She looked up at the dark sky sprinkled with twinkling stars and a huge full moon that glowed with the shimmer of the reflected sun. "Isn't it a beautiful night? If I could stop time, this is where I would want to be forever." Gretta exhaled.

Derrick moved closer to her and gazed up at the universe. "If you could make a wish upon any of those stars, what would it be?" Derrick quizzed, coming closer to her wet and shapely body.

Gretta paused for a moment, then she said, "It's so simple, Derrick, to have a man love me until the end of time."

They both tore their gaze away from the sky and peered into each other's eyes. An unsettling moment formed between them.

Where did that come from, and why did I say it to a total stranger? Gretta thought to herself. It was out there, though, and she couldn't take it back. She waved her hand to dismiss it. "Don't mind me, Derrick. I'm just a hopeless romantic tonight."

"There's nothing wrong with being a romantic," Derrick said as he continued to peer into her eyes.

"In this day and time, I think most romantics are dead, if not in body, surely in spirit," Gretta said with a tiredness to her tone.

"You sound so sad." Derrick cupped her chin with the base of his hand. He admired her beauty. There was something mystical about this woman, and he felt the need to fix whatever was wrong.

"No, just broken," Gretta said almost inaudibly.

"I think we need to lighten this mood up a little," Derrick said as he lowered his hand. "Let me ask you a question," he said, staring directly at her.

"Shoot," Gretta said with a faint smile.

"Well, for starters, let me ask you a personal question. Are you and Natasha related?"

Gretta paused a moment. "Why do you ask?" she said coyly as she kicked her leg at the water, making a small splash.

"To be honest, I heard it through the grapevine. But you know you can't always believe what you hear."

"Well, in this case, you can believe it, Derrick," Gretta said as she began to swing her arms and walk to the center of the pool. The water was warm and had a sultry feel as it caressed her body. Derrick followed closely behind her. They swam to the other end of the pool.

"Is it a problem for you?" Gretta asked breathlessly. Before Derrick could respond, she dipped beneath the water. Coming back up, she wiped the water out of her eyes. Derrick did the same as they faced each other.

"Why should it be a problem? I mean, with us being friends. Males and females can be just friends, can't they?" Derrick asked with a playful grin.

Derrick took another quick dip, and Gretta followed suit. Both came up again and wiped the water from their eyes.

"They most certainly can, and I would love to be your friend, Derrick Perkins," Gretta said with a devilish smile.

Derrick splashed water in her direction. She splashed it back, and they began to laugh. Gretta let out another squeal as they continued to splash each other playfully. Neither one noticed the shadow at the edge of the pool. Natasha was standing with arms folded, watching them. A surreal look formed on her face. After several more minutes of play, she yelled in a heated tone, "The pool party is over!"

The couple stopped and gazed at each other. With puzzled looks, they proceeded to get out of the pool. Gretta knew Natasha was irked that she was having such a good time with Derrick, but she didn't care. The pool party may have been over, but the chemistry between her and Derrick had just begun.

NATASHA

Wednesday nights were significant for Natasha, because she and Sloan called them their "platonic-date nights." They had done it for spent that night together for many years—no matter who they were dating at the time—that night was sacred for the two of them. It was on a Wednesday that they had met over fifteen years ago, so they had regarded that day as very special since childhood. Their families could never understand such craziness between them, and they were teased mercilessly about it. Natasha reflected back to her Aunt Queen singing an old hit song to them every time she quizzed them about their Wednesday ritual. Natasha couldn't really recall any of the lyrics from the song, however, she remembered her aunt telling them if they weren't careful, they were going to fool around and fall in love. Natasha had given her Aunt Queen a look at the time as if she thought her aunt had lost the last few marbles she had left.

But now, as she sat in front of her plasma television, she couldn't help but think that she was the one who had lost her marbles. How could she have let herself fall in love with Sloan? Since the party a couple of weeks ago, she and Sloan had barely spoken. Yes, they saw each other at work, but things were strange now. Something had changed between them. The bond that held them together for so long was slowly disappearing. Natasha exhaled as her thoughts rolled around in her head. She thought about all the women Sloan had dated over the years, and she thought about her own love life. They had shared some insights on how their relationships were going along the way, but neither of them had every had any long term relationships. That is, until Darin came into her life and she fell for his charm so easily. In a lot of ways, Darin reminded her a lot of Sloan. In fact, they even had similar features. Thinking back, she wondered if that was the reason her and Darin's relationship had lasted as long as it did. *Was he a counterfeit copy of the one she felt she couldn't have?* Natasha blew a puff of air out of her mouth. If she kept spinning her feelings this way, she would surely need help.

Getting up from her bed and heading toward her den, she thought she needed a drink, and it wasn't a Pepsi. After pouring a glass of wine, she was now settled on her sofa. She clicked on the plasma television. While clicking through the channels, her mind fell upon Sloan again. She just couldn't get him out of her head. Through the years, their relationship had never changed—ever. He still played silly little games with her, like walking up behind her, putting his hands over her eyes, and making her guess who he was. Or when they went places, like the mall, together, he would grab her purse and run away like a purse snatcher. She had told him plenty of times that one day that joke was going to cost him. Surveillance cameras were rolling everywhere these days, and she swore if he ever got caught, she was going to tell the police she didn't know him. She chuckled at the thought.

She missed that smile of his, which he still managed to give her at work. But gone was the closeness behind it. Their relationship was no longer the same, and there was only one person to blame for that—Essence Kirkland. She had stolen Natasha's best friend. She was the reason she and Sloan weren't together this Wednesday night. She was the interruption of everything. Natasha was starting to hate the woman. As the grandfather clock in the corner of the room chimed, she reminisced about her and Sloan's special night. Glancing at the clock, she noticed it was eight o'clock in the evening. Right now, they would have been sitting in their favorite restaurant, laughing, smiling, and enjoying themselves. He would be telling her some silly story, or they would be cracking up over something one of them had done that day. Her phone rang, and she nearly jumped out of her skin. *Could it be Sloan? Maybe he's on his way over. Maybe he remembered after all,* she thought as she ran to the phone and picked it up.

"Hello," she said excitedly. "Hello yourself, cousin," Gretta responded.

Natasha let out a disappointing sigh. "Gretta, what's up, girl?" Natasha said dryly.

"It sounds like someone is having a bad night."

"Yeah, I guess I am," Natasha muttered as she plopped back down on the sofa.

"I pretty much figured you would be. I was hoping I was wrong and you were out with Sloan, but…I see that you're not, so it must mean—"

"It means that Sloan and I have moved on with our individual lives, Gretta. Now, I don't want to talk about it anymore," Natasha quipped.

"Not talking about it is not going to make the situation go away," Gretta said with concern.

Natasha felt a twinge of anger seeping through her. "Gretta, there is no situation to talk about; okay? Sloan has found him a chick—an old chick, I should add." Natasha's shoulders slumped, but she held her voice evenly. "But I guess he wants to change the pace of things, so if that's he wants. Soon she will be just like the rest of them, Gretta. She will be history soon enough, and then things will be back to normal." Natasha's voice contained a ray of hope.

Now it was Gretta that let out the long sigh. Her cousin needed a heavy dose of reality, and she was the one who was going to give it to her. "Natasha, let me ask you something," Gretta began slowly. She knew she was about to tread into dangerous territory. "What is 'normal' to you? Having Sloan at your beck and call? Manipulating his time so he won't have any social life other than you? Do you think that is normal, Natasha?"

Natasha gasped with a distorted face. "What are you talking about, Gretta? Sloan had a slew of women—"

"Yes, before you and Darin broke up, that is," Gretta interrupted. "After that, you made it your business to keep him all to yourself on the regular."

Anger made its way into Natasha's voice as she gripped the telephone a little tighter. "Gretta, Sloan was helping me through a rough patch. The man I thought I was going to marry had just broken my heart for God's sake! Best friends help each other through things like that." Natasha's voice was high, almost like a child pleading to make her point.

Gretta spoke with a twinge of her own anger. "I could have been there for you, Natasha, but you wouldn't let me. The only comfort you wanted was Sloan Stevens'. You seemed to have preferred him over everyone else."

Natasha let a long breath escape from her throat. She wondered what Gretta was talking about. Surely she was delusional. "Gretta, I think you've had too many drinks tonight. Call me back tomorrow when your head is clear."

"My head is very clear. It's yours that needs some airing. Stop playing yourself, Natasha. You're all screwed up because Sloan seems to have found a woman he may not let go of this time. He and Essence seem to have a very close relationship. They may even move in together." Gretta held her breath momentarily, she knew she had let too much slip out, but it was better that Natasha found out now, rather than later. Just maybe she would do something about it.

"Just say it's in the wind that they may move in together. You know they practically spend all their free time together, anyway. And, as you can see, Sloan no longer remembers the 'special Wednesdays' you two used to share."

Natasha felt tears beginning to form in her eyes. "Is this the real reason you called me, Gretta, just to rub Sloan's relationship with *that* woman in my face?"

"I'm not rubbing anything in your face. I'm just trying to get you to see that Sloan is moving on."

Natasha exhaled. She wondered if Gretta was right. *Had Sloan met the woman of his dreams? How foolish of her to think there was even a chance...*

With a firm tone she said, "You know what, Gretta, you have opened my eyes. I think I do need a new man in my life, so I can squash these stupid accusations my family has about me and Sloan. It seems as if a woman can't just care about a man. It has to be something more," she uttered with a straight face, all the while knowing her heart was breaking in half. "Well, you know what? I'm calling Derrick, and if he is free, I will be going out tonight, after all."

With that, Natasha ended the call, and Gretta was left with a dial tone in her ear. Her intention had been for Natasha to see her true feelings for Sloan and go after him. Instead, she had just pushed her cousin into the arms of the man she wanted for herself.

SLOAN

Sloan soaped up his six-pack in the shower and then allowed the water to rain down on his golden, muscular body. As he closed his eyes, his mind revisited the night he had just shared with Essence. He'd had a lot of wine, a belly full of food, and a scrumptious night of sex on her king-size bed. The woman had his head spinning like a merry-go- round. She was exciting, invigoration, and very experienced at pleasuring her man.

Oh yes, he thought as he lathered his hair with his favorite shampoo, *I could get very comfortable with having someone like her in my life*. Shutting off the water, he stepped out of the shower. His body dripped water onto the tile floor. He silently reminded himself that he needed to buy a bath rug, and then his thoughts returned to Essence. There was so much about her that he liked. They had a lot of fun together; laughing, smiling, and joking around. It was almost like being with…Natasha. *Almost*. Grabbing his black velour robe, he put it on and walked into his bedroom. So much had changed in the past few weeks. He and Natasha exchanged pleasantries as if they were strangers. He and Essence were professionals at work, but after hours, it was one hell of a ride. He'd finally broken down and let his friend Ricky in on some of the things he was dealing with. He didn't tell him all of his business, but enough to make him gawk. Sloan remembered the conversation he and Ricky had shared at Cosmos a few nights ago.

"Ahh, man, you're lying like a rug," Ricky exclaimed after he told him how he and Essence had made love until the break of day.

"Get out of here, man. The girl I'm with now can barely hang on for an hour, and she's only twenty," Ricky bellowed. "What kind of energy drink is she clocking?" Ricky asked, laughing.

"I don't know, man, but I hope she has it stocked," Sloan joined in.

After their laughter died down, Ricky asked, "Is she a keeper, or are you still testing her out?" Ricky rolled with laughter, but then he noticed

Sloan had fallen silent. "Well?" he asked with raised eyebrows.

"I…uh…don't know, man. I mean, she is everything a man could want. Sweet, loving, good sex, but…"

"She sure sounds good to me," Ricky said, staring at his friend. But Sloan's eyes still held some uncertainty. Ricky took a gulp of his beer and then leaned into Sloan.

"Talk to me, man. What's really up?"

"I don't know what's up," Sloan exhaled.

"Dude, you said you were tired of playing the field. Now, you got you a chick who wants the same things as you do. Granted, she is a few years your senior." Ricky let a small smile crease his lips. "But if you don't have a problem with it…I say go for it. Hell, if I ever run into a woman as pretty as she is for her age, I may throw a ring on her finger myself." Ricky chuckled.

"Well, that must be the day when there's only one woman left in this world," Sloan snickered.

"You're sick, dude," Ricky chimed. "So, let's stop the tic-tac-toe. Spell the problem out to me. What's holding you back?"

Sloan picked up his glass of ginger ale and swallowed, yet remained silent.

"I think you need a real man's drink," Ricky said, holding up his beer. "Then, maybe you can see things more clearly," Ricky said as he watched his friend down the ginger ale.

"I don't need a beer to think straight, man," Sloan said, a little irritated. "I…just want to be sure…that's all. I mean, if I asked Essence to marry me…it's for life, man. She would be my friend for life."

"Yeah, and Natasha would definitely have to take a backseat. No more best friends, dude. A new sheriff would be in town." Ricky laughed.

"No, man, Natasha and I will always be friends," Sloan said pointedly.

"So you think?" Ricky asked as he raised his brows again. "Friends like the two of you were a while back, at the pool party? You remember, you told me about that situation."

A cold chill ran down Sloan's spine. The thought of Natasha never being in his life was unimaginable to him.

"People don't give up their best friends just because they get married," Sloan popped.

"Dude, you're talking about a red-blooded, pretty- as-hell woman. Do you think Essence would sit at home fiddling her little thumbs while you and Natasha are out catching up on old times? Somehow, I don't see that," Ricky pointed out as he took another swig of his beer.

Sloan quickly thought about Natasha's birthday and how they always celebrated together, even after the family threw her a big party. They would sneak off to a favorite spot, where he would have a chocolate cupcake with sprinkles and a candle stuck down the middle waiting for her. He would watch as she closed her eyes to make her second wish for that day and blow out the candle. Then, they each would take turns biting the cupcake until it was all gone. Sloan heard Ricky repeating his name.

"Dude, I don't know where you went, but you need to focus on reality. If you decide to marry Essence, you better be ready to give up Natasha. Having a wife as well as a female best friend is not going to work out. You can only have one or the other. Face it, man."

Sloan sat alone in the darkness of his bedroom with only the streetlight shining through the sheer curtains of his room. He dialed Natasha's number. He missed her like crazy, and he couldn't let another night go by without telling her so. As the phone rang not two, but three, and then four times, he wondered where in the hell she was. Another Wednesday had come around, and he was missing their special dates.

If he hadn't been spending so much time with Essence, he would have kept their dates each Wednesday. But Essence was having none of it. She made it plain and clear that they were together now, and those dates had to end. Essence was making demands of him, and they weren't even married yet. Well, tonight he informed her that he needed a breather. He had left Essence standing in the middle of her living room with a disturbed look on her face. But he'd had enough; he needed some space. For the past several weeks, he had been staying over at her place and doing everything she had wanted him to do. But tonight, he had returned home, to his solitude and to his peace and tranquility. He needed to think, and he needed to hear his best friend's voice. He hung up the phone—mid ring—in frustration. Looking out into the darkness, he could almost see her buttercup face.

"Where are you, Natasha?" he shouted into the empty room. He then proceeded to dial her cell phone number, which went straight to voice mail. He had already left several messages earlier, and, as of yet, she hadn't returned even one call. This was not like Natasha. She always returned his calls. But, then again, he hadn't been behaving like himself either. He wondered what had happened to them. Months ago, things were fine, and now it was as if their close friendship had never existed.

Sloan fell across his bed and stared up at the twirling ceiling fan. The image of Derrick Perkins flashed before his eyes. Natasha was with him; he could feel it in his bones. He rolled over and picked up his cell. Her voice mail came on again when he dialed her number. This time, he left a stern message.

"Natasha, call me, I don't care what time it is. Just call me!" Then he softened his voice and said, "Natasha, please call me…I'll be waiting, Me-Me," he murmured into the phone.

DERRICK & NATASHA

Natasha had not intended to be out so late, especially on a weeknight. But she and Derrick were having so much fun that she hated for the night to come to a close. The man saturated her with tales of his dubious encounters during his short-lived football career. Now, as she turned the key to enter her home, she could feel her date's breath on the nape of her neck. After unlocking the door, she turned to stare into Derrick's dark eyes. Derrick had been trying to persuade her to let him in for a nightcap ever since they had left the restaurant.

"Come on, babe, just one quick drink, and I promise I'll be on my way," Derrick said as he caressed her neck with his full lips.

Natasha pulled away and gave Derrick a skeptical look. Peering up at him, she had to admit her restraint was weakening. It had been a long time since she'd felt the hot-blooded body of a man next to her. Just thinking of the possibilities was sending S.O.S signals to her womanhood, which was crying to be rescued. Natasha placed her hand in the middle of Derrick's chest.

"Okay, Derrick, but it's going to be a quick drink. We both have an early day tomorrow. Don't forget that you have that proposal to present to Mr. Emerson."

"Natasha, the proposal is in the bag and so is Mr. Emerson," Derrick chuckled.

"Mmmm, sounds like someone is very confident."

"I am very confident," Derrick replied as he pulled her into him. The touch of his lips against hers made her body tremble. They broke apart as they entered the foyer. She dropped her Gucci purse onto the sofa and walked straight to the wet bar. She wasn't a drinker per se, but she needed something to calm her nerves. She poured two glasses of chardonnay and headed back to Derrick, who was perched on the sofa. He reminded her of an eagle waiting to spread its wings. The house was quiet and dark. Only the light in the foyer lit the area where they sat. Derrick took a sip of his wine. He didn't say a word, but his eyes spoke volumes as they stared into hers. Natasha stood up nervously.

"I think we need a little music. It's really quiet in here," she mused as she turned on her surround sound.

Luther Vandross's voice filled the air. Derrick stood and took her in his arms. They began to sway to the rhythm of the song. Derrick kissed her lightly on the neck, and then he nibbled on her earlobe, sending a trail of sensations spiraling down her spine.

"I want you, Natasha Jacobs," Derrick whispered into her ear with his steamy breath.

Derrick's hands cupped her butt cheeks, pressing her into him. She could feel the firmness of his manhood through his trousers. He had started a fire in her that needed to be quenched.

What about Sloan? her conscience replied. *Did he really care about her? Where were he now?*

Darin was living it up with the bimbo he had cheated with, and Sloan… well, he was probably in bed with Essence right now, and Natasha was probably the farthest thing from his mind. Both of their needs were being met. So was it right to deny her own? She leaned into Derrick and they both let out a lustful moan. Derrick picked her up and carried her to the bedroom. In the back of her mind, she wondered how he knew the way. But it really didn't matter now, for he had found the direction to her lonely heart.

SLOAN & NATASHA, DERRICK & ESSENCE

The board meeting began at 9:00 A.M. sharp in the conference room at Emerson & Stuckey. The huge room with its open-view windows and long, cherry wood table was almost like a scene from the movie, *The Godfather;* with Mr. Emerson as Al Pacino's character. Mr. Stuckey was seated next to Mr. Emerson. Mr. Stuckey was a few years younger than Mr. Emerson, and he traveled a lot more, so his presence was a surprise to the employees in attendance. Natasha was seated between Lisa Ray and another employee who had visions of climbing the corporate ladder. Essence sat across the table. Then there was Sloan, who was seated next to Mr. Emerson. Derrick Perkins—in his black, pinstriped Perry Ellis button-down shirt, black trousers, and mint-green and black silk tie—stood at the front of the room with his proposal posted on the screen behind him. The man looked like a breath of fresh air, and Natasha let her mind wander back to the evening—and morning—they had just spent together.

Derrick had awakened sensual feelings that Natasha had forgotten she had. She smiled inwardly as Derrick spoke to the group. Lisa Ray poked Natasha discretely in her side; she had noticed the morning glow on Natasha's face and could hardly wait to find the reason behind it. Natasha's eyes darted quickly at Lisa Ray, and she gave her a knowing smile. She also couldn't wait for the meeting to come to an end, so she could fill her in.

Someone else was sneaking stares, too. Sloan stole gazes at Natasha whenever he could, and the look he was giving her was none too friendly.

Derrick spoke professionally and strongly as he presented his proposal, as if he had done it a thousand times. No one had an inkling that he was new to the job. He carried himself well, and the board members seemed to be impressed; and so was Natasha. Memories of his hands roaming over her body made her shiver silently in her seat, so much so that she had to cross her legs.

Derrick noticed her discomfort and asked, "Do you have a question, Miss Jacobs?" Natasha's face flushed as she felt the presence of everyone's eyes staring in her direction.

She quickly cleared her throat and muttered, "No…Mr. Perkins, I don't." Natasha wondered why Derrick had called her out like that. It was bad enough Sloan was glaring her down. She didn't need the stare of the rest of the room, as well.

Sloan couldn't wait for Derrick to bring his act to an end. Even though Sloan had his own insecurities, he had to admit that Derrick was smart and articulate. He had already acquired three solid accounts after being at the company for only a few months. It was a record almost equivalent to his own, which made Sloan very uncomfortable. The threat of Derrick taking his job lingered with him daily. His job he could deal with, but the thought of Derrick taking away his best friend too wasn't feasible. He had stayed up until three o'clock in the morning, waiting to hear from Natasha. She hadn't returned his phone calls, and he knew the reason why. Sloan's mind continued to wander about just how far things had gone between Derrick and Natasha. Before the meeting had started, Sloan was about to approach Natasha in the corridor, but he was interrupted by Essence, who had a transparent look on her face. They'd had a small disagreement earlier, which ended with him promising to go back to her place tonight. Natasha greeted them both with a cool smile as she strutted by like a model on a catwalk.

He had to speak with her, so he left Essence standing with a perturbed expression while he ran after his best friend.

"Why didn't you return my calls?" he huffed. Natasha turned and folded her arms across her chest.

"I guess I was busy, Sloan. You know, I do have a life," she said with uplifted eyes. She was staring back at him with an amused expression.

He lowered his voice; he could feel Essence's glare on them. He whispered softly, "I called you several times last night, Me-Me. Where were you?"

"So, are you keeping tabs on me again? Don't tell me your old fling over there is beginning to lose its flavor," she smirked.

Now, Sloan was pissed and he didn't care if Essence was watching or not. "Stop this right now, Me-Me!" he insisted as he closed the distance between them.

"Stop what, Sloan? My life?" she asked with a trace of coldness in her voice.

"Were you out with him?" Sloan demanded.

"And…what if I was?" she said, raising her voice.

"Damn it, Natasha! Why can't you listen to me? The guy is trouble, and I want you to stay the hell away from him," he hissed.

They both turned as Essence approached them.

"It seems as if we have a problem here," Essence said, looking from one of them to the other. "Can I be of some assistance?" she asked as she gave them a questioning stare.

"Naw, baby…I…we…were just clearing something up," Sloan stuttered.

"Oh?" Essence said as her eyes darted between them. "Well, speaking of clearing things…honey, why don't we invite Natasha over for dinner this weekend? After that fantastic pool party she gave several weeks ago, I think it's time for me to show some of my own Southern hospitality," Essence crooned.

Natasha shifted her feet as she cut her eyes at Sloan. The last thing she wanted was to be entertained by Essence.

"Uh…I don't know about that," Natasha responded quickly.

"But, you must. I mean, you're very important to my sugar here."

Natasha cringed as Essence called Sloan "sugar" again. She was speaking of him like her child, not her man. "I can't shut out his friends, now can I?" Essence asked with a mischievous grin.

Sloan looked solemnly at the two women. He didn't particularly like the idea either, but thinking back to his conversation with Ricky that night at the bar, it would make a tremendous difference if Essence and Natasha could get along, maybe even be friends. Natasha gave them both a contemplative stare. An idea popped into her head.

"If you insist, but only if I can bring a date," she stated slyly.

"Why, of course," Essence retorted while Sloan gave Natasha a sidelong glance. Derrick's baritone voice broke into Sloan's reverie. He caught the ending of Derrick's speech. "Now, this concludes my proposal. Does anyone having any questions?"

Several questions were asked, and, in the end, Derrick's proposal was accepted. After the meeting dispersed, refreshments were served near the back of the conference room. Sloan noticed Derrick greeting Natasha. They smiled genuinely as if they both carried a precious secret, and it bothered the hell out of Sloan.

GRETTA

Gretta sat across from her cousin Natasha as they ate their evening meal. Natasha had invited her over earlier in the day, and she had accepted. Spinning her fork into the spaghetti, Gretta chimed, "So, you're really thinking Sloan is losing it because he thinks you're seeing Derrick?"

A smirk crept across Natasha's lips as she peered over at Gretta. "Think? There's no thinking in it, Gretta. I *am* seeing Derrick. That's why I invited you over here, silly," Natasha said with a roll of her head. "I wanted to tell you what happened after dinner a couple nights ago," she said with a playful smile.

Gretta wasn't so sure she wanted to hear the details, but she pasted on a fake grin and listened.

Leaning over her plate, Natasha said, "Gretta, Derrick and I slept together. And, girl, it was the bomb!" she chirped. Gretta choked and began to cough frantically. The spaghetti she had placed in her mouth hadn't quite made it down her throat.

"Girl, are you alright?" Natasha asked as she hopped up and gave her a couple of pats on her back.

Gretta's coughing soon subsided, and she swallowed a big gulp of her iced tea. Natasha returned to her seat and resumed eating. "So, I see you both didn't waste any time," Gretta uttered hoarsely.

Natasha raised her eyebrow. "I don't understand. Why should we have waited? It's not like we're preteens contemplating having sex. We've both been in the game for years and we know what we're doing, Gretta." Natasha's tone was a little harsh.

Gretta put down her fork and faced her cousin. "All I'm saying is, why are you moving so fast? I thought you were going to take some time before getting into another serious relationship," Gretta quipped. Gretta stared at Natasha, who was squirming in her seat. Pointing her fork at her cousin, she said, "In fact, I remember your exact words. You said you were taking the advice of that judge on *Divorce Court*: *Look deep before you leap*. So, did you look deep enough, Natasha?" Gretta was waiting patiently for her cousin's response.

Natasha wiped her mouth with her napkin and threw it onto her empty plate. With a surreal look, she uttered, "Well, you know, Gretta… sometimes opportunity knocks when you least expect it, and Derrick was an opportunity for me to get my life back on track. It's been almost a year now since Darin and I broke up. How long do you and Sloan expect me to keep my life on hold?"

"So, Sloan shares the same concern that I do?" Gretta asked.

"Yes, and I'm telling you the same thing I told him. I'm moving on with my life," Natasha said sternly.

Gretta gave her an impassive expression. "What about Sloan?"

Natasha rolled her eyes. *Why is everything about Sloan?* "Please, not again, Gretta," she said, waving both hands in the air. "I invited you over here tonight to talk about the new man in my life, and here you go throwing Sloan up in my face." Her voice was tipping on the verge of anger now. Natasha inhaled and then let out a slow breath. She refused to get upset again. "Look, Gretta, I'm going to say it one more time, and please hear me, will you? Sloan is living his life. He moved in with Essence, and they are a couple now. Derrick and I are a couple now. Hopefully, Sloan and I will remain good friends as we have in the past. I mean, this is not the first time we've both had other relationships."

"I know, but this is the first time you've acknowledged your true feelings for the man," Gretta muttered slowly.

Natasha's eyes grew slant as she returned Gretta's stern stare. "What… what are you talking about? I never told you anything of the sort."

"You don't have to tell me. It's written on your face every time you look at Sloan. We've all seen it, Natasha. Why can't you?"

Natasha dropped her head in frustration. She balled her fists and shrieked. "I give up! I mean, it's useless for me to keep talking to you," she said, standing and picking up her dish and silverware. She went to the kitchen, scraped the plate, and placed it in the dishwasher. Gretta followed the same routine, and then they returned to the dining room table in silence. Gretta stared at Natasha. There was so much she wanted to tell her, but couldn't. Instead, she opted for a piece of reasoning.

"Cousin, I heard you. Really, I did. Your mouth is saying one thing, but your heart is totally saying another." Natasha was about to explode, but Gretta held up her hand. "Please, let me finish."

Natasha scooted down in the chair and folded her arms. She felt as if she was about to be chastised for not doing an errand. Gretta spoke carefully. "If you're using your relationship with Derrick as a shield for your feelings for Sloan, you are going to end up in an emotional spiral, Natasha. I'm asking you—no, I am begging you to be honest with yourself and take a good look at what you're doing. Think about it now. Even when you were with Darin, Sloan was a big part of the picture. And to tell you the truth, and you may not like it," Gretta said with raised brows, "I think that's some of what helped break you two up."

Natasha squinted as she stared back at her cousin. Her heart felt as if someone was squeezing the life out of it.

Gretta had taken her seat and leaned forward in it. "You told me plenty of times about the fights you two had over Sloan. Darin said you were spending too much time with him."

Natasha straightened her spine and sat upright. "Darin was always exaggerating. And wait a minute," Natasha's eyes widened. "When did Darin tell you this lie? Was it after his indiscretions?" she said, almost screaming. "I've spent more time with Sloan, because his ass wasn't here with me. Where was Darin, Gretta?" she asked with narrow eyes. "I'll tell you where! In some other woman's bed," Natasha cried out.

"Maybe that's what drove him there," Gretta said, barely audible.

"What? What did you say, Gretta?" Natasha's eyes grew red with anger. She stood up and pushed the chair into the table. "Are you saying that I drove Darin away? That I pushed him into somebody else's bed?" she spewed.

Gretta stood up and backed away from Natasha, who had made her way to her, invading her personal space. "Look, I'm sorry, Natasha. I didn't mean to upset you."

"But you did," Natasha uttered with her hands on her hips. "Here you are, making crazy accusations about what went on between me and Darin. You don't know anything about my business!" Natasha shouted. Her voice made Gretta jump. "I know what this is all about, Gretta. You're just jealous of me. I've had a good man in my life for quite some time…and

Sloan has always been there for me every step of the way, but you…you have no one. All of your relationships dissolve like the dew on a hot sunny day and you're just jealous."

Now, it was Gretta's turn to get upset. It was past time that her cousin knew the truth. "I damn well know what I'm talking about, because Darin confided in me!" she yelled. Her eyes were as round as saucers as she spoke to Natasha. "He told me he thought you two were screwing each other, and he couldn't take it anymore. He was sick of the way you both behaved. 'Like lovesick puppies' he described it. He said he woke up many nights to hear girlish giggles coming from you while you were on the phone with Sloan. He said he felt more like the other man in your life," Gretta continued.

Natasha covered her ears and shook her head from side to side. She didn't want to hear another word. "Gretta, you need to leave. Right about now!" she shouted.

"Yeah, I better go, and maybe you should sit yourself down and really think things through before you ruin your life, yet again," Gretta huffed as she slammed the door behind her.

Natasha sailed to her bedroom and threw herself across her king-size bed. Tears burned her eyes as the memories of her fights with Darin came crashing back. Gretta was right. They had fought constantly in the second year of their relationship. Was it really her fault Darin had done what he had done? Did she push him into the arms of another woman? Did Darin really think Sloan was the other man? And most importantly of all, did he truly believe that she was cheating on him with Sloan? All of those questions entered her mind as she thought about her torrid relationship with Darin. Natasha revisited the last argument they'd had. "Natasha, who are you talking to?" he asked as he sat his briefcase down on his desk in the home office.

"Oh, baby, it's just Sloan," she said as he glanced over her shoulder. He heard a giggle, and then more giggles, and then an outburst of laughter that felt to Darin like chalk squeaking on a blackboard. It wasn't the laugh itself that irritated him. No, not at all, because Natasha had a wonderful laugh—a laugh he enjoyed hearing. It was just that he knew who was sharing her laughter, and he'd had enough.

"Why did I even ask?" he huffed as he left the room. She followed with the cell phone in her hand as he entered the kitchen. He rummaged through the fridge and then pulled out a slice of cheese and a celery stick. Then, he picked up a can of beer and popped the top. As he turned,

she could see the expression on his face. His forehead held a deep crease line as he looked at her.

"Is it too much to ask for a man to have his woman's attention when he comes home from work?" Darin yelled. The laughter stopped.

"Sloan, I'll call you back later," she uttered as she ended the call. "Darin, what is your problem?" she said, getting an attitude of her own. "Sloan and I were just talking about an incident that happened with Mr. Emerson today at work. It was so funny, Darin, you should have—"

Darin held up both hands, cutting her off. "Natasha, you work with the man five days out of the damn week. You're on the phone with him all times of the night. The only time I have your undivided attention is on the weekends, and, even then, you two find a way to talk to each other. What's up with the both of you? Is he getting what I'm getting?" Darin lashed out.

Natasha slapped him across the face. How dare he even go there with her? "You're so pathetic, Darin," Natasha yelled. Darin rubbed his cheek, but the sting of Natasha's hand remained.

"Well, there is something going on here, and it's not normal. I'm sick of it, Natasha," he said through clenched teeth, "Where do you two draw the line?"

"Oh, so you're saying that you want me to stop seeing my best friend?" she asked as a hint of tears threatened the surface of her eyes.

"No, what I'm saying is, let *me* be your best friend. For God's sake, we're…engaged." He exhaled. Darin had a defeated look in his eyes as he stared at her. "Natasha, baby, I'm supposed to be your best friend now, not him!" Darin shook his head and exhaled.

Natasha put her arms around him and kissed him softly on the lips. "Baby, you are my best friend, and I love you so much," she uttered as she stared into his eyes.

Darin held her in his arms. "So, why do I feel like a third party here? You got to make up your mind which one of us you want," he said as he pulled away from her.

Natasha dropped her hands to her side. "Are you saying that I must choose between the two of you?" Natasha asked in disbelief.

"Exactly," he said with the sternest look she had ever seen.

"This is crazy, Darin. Sloan and I have been friends since elementary school, and you are very aware of this."

"And I understand all that, Natasha. But you're not kids anymore. You are a grown woman in a relationship with a grown man now. You two can't behave as if you are still seven or eight years old, running around having fun on the playground."

"So, now you're playing on my intelligence," she blared, turning away from him. "There's nothing going on with me and Sloan, and you're just using him as a scapegoat to cover up what you're doing behind my back."

Darin's voice grew rigid. "And what am I doing, Natasha?"

"I don't know, Darin, but I have my suspicions."

"Natasha, I only want you, baby. All of you."

"Darin, you have all of me."

"Prove it."

"How?" Natasha looked at him long and hard. "You want me to cut ties with Sloan?" she uttered. A bad taste formed in her mouth. "I…can't. I…won't do that, Darin. He's my best friend," she exclaimed as tears filled her eyes.

Darin didn't say another word. Instead, he picked up his keys and left. After that, things between them were never the same.

The doorbell chimed, and Natasha sat straight up on her bed. She wondered if it was Gretta coming back with more venom to heap on her. Natasha rushed to the door, wiping tears with each step. As she peered through the peephole, her heart did a flip. She hesitated to open the door as Sloan leaned on the doorbell.

"Open the door, Me-Me. I know you're in there," his voice beckoned.

Natasha slowly opened the door, and with a false smile, she said, "I see your mommy let you out of the house for a while." She had to use humor to cover the turbulent emotions that ran through her. Peering around him, she uttered, "Are you alone, or is the ball and chain waiting for you in the car?"

"Cut it out, Natasha." Sloan smirked as he headed into the living room.

Natasha sat down on the sofa and curled her legs up on the couch, a move she always did when she was apprehensive. Sloan dropped his long frame down beside her.

Staring into her eyes, he said, "This has gone on long enough. We have to resolve this thing between us, right here and now."

"I don't understand, Sloan. Where are you going with this?" she said with a blank look.

"What's wrong with us?" he asked.

Natasha lowered her eyes from his intense stare. "I think you need to ask yourself that question, Sloan. I mean, there is nothing wrong with me."

"Stop it, Natasha," Sloan quipped. "We have been friends too long to be behaving like this. We have had relationships with other people along the way, and never has it affected us like it's doing now. I don't understand why you are giving me such a hard time with my relationship with Essence. I've had women before in my life that you didn't necessarily approve of, but you respected my space. Why can't you now?"

Natasha uncurled her legs and sat up straight. "You're right, Sloan. You always respected my space, even when Darin and I were going through our problems. So, why won't you do the same with Derrick? You want me to accept your relationship with Essence, so you need to do the same with me and Derrick."

Sloan lowered his head and exhaled. A moment of silence passed between them. Then he looked up. "Natasha, if I thought for one minute he had your best interest at heart, I would back off. But I know he doesn't. He will use you and then run off to another woman waiting in the wings."

Natasha's feelings were hurt, and she lashed out. "You know what I think, Sloan? I think you are just jealous of Derrick. He is just as smart as you are. He's already moving up at Emerson & Stuckey, and you're afraid that he may just have your job before it's all said and done. Now that he has my attention, you can't stand that either."

"Me-Me, you got it twisted."

"Oh, do I? So everything is perfect in your world with Miss Oldie? Does she have your best interest at heart? What kind of snow job are you running here, Sloan? That woman wants you because you have money and you're young. She probably brags to her old friends about her boy toy," she said with uplifted eyes.

"This is not about me, Natasha. I can take care of myself."

"And so can I," Natasha said defensively.

"Why can't you see that he is a playa? He's playing you, Natasha."

"What if I'm playing him as well? You know we women can play the same game. What if I just need a man in my life right here, right now, to ease my lonely nights? Is that so bad, Sloan?"

With slumped shoulders, Sloan uttered, "You don't have what it takes to play the game, Me-Me."

"And what does it take? Surely you have the recipe for it. Fill me in with the ingredients, Sloan. You're the expert, right? Share your prize-winning recipe with me," she yelled. Her face took on the look of a wayward woman.

Sloan's expression grew hard, but his voice was soft when he uttered, "I don't know what has gotten into you, Me-Me. But you're not the same girl I used to know."

Natasha felt a rush of fresh tears coming to the surface of her eyes. She tried to blink them away. "Why do you insist on running my life?" Natasha said with an angered look. "You're having your fun, playing house with Mrs. Robinson. How long will you play her, Sloan?" He grimaced. Before he could respond, Natasha continued. "I know she's playing you, as well."

"Just stop it, Me-Me," Sloan muttered as he faced Natasha. "There is another reason I came over here tonight. I need to tell you something."

There was seriousness in Sloan's voice, and it scared her. He wiped away the single tear that fell onto her cheek. His touch made her tremble inside.

Sloan peered into her hazel eyes. "You know, I miss the conversations we used to have about our dates. We shared so much over the years, and I don't want it to stop now." Sloan wrapped his arms around her and held her ever so gently. He missed her smell, her warmth. Natasha's mind was racing. What was he going to tell her? She needed to hear it now. Natasha pulled away from him with a frantic look upon her face.

"Tell me what you came here to say." She sounded almost childlike.

"I'm falling in love with her, Me-Me, and I'm thinking about asking her to marry me."

Natasha gasped as if someone had stuck a knife in the middle of her chest. Sloan's words kept coming as she struggled to listen.

"Me-Me, she is everything I ever wanted in a woman. She's intelligent and warm, and she makes me laugh. And most importantly, she wants to settle down and have a family, and that's what I want as well."

Natasha forced herself to breathe. Of all the women she had ever known Sloan to date, not one had ever inspired him to mention the word love. And now, he was talking marriage. He rattled off all Essence's good qualities, and Natasha wondered if she should tell him the truth about her own feelings. She held the same love for him. Sloan reached for her again, but she pulled away.

"Natasha, what's wrong?" he asked, his voice filled with concern.

"Nothing. I need you to leave now, Sloan."

"But I'm not finished."

"Yes, you are."

"Me-Me, there's more I want to tell you about Essence."

"Sloan, I don't want to hear another damn word about her or your relationship with her, alright!" She almost screamed. Natasha folded her arms and took in a deep breath. In a firm tone, she said, "In fact, from this night forward, I think we should keep our personal relationships to ourselves." She looked at him with as much conviction as she could muster. Her warm hazel eyes looked cold and barren as Sloan stared into them.

"You don't mean that, Natasha."

"Yes, Sloan, I do."

Sloan gazed at her one last time as he headed for the door. He remembered the mantra they had always repeated as children. *Best friends until the end of time*. Had their time come?

G STREET CHRONICLES
A LITERARY POWERHOUSE
WWW.GSTREETCHRONICLES.COM

SLOAN

Sloan leaned back in his seat at Oscar's Bar. It was way past midnight, but he just didn't feel like heading home. His head was all screwed up thanks to Natasha's odd behavior. Sloan stared at the bottle of Hennessey. He wondered if the alcohol could help ease the turmoil within him. He picked up the bottle, bringing it close to his lips. Then, like an impulse he couldn't control, he sat the bottle back on the table. Drinking had never solved his father's problems, and he knew it wouldn't solve his either. Sloan rubbed his eyes and let out a long sigh. He'd never thought, in a million years, that he and his best friend would be at such drastic odds. Sure, they had argued during the past years, but that had never threatened the foundation of their relationship. His conversation with Natasha played before him like a video. He had never seen her so cold and callous. Her last words haunted him: *From this night forward we will not discuss our personal relationships.*

"What is that?" he said aloud.

Their friendship had been personal from the very beginning. They talked over everything that had ever concerned them. *She didn't know what she was saying*, he thought to himself. *I'll give her a few days to cool off. Yeah, that's probably what we both need, a little time to get things back on track.* Sloan pushed the Hennessey bottle aside and waved to the bartender.

"Give me a ginger ale, my man."

The bartender gave him a funny look, but didn't say a word. He placed a tall glass of ginger ale in front of Sloan. "Thanks," Sloan uttered as his thoughts continued.

He was now thinking of his homeboy's words. He wondered if Ricky was right. Was Natasha feeling him, really feeling him? He just couldn't wrap his mind around that. They'd shared so much over the years, and not once had she ever mentioned any feelings for him other than basic friendship. *Why hasn't she said anything?* his inner voice asked. *Why haven't you?* the inner voice responded. Sloan refused to acknowledge his thoughts. He looked around the bar. It was really crowded for a weeknight. He wasn't the only one that wasn't in a rush to get home. His cell phone vibrated on his side. He retrieved it and stared at the flashing number. It was Essence. He pressed the talk button.

"Sloan, where are you, honey? You had me worried," she said in a single breath.

"I'm fine. I just needed some time alone," Sloan replied.

"Alright, so I'll just keep the bed warm for you," she crooned.

"Essence, I'm not coming home tonight."

Sloan braced himself for the attitude he knew was coming. Essence could be very aggressive when things weren't going her way.

"And would you like to tell me why?" Her voice went from warm and cozy to as cold as ice. "Like I've said, I need to be alone."

"What's going on, Sloan?" she almost shouted.

"Essence, there is nothing going on. I just need some time to think!" he countered.

"To think, or to screw around with some other woman?" she retorted.

"Look, Essence, I'll see you tomorrow." Sloan didn't wait for her response before hanging up the phone. Sloan took a big gulp of his drink, and, as he did, his cell went off again.

"Essence, I'm not coming home tonight," he hissed when he answered.

"Hey, dude, that's fine with me." Ricky chuckled.

"I'm sorry, man, I thought you were…"

"Yeah, yeah, mistaken identity." Ricky chuckled again. "So, dude, what's up with you and her? Don't tell me there's trouble in paradise already."

Sloan exhaled. "Essence is not really the problem, Ricky."

"Then what is?"

"It's me, man. I feel confused right now," Sloan lamented.

"Confused? Dude, you got a fine woman waiting for you to get your ass home. And from what you told me the other day, wedding bells may be ringing pretty soon."

"Well, I'm not even sure about that anymore," Sloan uttered.

"Where are you, dude?"

"Oscar's Bar."

"Feeling some company?"

"Sure, man, why not."

"I'm on my way," Ricky said as the call ended.

DERRICK

Derrick walked toward Natasha's desk. He paused for a moment as he took in her natural beauty. She wasn't the type to wear a lot of makeup. Her natural glow shone on her face as her long cinnamon-colored hair flowed freely around her shoulders. She turned her head in his direction and smiled.

Derrick mouthed the words, "Have lunch with me." And she nodded her head. Derrick returned her smile and continued down the corridor. Lisa Ray's desk was across from Natasha's, and she caught what had transpired between the two. Smiling, she turned off her computer; and Natasha did so as well. The women entered the break room. After filling her cup with coffee, Lisa Ray joined Natasha where she sat at the corner table in the back of the room. Natasha was sipping a Pepsi when Lisa Ray took her seat.

"I caught that lunch invite, and, girl, you must be in seventh heaven," Lisa Ray chimed.

Natasha gave her a weak smile. "Mmmm, not exactly."

"I don't get it. You've been seeing the man for weeks now, and you just accepted lunch with him. So, what's the deal?" Lisa Ray asked with raised brows.

"You don't miss a trick, Lisa Ray," Natasha said with a roll of her eyes.

"Well, I try not to, girlfriend. Especially when it comes to fine men, and, girl, you got yourself the cream of the crop," Lisa Ray quipped as she smoothed back the edges of her long weave.

Natasha gave her another small smile and shook her head.

"Oh, so you don't think so?" Lisa Ray said. She paused as her brown eyes scanned the break room as several young ladies pivoted around. "Mmmm, some of these women in here would give their best pair of panties to go out with Derrick Perkins and you know it, girlfriend."

"Yeah, girl, I know you're right. And Derrick is a nice guy, but…"

Natasha gave her an exasperated look.

Lisa Ray raised her hands. "But what? There are no buts when it comes down to a gem like Derrick."

Natasha lowered her voice and said, "Lisa Ray, you know Derrick has a reputation when it comes to women. He even admitted that to me himself." She took another sip of her soda. Lisa Ray leaned in.

"And tell me, girl, what male species who looks like him wouldn't have some mileage with females?" Lisa Ray gave her a questioning look. "Not unless he walks on the other side, if you know what I mean," she whispered with a wink.

"Girl, you are so stupid. Derrick is straight as a line in the middle of the road," Natasha said. She chuckled, and Lisa Ray joined in.

"Well, maybe you are the one to tame that tiger. Bring him out of the jungle and get him into your cage, girl."

With a skeptical look, Natasha said, "Mmmm, I don't know about all that. Men who play like that leave a long list of broken hearts, and I don't want to be one of them."

"Natasha, there's no guarantee in love, girl. You can date one or two men and still have your heart broken. Loving is like the game of life… sometimes you win and sometimes you lose," Lisa Ray said, sounding like a commercial. "You know you two look good together, and I bet you both have a lot in common."

Natasha nodded her head slowly while saying, "I guess we do, and Derrick is funny. He makes me laugh all the time." Natasha's eyes brightened for the first time.

"Since we're talking about playas, I see Sloan got his wings clipped by that cougar, Essence, and if she could do that to him, Derrick should be a piece of cake for you," Lisa Ray chimed.

A stream of anger flared within Natasha. If Essence Kirkland had never entered the picture, her relationship with Sloan would still be intact. There wouldn't be any bickering or distance between them. "You know, Lisa Ray, that's just a phase Sloan is going through. I don't believe for one minute that anything will come of that relationship. Essence is an older, mature woman, and I think Sloan is just caught up in the fantasy of having an older woman stroking his ego." Natasha smirked.

Lisa Ray was speechless. Natasha was speaking as if she were a jilted wife. Lisa Ray was about to respond when Sloan and Essence entered the break room. Both women's eyes were drawn to the couple, who wore bright smiles. They watched as Sloan pulled out the chair for Essence as they sat a few tables away. The cat suit Essence was wearing barely passed the office dress code. The navy-colored skirt was so tight, Natasha was sure part of her circulation was compromised. Natasha's eyes darkened. She envisioned herself walking over and pulling the chair right from under Essence's high-maintenance, over-the-hill ass. Natasha stood abruptly.

"I'm going back to work," she snapped.

"But we have ten more minutes," Lisa Ray quipped, looking down at her watch.

"Well, you can stay. I'll see you back at the office," Natasha said, picking up her empty Pepsi can. As she was leaving, she caught a glimpse of Sloan's stare. She didn't acknowledge him as she hurriedly left the break room.

SLOAN & NATASHA

Natasha wondered how in the world she was going to get through dinner with Sloan and Essence. She hated herself for being so gullible. She wanted nothing to do with Essence and her fake-ass hospitality. In the beginning, she'd had her doubts about Essence, but then she began to like her—a little. That was before she pounced on Sloan like a soaring eagle snatching its prey. Natasha slid her black panty hose on over her round hips. Standing in front of the full-length mirror in her master bathroom, she took in her reflection. The Donna Karan, after-hours black dress with its chain-link belt fitted her curves perfectly. Taking in her freshly-done up do hairstyle and Fashion Fair makeup, which accented her skin coloring, Natasha knew she would blow Essence out of the water. Looking into her jewelry box, she selected the sterling silver cross Sloan had purchased for her as a birthday gift a few months ago. With a touch of cocoa-colored lipstick and a quick spray of J. Lo perfume, she was ready for her enchanting evening.

A mischievous idea popped into her head. *Since Sloan seems so smitten with his new love, or should I say "old love", why not play his game?* Thinking back to their conversation a few days ago, he had accused her of not having what it takes to be a playa. Just thinking about it made her angry. Well, tonight she would show him that he didn't know her as well as he thought he did. Natasha slipped on her black three-inch pumps, grabbed her matching designer purse, and headed out the door. She couldn't wait for Sloan Stevens to see the new side of Natasha Jacobs.

SLOAN, ESSENCE, NATASHA & DERRICK

Sloan stared in awe at the elegant table setting for four. Opulent candles were burning in sterling silver candleholders. Fresh-cut flowers were centered in the middle of the oval mahogany dining room table. A delicious aroma filled the room. Sloan was wearing a black double-breasted Kenneth Cole suit with matching Italian loafers. Essence had insisted upon a formal affair.

Sloan poured himself a nonalcoholic drink. He heard Essence tinkering in the kitchen. A few minutes later, she was by his side. He thought she looked good enough to eat as he peered into her dark, slanted eyes. Essence wore a pearl-white shimmering evening dress that accentuated her curvy body. Her long, fine dark hair hung pleasantly around her shoulders. Essence reached for his glass and placed it on the coaster on top of the wet bar.

"You're looking mighty handsome tonight, sugar," Essence crooned as their lips touched.

"And you are very beautiful, as usual," Sloan uttered as they shared another kiss.

"Oh, Sloan, I am so excited about tonight. I can't wait for our guests to arrive," Essence said with a sparkle in her eye. She walked around as if she were on a cloud.

"You're acting as if President Obama and his wife, Michelle, are joining us tonight, Essence," Sloan said with an irritated voice.

Essence stood silently, taking in his distress. Essence was in awe as his demeanor suddenly changed. "Is there something bothering you, Sloan? Something we need to talk about?" she asked with a questioning stare.

Sloan retrieved his glass. After taking a sip, he shook his head. "No."

Essence walked toward him and met his eyes. "You haven't been yourself lately."

"Essence, please don't start that again. Since I moved back in, things have been going pretty well, don't you think? Let's not rock the boat tonight." Sloan glanced at his watch. "Our guests should be arriving any minute now, and we both need to be on our best behavior."

"You're right. I'm going to freshen up," she said as she left the room.

Shortly afterward, Essence greeted Derrick and Natasha with a warm, pleasant smile.

"Come on in," she uttered as they entered the foyer. "You both look wonderful tonight." She gave them both a once-over stare.

"Thanks, and so do you," Derrick said with a smile of his own.

"Yes, Derrick is right. You look absolutely stunning," Natasha chimed in as they made their way into the livingroom.

Sloan stood in the middle of the floor. He greeted the couple with a small, short grin. Natasha's gaze met his. It seemed as if she was seeing him for the very first time as a man and not her best friend. But not only as a man, but as a man whom she was attracted to. His smile widened as he stared back at her. She felt her pulse quicken as he took her hand.

With a slight squeeze, he said, "I'm glad you two could make it, and I hope this evening will go well. Essence has spent many hours making sure everything is perfect." He gave her his popular smile.

"Oh, I'm sure we will have a wonderful time," Derrick said with a richness in his voice, interrupting the connection between Sloan and Natasha.

The evening flowed nicely as the foursome dined on calabash shrimp, rice pilaf, and asparagus with red wine. The conversation was light and airy. Sloan could hardly keep his eyes off Natasha. He had never seen her look so beautiful. Derrick and Essence tried to keep the conversation flowing, but there were several uneasy moments.

"So, Sloan, I've heard the Norris account folded. What happened, man? I thought you had it wrapped up," Derrick asked.

Sloan shot Derrick a frozen stare. "In this business, Derrick, you will eventually learn that even if you get almost to the finish line with a client, there is still time for them to stop the game."

"I see," Derrick uttered as he peered over at Natasha. "Well, I got some good news. I've landed the Alex account. You know, the one you said was a downer. Turns out the old man's son had different ideas. I contacted him several days ago. We had dinner last night at Michael's." Derrick was smiling from ear to ear. "And I'm happy to say we've signed the contract this afternoon. Mr. Emerson couldn't believe I bagged the deal so quickly.

He was so impressed, he gave me a bonus," he said, turning to face Natasha. "I'm taking this young lady on a much-needed vacation."

Natasha caught the icy stare coming from Sloan.

"Well, congratulations, Derrick!" Essence exclaimed. "You two are leaving the city? How soon?" Essence couldn't help but prod.

Natasha's eyes quickly met Derrick's. "Next week," Natasha said smoothly as Sloan's glare made its way to her warm face. She quickly turned and peered at Derrick. "I can hardly wait," she uttered with a smile.

"Same here, babe," Derrick responded, taking her hand in his.

Essence noticed the tension in the air as everyone's eyes traveled around the table. She had to do something—and quick.

"Come, everyone," she said, standing. "I think we all could use some fresh air after a feast like this." She waved her hand, gesturing for everyone to follow her.

The foursome retreated to the balcony of Essence's high-rise condo. The night was so lovely. The full moon shone brightly as a cool breeze blew gently enough to keep everyone comfortable. Natasha and Derrick were surprised to see the patio table set just as beautifully as the dining room table. Essence had placed flowers and heart-shaped candles floating in miniature glass bowls in the center of the table. She sent Sloan back inside for drinks and dessert. When everyone was settled, the conversation flowed once again.

"I am very happy both of you came tonight. I'm beginning to feel more at home in Atlanta," Essence said, taking Sloan's hand and giving him a warm smile. Turning her gaze to Derrick, she asked. "What about you, Derrick. Do you miss Texas?"

Derrick smiled, "I will always miss my home, but I agree with you concerning Atlanta. Since I've been here, I find Atlanta growing on me, especially since I've met this sweet young lady." Derrick smiled broadly as his eyes met Natasha's.

"Well, I think we've both been blessed in finding a wonderful place to work and such charming people to spend our lives with," Natasha crooned as she looked around the table. "Would you care to elaborate, Natasha?" Essence quizzed as she looked into Natasha's eyes.

"Um...sure," she stumbled. "It's very nice to have you and Derrick on board with us at Emerson & Stuckey. And I hope you both will have long employment with the company and…" Natasha paused as her gaze met Sloan's stare. "I hope you and Sloan will be very happy…together. Just like Derrick and me."

Sloan gave her an empty smile. Natasha knew she was beginning to get to him, and she wasn't finished, to say the least.

"Derrick, you have made great strides since you've been with the company. But being a smart man like you are, I knew it would only be a matter of time before you rose to the top," Natasha said as she stroked his ego. Sloan remembered Natasha saying something similar to him a few months ago, before their relationship took a nose dive.

"Thank you, babe, for believing in your man," Derrick beamed.

Sloan had had enough of the "babe" line. He wanted to shove the words down Derrick's egotistical throat.

"I will always believe in you, Derrick. You just have to know what it takes to get what you want. Isn't that right, Sloan?" Natasha asked as her eyes danced.

A thin line formed across Sloan's forehead. He wondered what kind of game Natasha was playing. Sloan didn't respond. Instead, he picked up a butter-flavored cracker and a single cube of cheese and placed them in his mouth. As he chewed, he gave Natasha a disapproving look. Natasha's eyes were glued to Sloan's full lips as he chewed. For a moment she got a vision of her lips kissing his and a warm sensation crept down her spine. Natasha tuned out the conversation between Derrick and Essence.

"Babe, isn't that great?" Derrick asked.

Natasha gave Derrick a questioning look. "Isn't what great?" she asked, slightly embarrassed by her momentary fantasizing.

"Essence just invited us to go camping with them. Doesn't that sound like fun?"

Natasha cringed. "Sorry, Derrick, I don't do camping," she said firmly.

Sloan let out a small chuckle. "She's telling the truth. When we were kids, Natasha's cousins and I pitched a tent in her mother's backyard one hot summer night." Sloan's eyes glowed as he continued the humorous story. "We had the campfire going and were roasting marshmallows as everyone sat around in a circle. Barry was telling one of those creepy ghost stories, and we all were sitting very quiet with our ears hanging onto to his every word. When Barry was about to give us the scary ending, Natasha stood up like her pants were on fire. She ran so fast I thought a ghost was really chasing her." Sloan threw his head back as he laughed. "She was so scared, the rest of the night she slept in the tent with…me." Sloan faltered to a stop. He relished the memory of holding Natasha in his arms all night long.

He could smell the fresh scent of her hair and the softness of her smooth skin as if it had happened yesterday. The air grew thick in the room as everyone but Natasha stared at Sloan. She couldn't look at him, because the memories were as clear as day to her as well; and it tugged at something deep inside of her. Pandora's Box was beginning to open as she remembered that night. What Sloan didn't say was how they had kissed, really kissed—a kiss so deep that it had shattered their very souls. Nothing had happened, but they were very afraid of the unfamiliar feelings that flowed through their veins. They promised not to tell a soul, and they also promised to forget it had ever happened. And somehow, they did…until now. When Natasha found the courage to look into Sloan's face, she was certain of what he was thinking and remembering.

"Umm…well…I'm sure we can do other things together," Essence said, breaking the awkwardness of the moment.

Clearing his throat, Derrick muttered, "Yes, I agree. Maybe we can hang out on the beach."

"Oh yes…I love the beach," Essence flared. "Let's toast, everyone!" she said, holding up her glass of wine. The foursome held up their glasses.

"To all of us, may we stay the best of friends." The tinkling sound of their glasses filled the air as their eyes scanned each other's faces. Derrick's cell phone went off. Glancing at the number, he uttered, "I must take this" and he quickly left the table.

"Well, I'm going to get us some coffee," Essence announced as she headed back inside.

Natasha and Sloan made their way over to the balcony, where they both stared out at the glimmer of the city night's lights. Atlanta seemed to burst with flares as the lights shone brightly. Slowing turning to face her, Sloan took in Natasha's elegant beauty. His eyes lowered to her chest, where a sterling silver cross gleamed in the moonlight. He reached out and touched it gently with his fingertips. Natasha flinched as if his fingertips were a match that burned her delicate skin.

"I see you still have it," he said softly. She could only nod her head. Natasha wasn't sure if she trusted herself to speak. "I miss you, Natasha," he whispered so gently.

She let out a whiff of air. "Don't, Sloan," she muttered.

"Don't what? Don't fight to save our relationship, Me- Me. You act as if you don't care about us anymore," he said as his voice rose slightly.

Did he just say the word, 'care'? Natasha questioned silently. What she felt for him was a hell of a lot more than caring.

"Do you hate me, Natasha?" He had moved so close to her that she could feel the warmth of his breath. The sexy cologne, which was her favorite, tingled in her nostrils. Natasha gasped as she fought for control.

"Hate you? Sloan, I could never hate you."

"What is it, then? Just tell me, and you know I will make it right. I want you back. I want us back like we used to be."

Natasha attempted to respond as she peered into Sloan's pleading eyes, but the sound of Essence's voice startled them.

"No fair, you two. Whatever you are talking about over there, I think we all should be a part of it."

A haphazard smile formed across her lips. "It's nothing, Essence. Natasha was just giving me a piece of her mind about ragging on her with the campfire story."

"Sloan is always telling things he shouldn't," Natasha added, trying to sound convincing. Derrick returned to the group. They drank coffee and conversed as friends as best they could.

ESSENCE

Sloan stood next to the dishwasher after he had placed the last plate inside and turned it on. He was lost in deep thought while the dishwasher hummed. Essence startled him as she wrapped her arms around him from behind.

"Oh, honey, I had such a great time tonight. Everything went just as I planned!" she exclaimed as she gave him a warm squeeze. Sloan released her grip and then turned and peered into her eyes.

"Essence, please tell me why you are so hell-bent on creating these little get-togethers? You know how I really feel about Derrick, and I know you are not a fan of Natasha's, as you claim to be. We all work together, and now you want to include Derrick into our personal lives."

"Are you saying that it's okay to leave them both out of our lives? Well, if that's what you want, it's fine with me."

"No, that's not what I'm saying," Sloan said absently.

"Oh…I get it," Essence said with a raised brow. "It's only Derrick you want to leave out," she smirked.

Sloan grimaced at her remark. "Look, I just don't trust the guy, alright. I've spoken to him several times, and I know where he is coming from. He is a womanizer, and I don't want Natasha being one of his victims."

Essence felt herself growing a little agitated with Sloan's over-concern for Natasha. After all, the woman wasn't green behind the ears.

"Sloan, I'm sure Natasha is capable of taking care of herself. She doesn't need you to hold her hand."

Sloan shot her a patronizing look. "I'm not trying to hold her hand. I know what she's been through," Sloan asserted.

"And she's gotten over it. You know, she is not the first woman to ever get her heart broken!" Essence almost screamed. She pulled her hair back and gave Sloan a tired look. "It seems to me you didn't have a problem with Derrick until he and Natasha started dating. Now, you tell me what's really going on here, Sloan," she said, folding her arms across her chest.

Sloan looked at her and frowned. "I think you're missing my point."

"And I say it's all bologna," Essence spat. "I think you're afraid that your little best friend is moving on with her life and she doesn't need you to play hero anymore."

Sloan felt a roar of anger rise in his chest. "You are twisting things, Essence! You don't know anything about our friendship. She is more than a friend… she's like my…sister," he stammered.

Sloan could have kicked himself for stuttering. He didn't understand why he behaved in such a way when he spoke of his feelings for Natasha. Essence's nostrils flared.

"Well, if she is just like a sister to you, why did you keep giving her those funny looks over dinner? And when Derrick was showing her affection, you acted as if he had stolen your wife."

"Now you're being pathetic!" Sloan retorted as he entered the living room. Essence followed him closely as she cringed at his malicious remark.

Standing in the middle of the living room floor, Essence bellowed, "So, was I being pathetic when I saw you two on the balcony, huddled together like football players getting ready for a play? And don't think for one second that I bought into that explanation you both managed to chisel out when I confronted you."

Sloan's face hardened. "I care about Natasha. I always have, and I always will."

"Are you sure you two are not sleeping together?" Essence stormed with rage. "Because if you are, it better stop, and I mean right now!" she yelled.

"I don't like the sound of this," Sloan hissed. "First, you're accusing me of something that is totally ridiculous, and now, you're threatening me as well. Who do you think you are?" Sloan asked as his eyes narrowed.

Essence walked over to him. She circled his lips with her fingertip, and then she kissed them softly. Peering into his dark-brown eyes, she whispered, "I'm your woman now. That is who I am; and you are mine, Sloan Stevens. And no one is ever going to come between us, past or present. Do you understand me, sugar?" She attempted to pull him into her, but he withdrew her arms and held them to her side.

"I don't know what planet you came from. But you are on Earth now, and in my world, I don't respond to threats."

Essence gave him a daggered look. "Sloan, you're not speaking to an inexperienced schoolgirl. I'm not one to be played with. You said you loved me and you wanted a family with me," she said as she pointed her finger at him. "And this is where you're going to stay."

She pulled him into her and began tearing off his clothes. She ripped the buttons off his Kenneth Cole shirt and reached down and began to undo the belt buckle of his matching trousers. She embraced him with a fiery kiss. Sloan couldn't help but respond with a fire of his own as he followed suit. The evening dress she wore was torn from her shoulders, exposing her dark caramel colored breasts. Within seconds, they both were freed from their clothing. Dropping down to the thick, tan carpet, Sloan entered her. He pumped into her wildly, taking their lovemaking to greater heights.

As he made love to Essence, something scary was happening to him. He saw Natasha's face, but he was Essence's body. He was physically making love to Essence, but he fantasized that he was making love to Natasha. After several moments, Sloan and Essence both reached climax; exploding in unison. Sloan lay spent on the floor with his eyes closed, breathing deeply. Essence laid her head in the crook of his shoulder as she panted for breath.

"You're one hell of a woman," Sloan mumbled after his heavy breathing subsided.

"I know, sugar, and don't you ever forget it," she said between quick breaths. Essence stood. "Let's continue this upstairs, shall we?" she uttered lustfully. Sloan took in the sight of her sweaty body. Her full breasts dangled before him like diamonds as she extended her hand. Without saying a word, he took her hand and they headed toward the staircase, leaving their clothes behind.

DERRICK & NATASHA

Derrick found himself in unfamiliar territory. Women had come and gone since his divorce a couple of years ago, and he felt nothing for them. To him, they were just little trinkets purchased along the way and discarded when a newer one took its place. Watching Natasha's long lashes flutter as she slept in his arms stirred up feelings he thought had been buried long ago. He began to revisit a place he never wanted to see or feel again, but the quietness of Natasha's warmth lured him there.

Falling head over heels was an understatement where his marriage was concerned. No woman had ever possessed his heart the way his ex-wife had; and he showered her with affection, emotionally, physically, mentally, and sexually. Their world was a fairytale, but he soon woke up to reality when he came home to find her gone.

Natasha stirred in his arms. He kissed the top of her head as her eyes flickered open.

"Good morning, sunshine," he said as they snuggled under the cool bed sheet.

"What time is it?" she asked as she propped herself up on her elbows.

"It's still early, babe, and it's Sunday. Unless you're going to church, I say let's go back to bed," Derrick suggested.

Natasha thought going to church was a good idea. Lord knows, it had been a while since she'd stepped foot in New Jerusalem Baptist Church, and she felt a twinge of guilt. Maybe church is where she needed to be, to cleanse her mind, her soul, and her heart. Hopping out of bed, she looked around for her clothing. After leaving Sloan and Essence's place last night, she'd really tied one on at Derrick's place. She sure as heck hadn't planned on spending the night and ending up in his bed.

"Babe, come on, I know you're not leaving me," Derrick grumbled as he pulled back the mauve-colored sheet and stood up. Natasha swayed as her eyes focused on the black Adonis that stood tall and lean before her.

Derrick's body was screaming sex and pleasure. For a moment, she was tempted to stay. But her inner spirit won. She was going to church.

"Sorry, Derrick, but I promised my mother that I would attend church with her this Sunday. I already missed two Sundays in a row, and I'm kinda feeling like a wayward sinner right about now."

Derrick's expression grew dim, and then it brightened. "I can go with you. I'm a little ashamed to say that I haven't been in a while myself. And I would love to meet Mom," he said, smiling.

Natasha gave him a smile of her own and chuckled. "Okay…but we must hurry. I got to stop by my place and get dressed," she said as they both headed for the shower. On the drive to her place, she pondered why she felt as if she had been railroaded.

New Jerusalem Baptist Church was filled to capacity when they arrived at the front of the church; but, as usual, it was a hot, yet beautiful Sunday morning. The audience was sprinkled with ladies adorning stylish suits, some with matching hats. It was like looking into a beautiful, colorful garden. Even though most of the hats were fashionable, she found them a nuisance at times, especially if you found yourself sitting directly behind a lady wearing an outrageous one. Mrs. Jenkins's black-and-white-spiral hat was so wide it looked like a spaceship, instead of a

hat. Natasha had to keep looking around the sides of it just to get a glimpse of Pastor Austin as he preached the Word. Her mother sat on her left, and Derrick was seated on her right; neither seemed to notice her dilemma.

Natasha peeped at Derrick, and as she did, her heart skipped a beat. The man was gorgeous in his light-blue pinstriped Armani suit. He gave her a slow and sexy smile as he returned her gaze. Goosebumps popped up on her arms as she noticed the stares of women who also took notice of Derrick. Their eyes were filled with the age-old questions women in heat would ask. *Who is he? And how do I get next to him?* Natasha concluded that maybe it was time she let go of any feelings other than the feelings of friendship for Sloan. Maybe she was just mistaking feelings of loneliness for love. It was crazy, and it was time to stop it. Darin was gone, Sloan had moved on, and here sat a man who could be her future.

A slow heat rose to the surface of her neck. She felt as if she were having a hot flash. She retrieved the fan, that was adorned with Martin

Luther King's face on the front, from the pew in front of them, and she began to fan herself vigorously.

"Are you alright, chile?" Florene asked, eyeing her suspiciously.

"I'm fine, Momma. It's a little stuffy in here," she mumbled.

"That's weird," Derrick chimed in. "I have on a suit, and I'm not hot at all. You are wearing a chiffon dress with no sleeves. Are you sure you're okay?"

Natasha's temper flared. "Derrick, I'm fine. Drop it," she uttered through clenched teeth.

"Okay, okay," he relented as Pastor Austin finished his sermon.

NATASHA & FLORENE

Natasha spent the night with her mother. And while lying on her mother's blue-and-yellow floral sofa, she decided not to go to work on Monday. She just needed a break. *A break from both Sloan and Derrick,* she thought as she closed her eyes. She thought about the trip she and Derrick had planned for the next week. Actually, it wasn't a plan. It was something thrown together for the sake of making Sloan jealous. Now she wanted—no, she *needed* out of it. Even though Derrick was as fine as they came, her feelings for him weren't what she thought they should be.

Noticing her daughter's restless demeanor, Florene walked over to her. Tapping the calf of Natasha's leg, Florene motioned for her to scoot over so she could sit next to her.

"Honey, what's the matter? You hardly said a dozen words tonight," Florene observed as she stared into Natasha's troubled face.

Natasha scooted over, repositioning herself on the couch; she looked back at her mother. Then she placed her head on her mother's lap as if she were a child. Her mother stroked her spiral curls, but didn't say a word. They both sat in silence for a moment.

"Momma, how do you know when you really love someone?" Natasha asked in a childlike voice.

Florene let out a long sigh, and then she giggled before saying, "When I met your father, Natasha, I knew right away it was love. Real love, that is, and not just lust. You do know there is a difference, right?"

"Yes, Mother, I know that," Natasha responded.

"Anyway," Florene continued, "Your father had a way of making me feel as if I was the only woman in the world. He would hold me in his arms and tell me how pretty I was. And then he would tickle me into tears. I begged him to let me go, but do you know what your father said?"

Natasha shook her head no.

"He said, 'Woman, I'm never letting you go.' And then he gave me a kiss that touched my very soul. And even after thirty years of marriage, through our ups and downs, he still makes this old heart of mine flutter," she chuckled.

Natasha had a mist of tears forming in her eyes. She sat straight up. "Oh, Momma, that's how I feel about…"

"Derrick," Florene finished. "He seems to be a nice man. He is so handsome and very well spoken. A man like that, I'm sure, has had his share of fruits."

"Momma, what are you getting at?" Natasha asked with a raised brow.

"Honey, men like that have to be carefully watched. You know a snake can be charming when it wants to be, but its bite is ready to strike at a moment's notice. Lord knows, you don't need another Darin in your life. Now, I'm not trying to tell you how to run your affairs but…"

"I know, Momma, and he is not who I'm talking about."

"Oh," Florene said with a perplexed expression. "Well, who are you talking about chile?" Florene asked, peering into her daughter's eyes. Natasha was silent. "Oh my Lord, are you saying what I think you're saying?"

Natasha's bottom lip quivered. "Momma, I think… no…I know that I am in love with him. I have been for a very long time, but—"

Florene reached out and grabbed Natasha by her shoulders. Looking squarely at her, she said, "After all this time, your brain is finally accepting what your heart has known for years." Natasha stood up and started pacing the floor.

"I've been going over everything in my mind, Momma. Sloan and I have been friends since third grade. I keep asking myself when our friendship turned from its innocent, childlike relationship into feelings that a man and woman would share. I mean, it's like one morning I just woke up in love with him. No warnings, no nothing. And now I'm scared, Momma. What if his feelings are totally different from mine? I mean, he's in a relationship right now, and what if he…doesn't love me?"

Natasha began to sob. Florene walked over to her and took her into her arms. Once Natasha's sobs subsided, Florene said, "You need to tell him."

Natasha pulled away from her. "I can't, Momma," she whispered.

"Natasha, you have to. You two have shared so much over the years. And you know there is a chance that he might feel the same way. Don't be afraid, honey. If it's meant to be, it will be," Florene answered softly.

GRETTA

Gretta trotted in the direction of her black Toyota Avalon and pressed the remote lock. The car came alive as the lights flashed. Gretta opened the driver's side door and threw in her leather bag. She was about to slide in when she noticed the tall figure of a man in the shadow of the underground parking lot. A scream was preparing to escape from her throat as her thumb located the small can of pepper spray on her key ring, when the man stepped into the light.

"It's me, Gretta," Derrick said, coming forward.

"Oh my God, you scared the heebie-jeebies out of me," she spouted as she grasped her chest. Her racing heart began to slow.

"Sorry about that," he said, draping his arms around her shoulder. "I just wanted to see you again. I remembered you telling me where you worked, but ITT is a large corporation. I've walked my legs off trying to find your car," he chuckled as he gazed into her eyes. "I was about to give up when I saw you coming this way. You're looking mighty fine, Gretta," he said with a slow grin. Gretta let out a soft giggle. She knew she was hot in her newly-purchased, tan Donna Karan business suit that caressed her curves perfectly.

"How about having dinner with me tonight? I mean, that's the least I can offer you since I almost gave you a heart attack."

Gretta paused for a moment as she stared back at his handsome features. Then she smiled. "Alright, but I will follow you," she said firmly.

"Fine, I'm parked right over there," he said, pointing to the other end of the parking lot.

Gretta felt a tingle run down her spine as she followed Derrick out of the parking garage. She was attracted to this man like flies to honey, and she couldn't wait to taste his sweetness.

Minutes later, they were seated across from each other at Ray's In the City, an Atlanta restaurant that was famous for its delicious foods. Gretta sipped on her glass of red wine as soft music filled the air.

"Dinner was wonderful," she mused as she gazed into his eyes after they had finished eating.

"Not as wonderful as what I'm seeing before me," Derrick flirted.

"Cut to the chase, Derrick. What's this really all about?" Gretta said, placing her glass on the table.

"Mmmm, I see you are very direct."

"Very," she responded.

Derrick leaned in. "Ever since the pool party at Natasha's, I can't seem to get you off of my mind." Derrick took her small hand in his. He rubbed the back of her hand with his thumb. Gretta's panties became wet at his gesture. She wanted this man, and she was sure he wanted her as well. But she couldn't cross that line. Or could she? She cleared her throat and gently pulled her hand way from his.

"Yes, the pool party was very entertaining," she managed to say. Looking into his eyes, she muttered, "But I thought I would have been a faded memory in your world by now."

"Gretta, a woman as beautiful as you are could never be a faded memory," Derrick said, giving her a charming smile.

"I bet you run that popular line on multiple women," Gretta snapped with a quick roll of her eyes.

"Feisty are we?" he retorted as he enjoyed her stab of attitude.

"No, I'm just not stupid," she retaliated, her gaze never leaving his. She wanted to down her whole glass of wine, but she forced herself to take another sip. Derrick was making her very nervous, and his vibes were playing tricks with her mind. But she was going to force herself to keep a level head.

"I really want to get to know you better," Derrick said, giving her a sensual smile that most women couldn't resist.

Gretta couldn't decide whether the room was getting hot or if it was just her temperature that had gone up a notch. She looked down at her designer watch. "You know, it's getting really late, another work day is on the horizon," she mumbled as she stood up.

"I hate for our evening to end so soon," Derrick said with an air of disappointment as he stood.

"I know…but a girl has to pay her bills," Gretta chuckled as she reached for her purse.

Derrick retrieved the bill from the table, and they both headed for the front door of the restaurant. After paying the bill, they walked to their cars. Derrick pulled Gretta into his arms and planted a sizzling hot kiss on her lips.

"I wanted to do that from the minute I laid eyes on you," he said as he peered into her eyes. Gretta felt as if she had just stepped off a merry-go-round. Her head was spinning.

"Derrick, we can't do this," she murmured. Derrick pulled her into him again. This time, she felt his manhood rise as they kissed deeply and the flames of passion rose in them both.

"Wait…wait," Gretta gasped. "What about Natasha?"

"I'm a free agent, Gretta. And if it makes you feel any better, she doesn't have to know," he whispered as he ran his fingers under her dress. Gretta wanted this man like a drowning man wants to be saved. They barely made it through the door of her apartment before they discarded their clothing. Gretta's mind said, *This is my cousin's man,* but her heated body said, *At this moment, he's mine.* She inhaled the scent of his spicy cologne, which drove her wild with desire. She shivered as his fingers walked across her body like someone looking through the phone book. When he finally entered her, the rhythm began like drums beating far away. They grew louder and louder and louder and louder, until the peak was reached.

A volcano had erupted, bringing the utmost pleasure to them both. Derrick lay breathless on top of her. Silence blanketed the room. Only the tick-tock of her alarm clock broke the silence. As reality set in, so did revelation. Gretta pushed him away and sat up in her bed. "I can't believe we did this, Derrick." A ton of guilt washed over her.

Derrick rolled over and propped himself up. "I'm not married to your cousin, Gretta. So, why are you tripping?"

"I know, but you're dating her," she said with a roll of her head.

Derrick decided to lay his cards on the table. "Gretta, let me be totally honest with you. I'm not big on relationships—long lasting relationships, that is," he clarified. "I've been hurt deeply in my past, and I don't think I'll ever love again. So, for me, relationships are like seasons. They come and they go."

Gretta couldn't believe it. This man had just bedded her, and now he was discarding her as if she were trash. Gretta jumped out of her bed.

"So, is this all I was to you? A season?" she asked with ice in her voice.

Gretta felt like a fool. *Why do I always fall for the trap?* she asked herself furiously. It was as if she were walking in the dark forest, always being caught in an animal trap.

Derrick got out of bed and walked over to her. Placing his hands on her shoulders, he uttered, "I'm sorry, Gretta. That came out so wrong."

Gretta stepped away from him, pulling the bed sheet around her even tighter, and exhaled.

"What about my cousin? What season are you in with her?" she smirked as she peered into his eyes.

Derrick cupped his goatee, a habit he had when he felt he was cornered. "As I told you before, I'm a free agent. I'm just having a little fun."

"Yes, fun, but at whose expense?" Gretta asked wildly.

"Gretta, I like your cousin a lot. I could even fall in love with her…"

Gretta's face crumbled. Now, she felt like a cheap thrill. *I must be a glutton for punishment,* she thought as she folded her arms across her chest. She wanted this man out of her house and her life. "Derrick, I think you should—," she began.

"But, I'm more attracted to you," he interjected. Gretta took in a deep breath as her throat tightened.

"Uh…what did you say?" she stammered.

"You heard me, Gretta," he said with a sexy smile. "I'm more attracted to you, baby."

He closed the gap between them and pulled her into his arms. The fire started again as Derrick kissed the nape of her neck, the roundness of her shoulder, and between her breasts. Her soft skin was like butter to his touch. He continued his trail of heat as his tongue found its way to her sensual spot. A moan escaped from the bottom of her throat.

"Derrick, you're driving me mad crazy."

"Before I'm finished with you, baby, you will be insane," Derrick said, caressing her womanhood. The shrill sound of the phone made Gretta freeze.

"Let it ring, baby," Derrick said huskily.

"No, it might be my boss. I'm expecting a call from her," she uttered as she wiggled out of Derrick's grip.

Gretta picked up the phone and muttered, "Hello."

"Hi, Gretta, it's me, Natasha. What are you up to tonight?"

Gretta peered over at Derrick's naked body. *If she only knew,* she thought silently.

NATASHA

"Girl, what happened to you tonight? I thought you told me we were going to hook up."

"Uhhh…yeah, but something came up," Gretta responded as Derrick licked the dark nipple of her breast.

"Well, at least you could have called me, Gretta. I got dressed and waited on you for hours," Natasha bellowed.

"Ummm, sorry about that…" Gretta mumbled.

"Gretta, is something wrong? You don't sound right. Is someone there with you?" Natasha quizzed.

Gretta pushed Derrick's face away from her chest and sat up straight. "Natasha, I'm real busy, okay. Can we finish this conversation later?"

"Gretta, the reason I'm calling is to tell you I'm leaving the city for a while."

"Leaving?" Gretta gulped as her fingers gripped the receiver a little tighter.

"Yeah," Natasha responded.

"Where are you going and, Natasha…why?" Gretta probed.

"I don't exactly know where I'm going, maybe Florida. I…just need to get away for a while to clear my head. You know, get some perspective on things," she explained. Gretta looked over at Derrick, who was now in a sitting position. Gretta thought he was looking sexier by the minute.

"Have you mentioned this to Derrick?" Gretta asked cautiously.

"No."

"What about Sloan?" Gretta asked with a raised brow.

"No," Natasha replied again.

"Well, are you going to tell them?" Gretta asked.

"Of course I am, Gretta, but not until I know where I'm going. You know, I think I've changed my mind about telling Sloan."

"And why is that?" Gretta inquired.

"Mmmm, he's probably so caught up with Miss Cougar, he won't even notice I'm gone."

"You know, I don't agree with you on that, but maybe a getaway is what you need," Gretta said as selfish thoughts crossed her mind. This meant she could spend more time with Derrick. And that was something she knew she would enjoy doing. "Gretta, are you there!?" Natasha's voice boomed through the phone.

"Yeah, I'm here. You don't have to blast my eardrums."

"Gretta, is someone there with you? You seem very distracted."

"No…there's no one here, already. Look, I gotta go. Talk to you later, cousin."

The phone hummed in Natasha's ear. Natasha thought as she dialed the digits to Emerson & Stuckey.

SLOAN

Sloan walked out of his office and down the long corridor. He passed a couple of male coworkers dressed in the usual office attire: crisp, white designer shirts with matching dark trousers. One mumbled, "good morning" while the other only nodded his head. The women, on the other hand, had brought spice to the company's business attire. Some wore stylish suits that screamed sex appeal; their blouses were lacy and their skirts were just long enough to appease the company dress code. Long legs and spike heels made working very interesting, but, at the moment, girl-watching wasn't on his agenda. He was looking for one lady only, and as he approached her desk, he saw that she wasn't there. He had practically searched the whole building, but Natasha was nowhere to be found.

"Good morning, Mr. Stevens," Lisa Ray said, coming up behind him. Sloan turned to face her. Lisa Ray wasn't the finest chick he had ever seen, but her body made up for her almost plain-Jane look.

"You must be looking for Natasha," she said as she stared into his eyes.

"Yes, have you seen her?" he asked. Lisa Ray gave him a strange look.

"Mr. Stevens, Natasha is not coming in today."

"Oh," he responded. "I hope she's not sick."

A thin line formed across his forehead. He made a mental note to stop by her place after work. Lisa Ray gave him a puzzled look. She chuckled. "Mr. Stevens, Natasha is not sick at all. She has taken a few vacation days. I think she's going on a trip."

The line on Sloan's forehead deepened. "Are you sure about that?"

"Positive," Lisa Ray replied.

Sloan remembered a time when he knew exactly where Natasha was at any given moment of the day. He knew what she was thinking. They always kept in touch, if only to say hello and ask how the day was going. Oh, how he missed those times. For the past few months, Sloan felt as if they were only casual associates. His heart began to ache. The sharing, the laughter, and the bond between them was now gone.

Coming out of his reverie, he asked, "Do you know if she left already?" A hint of desperation crept into his voice. Lisa Ray felt as if she had said too much, but she concluded that there was no reason to stop now. The cat was already out of the bag.

"No, but she will be in about an hour," Lisa Ray said, glancing down at her watch.

"Thanks, Lisa," Sloan said, giving her a light tap on the arm. She watched as Sloan took long strides down the corridor.

NATASHA

Natasha had placed the last suitcase in the trunk of her car. As she headed back up the walkway to her home, she saw Sloan's Navigator turn sharply into her driveway. The bright rays of the sun casted a reflection that prevented her from seeing his face, but from the way he stopped the vehicle, she knew he was upset. Sloan flew out of the Navigator and raced toward her. Sloan's usual warm smile failed to greet her as he approached the steps of her home, and for the very first time in their relationship, she felt vulnerable.

"Were you going to leave without telling me?" His voice held a spark of anger as well as hurt.

"Sloan…I needed to get away," she mumbled.

"Get away or runaway, Me-Me!"

Natasha turned away and headed inside. Sloan followed her. "I was making some coffee. Do you want some?" Natasha asked as she walked into the kitchen.

"No, Me-Me, what I want are some straight answers," Sloan retorted as he stared into her eyes. "We don't have to argue. Just be honest with me. Tell me what's really going on."

Natasha lowered her eyes as she leaned against the coolness of her stainless steel fridge and let out a low breath. She knew Sloan had her cornered. Natasha forced herself to look into the eyes of the man she loved and craved with her whole inner being. Her mother's words echoed in her ear. *"Tell him how you feel."* But she just couldn't. "Sloan, I do owe you an apology for the other night at dinner. I was rude. I shouldn't have made the snide remarks about you. We…both are adults now, and we shouldn't be behaving like children. We've grown up now, and we have separate lives to live." Natasha paused. Her voice was tight, but she had to go on. "So, if Essence is the woman for you…I wish the both of you all the happiness there is." Tears formed in her eyes, but she managed to blink them placing his hands on her shoulders.

"You're acting as if I asked her to marry me."

Natasha moved away from him. Being that close to him threatened the wall she was putting up and was determined to hold on to. "Well, isn't that the next step? I mean…you said that you…loved her."

Her words came out thick. Sloan walked up behind her and turned her around. For the first time, Natasha noticed how tired and strained Sloan appeared. Her heart went out to him. He was not only her best friend, but the man she cared deeply about. He was hurting; she could feel it, and she knew it wasn't all because of her.

"Sloan, something is wrong. What is it?" she asked. For the first time in months, she touched him. She cupped his face with her small hands. Sloan pulled her into him and held her. For a brief moment, there was silence, and then he began to speak as they pulled away from each other. They took a seat at the breakfast table. Sloan's head dipped. His voice came out heavy.

"When Essence and I first started dating, Me-Me, things were fine. I really thought I'd found the woman I would spend the rest of my life with. Everything was good between us. But slowly, things began to change. Essence started to get possessive. She had to know where I was and who I was with every minute of the day."

Natasha managed a weak chuckle. "Sloan, you had a girlfriend like that once before. What was her name?" Natasha's eyes flickered as she sought the memory.

"Bonnie Fairchild," Sloan uttered.

"Yeah, you told me she was like a sponge." Natasha smiled. Sloan gave her a strange look. "What?" she asked. Sloan's inner voice tugged at his heart.

"Mmmm, nothing," he said.

"I'm sorry, Sloan, go on and finish telling me about Essence," Natasha apologized.

"Natasha, Bonnie was a walk in the park to compared Essence. She gets this crazed look in her eyes as if she's in another place. I've never experienced anything like this before."

"I knew there was something strange about her from the very first time we met," Natasha admitted. "And, you know, every time she sees us together, she gives me this hateful look when she thinks no one is watching," Natasha added.

"Don't read too much into that, Me-Me. After all, she knows you're the only other woman in my life," Sloan said, giving her that heart-stopping smile of his.

Natasha playfully hit him on the shoulder and they both fell out laughing.

"It's been too long since we've done this," Sloan said as he wrapped his arms around her. "Me-Me, I need you. My life won't ever be the same if you're not here for me. I want us back like we used to be."

"And that's it?" Natasha asked slowly and firmly as they looked into each other's eyes.

Sloan gave her a puzzled stare. "What do you mean by 'and that's it'?" he asked.

Natasha knew she was about to open Pandora's Box. She stood up and decided to keep it closed. Looking at the clock, she uttered, "I got to get going, Sloan. I was about to take a shower when you pulled up."

"You haven't answered my question."

"Sloan, come on; don't make me miss my flight. I will call you when I get settled."

"Natasha, you haven't even told me where you're going or when you're coming back."

"Sloan, what does it matter?" Natasha gave him a cold stare.

He didn't understand. One minute they were laughing like old times, and now it was as if none of it had ever happened.

"I guess you're right. Our lives are separate now. I have no right to question anything you do." He walked over to her and pulled her into him. The scent and firmness of his body made Natasha feel faint as they embraced. Her eyes fluttered as he held her as if he were holding her for the last time. "Me-Me, I don't know what went wrong with us. But I do know that you will always be important to me. Take care of yourself, you hear." He let her go. Tears welled up in her eyes.

"I will, Sloan."

He turned and headed for the door. "I'll be waiting for that phone call," he said with a crooked grin.

"I'll call. I promise."

Natasha watched from her bay window as Sloan entered his vehicle and sped away. Fresh tears made their way down her cheeks. Why hadn't she told him how she really felt? She realized that Sloan wanted things back to where they used to be between them, and that was not the answer she was looking for. He saw them as what they had always been—best friends. And that's all they would ever be.

DERRICK & ESSENCE

Derrick sat behind his desk with his head buried in files when she entered the office. He lifted his head, and with a scowl, he demanded, "Don't you know how to knock?"

Essence gave him a surreal look as she took a seat on the cherry-colored chair adjacent to his desk. "There isn't any time for pleasantries, Derrick."

Derrick walked over to the office door and closed it. "Make this brief, Essence," he instructed as he took his seat again. Essence's slanted eyes darkened.

"What I want to know, Derrick, is why you didn't join Natasha on her trip?" she asked as she leaned forward. Derrick grimaced.

"I couldn't. I had too much work to do here," he said as he closed a file and placed it neatly on another stack at the corner of his desk. "Derrick, everything would have worked out perfectly if you had left with her," Essence said with irritation in her voice.

"Perfect for whom, Essence? You or Sloan?" Derrick asked as his eyes focused on her.

"You just don't get it, do you?" Essence spat.

"No, you're the one who doesn't get it," Derrick said as his voice took on a deeper tone.

"Derrick, we've had our fun and games," Essence began.

"And we're still playing them, aren't we?" Derrick uttered, glaring at her.

Essence stood. "What are you saying?" she asked.

"I'm saying that we should have been straight with everyone from the very beginning," Derrick said, leaning back in his leather office chair.

"It would not have been in our best interest," Essence replied, trying to control her anger.

"Oh yes, you're quite right about that. If Sloan knew the real you, he would run like hell." Derrick chuckled icily.

"You're the same bastard you always were!" Essence screamed. "Tell me, Brandon, why have you followed me here?" she asked as she stared down into his eyes, calling Derrick by his real name.

"Did you honestly think I was going to let you get away with destroying my life? You left me high and dry. I gave up my whole life for you, Essence." His voice had an eerie shakiness about it. Derrick's eyes shot daggers at her as he stood from his seat.

"I had a wife who loved me, but I threw it all away for you!" he spat as he pointed at her. Essence held his angry stare. "And what did you do for me, huh?" he asked. Essence took a deep breath as Derrick stood just inches away from her face. "I tell you what you did. You took and took and took, until there wasn't anything left." Essence took a step back. Derrick's distorted face was scaring her.

In a quiet, but firm voice, she asked, "So, what are you going to do now?"

"That, I don't know yet," Derrick said as he let out a deep breath.

Essence squared her shoulders and said firmly, "Brandon, we have a good opportunity to begin our lives again. You know, a fresh start for the both of us. Natasha is the perfect woman for you. Marry her and let all the hurt and pain of the past die," she practically begged him.

Derrick let out a sinister chuckle, and with a stony stare, he said, "That would make it too easy for you, Essence." He entered her space and she could feel his faint breath upon her face.

"No, I want you to feel the same pain you inflicted upon me. I want you to experience what it is like to have part of your life ripped away," he hissed.

Essence's throat went dry as she gripped her purse. Hoarsely, she uttered, "Hurting me, Brandon, will not make you happy. Revenge never does."

Derrick stared into her. "Maybe not, but it sure as hell will help me sleep better at night knowing that you didn't get what you so desperately wanted. And I know how much you want Sloan, Essence. You will go to the bottom of the Earth to get what you want. But, this time, you may just come up empty handed."

"Brandon, I'm sorry. I told you before how badly I felt about what I did to you. Please, Brandon…" she pleaded.

"Essence, get the hell out of my office, and I mean right now!"

"Listen to me, Brandon," she said as she approached the door. "This should be a healing time for the both of us. Just think about it, please," she said as she closed the door.

Derrick stared out into the darkness of his office. Everyone had left for the day, and he was just sitting and staring out into the glimmering lights of Atlanta from his high-rise office with memories of his past looming before him. He had lost the one and only woman he had ever loved. A woman he knew had loved him deeply as well. A woman he had cheated on for the lust of Essence Kirkland.

Memories of their torrid love affair came crashing to the surface. There was a time that he couldn't get enough of Essence. It was as if she had him under some kind of spell. She was as beautiful as an angel sent down from heaven. Her lips were as sweet as cotton candy, and when they made love, it was like a symphony of music thundering through the clouds. Derrick closed his eyes tightly as the lies he'd told his former wife danced in his mind. Miesha had been so young, so trusting.

"Ohhhh!" he screamed into thin air; his hands were balled into tight fists.

How could he have been so blinded by Essence's attention? She never truly loved him. As soon as the newness wore off, she discarded him like a cheap suit from a thrift store. After Essence left him, he went crawling back to Miesha with his tail tucked between his legs. He begged her to take him back, but she stood her ground. She wanted nothing to do with him. And for that, he hated Essence. He swore he was going to make her pay. And it looked as if his opportunity wasn't far away.

SLOAN

It had been almost a week since Natasha had left, and Sloan was feeling the effects. A part of him felt empty. It was so weird, but he had to admit that they had never been far away from each other, even when they were involved in other relationships. If they needed to see each other, they were always minutes away. Sloan walked around Essence's apartment. She wasn't home yet, and, truth be told, he was relieved. He retrieved a sandwich Essence had prepared for him earlier that day, and he grabbed the last can of ginger ale from the bottom of the fridge. Taking a bite of the sandwich, Sloan's mind fell back to Natasha. He remembered so well the breakup between her and Darin. Natasha had called him late that evening. She was crying and mumbling into the phone. Within minutes, Sloan was at her place, but, thankfully for Darin, he had already left. Sloan was prepared to kick his ass until the sun came up the next day.

Another memory flashed before him; one he had never shared with Natasha. Before the breakup, Darin had come over to his place. He had just gotten in from work when he heard a loud banging on his door. He thought it was the police as he ran to open it. Lo and behold, there stood Darin with a screwed-up look on his face.

"Hey, dude, what's up?" Sloan said as he waved Darin inside. "I just got in, man. I'm going to get me something to drink. Want anything?" he asked over his shoulder as Darin stood in the living room.

"Naw, man, I'm fine," he said in a tight tone.

Sloan came back into the living room. "Sit, man, and tell me what's up," he said as he popped open the soda can and took a swallow.

"Look, man, I'm not here for buddy bonding. I just want to know one thing," Darin huffed.

Sloan took on a disturbed look. "Hey, man, I don't know what's going on, but how about putting it on the table," he said, placing the half empty can of ginger ale on the coffee table.

"What's up with you and my girl?" Darin lit into him.

Sloan's face held a puzzled look. "Huh? Darin, man, I don't know where you're going with this," Sloan retorted.

"Don't play stupid, man. You know exactly where I'm coming from," Darin growled. "Natasha eat, drink, and sleep you, man. Every damn time I turn around, I'm looking in your face, man." Darin's eyes grew wider.

"Look, Darin, I don't know what to tell you, except me and Natasha is close. You knew that when you came into the picture, man."

"Save the best-friend theory, man. Natasha drills that shit in my head every time she and I get into an argument about you." Darin was breathing into Sloan's face now. "I feel like you are in the center of our relationship, and where I come from, man, three is a damn crowd," Darin huffed.

Sloan took a step back. "Hey, Darin, man. What are you trying to say?" Sloan copped an attitude of his own.

"I ain't trying to say nothing, man. I'm telling you to stay the hell away from Natasha!" Darin yelled.

Sloan gave him a sarcastic chuckle. "Dude, you're crazy. That's one thing I will never do," Sloan said as he stared at Darin.

With a swift raise of his hand, Darin's fist connected with the bridge of Sloan's nose. The impact knocked him over the blue La-Z-Boy chair. A crashing sound filled the air.

"I mean it, Sloan! Stay away from her!" Darin shouted as he headed out the door. Darin brushed by Ricky so fast he almost knocked him down.

"Hey, dude, what happened here?" Ricky asked as he entered the apartment.

Sloan heard Ricky's voice, but, at the moment, he couldn't answer. His nose felt broken, and he was seeing stars. He made his way to the sofa. Once he was seated on the sofa with an ice pack to his face, Sloan relayed the blurred order of events to Ricky. They were watching sports on Sloan's wide-screen while Ricky listened.

"Man, he must have had it in for you for a while. I mean, for him to come all the way over here and explode like that," Ricky observed as he took a swig of his beer. "Sure you don't want some?" He offered Sloan a beer. "It might help with the pain," Ricky said and then chuckled softly.

"Naw, man, and you can hold the jokes, alright."

"Man, you know I'm just having a little fun. Look, it's not every day you walk in your homeboy's apartment and find him spread out on his living room floor with a bloody nose." Ricky let out another chuckle.

"The dude is sick, man. Natasha needs to get rid of his ass," Sloan responded. "The dude thinks something is going on between me and Natasha just because we talk all the time. Man, I've been in the picture when he wasn't even a thought," Sloan quipped.

"Well, you know the dude does have a point."

Sloan put down the ice pack and stared at Ricky as if he were unrecognizable. "What point?" Sloan asked with a twinge of attitude.

"Come on, man! How would you like it if your girl spent most of her time talking to another dude when you and her were together? And I don't care if she told you the guy was just a friend. Now, how would you feel about that?"

"So, you think I'm sleeping with my best friend?"

"Naw, man. Now, don't go off the deep end at me. Let me explain myself, alright. You and Natasha have a tight relationship, and I respect that. You've both known each other since childhood and that's cool. But you're adults now, with adult relationships. Natasha is *his* woman now, and there shouldn't be any man on her mind like that except him."

"So, does that mean there is no more room for me in her life?"

"No, dude. It just means that you should be less in her life now," Ricky relented. Sloan picked up the ice pack and placed it back on his nose.

"I bet if I was a woman, we wouldn't be having this conversation. But I guess some ignorant folks think that a man and a woman can't just be friends. They have to be screwing each other," Sloan protested.

Ricky took another gulp of his drink. He had lost the count of the game's score a long time ago. "Well, I've said my piece," he uttered lightly.

"No, let's continue this. You opened this can of worms, so let's finish it," Sloan bellowed.

"So, you want to know if I think a man and woman can just be friends?" Ricky asked as he scratched his head.

"Exactly," Sloan stated, taking the ice pack away from his face and staring into his homeboy's eyes.

"Mmmm, no I don't."

"And why is that?" Sloan asked, continuing to stare at him.

"Sloan, I believe somewhere down the line, they would either end up sleeping with one another or either ending the friendship all together because of the fear of ruining it all."

"Man, that's crazy. Natasha and I have been friends for over fifteen years and our relationship is still strong."

"Are you telling me you never thought about sleeping with her? Come on, man. You got eyes. The woman is beautiful," Ricky insisted as he leaned forward in his seat. The conversation had shifted, and Sloan wasn't sure he wanted to answer that question. "Hey, dude. You don't even have to say another word. It's written all over your face." Ricky chuckled.

The ringing of his cell broke Sloan from his thoughts of the past.

"Hey, you," Natasha said as Sloan answered.

"Hey, Me-Me. What a surprise. I was just sitting here, thinking about you," Sloan responded.

"Good thoughts, I hope," she snickered.

"Whenever I think of you, Me-Me, it's always good," Sloan uttered as the sweetness of her voice lifted his spirits.

"Sloan, I wish you were here with me," she said quietly.

"I would have been, Me-Me, if you had given me the chance." Silence hung in the air like a dark cloud casting a gloomy shadow.

"I'm sorry about everything, Sloan."

"I'm sorry, too, Natasha." Sloan paused for a moment. "I tell you what. Why don't we both stop being so sorry and start acting like ourselves?"

"I think I would like that," Natasha relented.

"Are you having a good time?"

"Yes, I am. I've taken so many pictures. And, oh, I got so many souvenirs to bring back home. I even have something special for you," she cooed.

"Well, I have an idea," Sloan said as a smile creased his face.

"Go on."

"When you get back, I'm going to take you someplace special, just the two of us. And, Natasha, it will be a night we will never forget," he finished softly. His words made her tingle inside. She could almost smell him, almost feel his lips as he spoke to her. "Natasha, did you hear me?"

"I heard every word, Sloan. Uhhh…I got to go now, but I'll see you in a couple of days."

"I can't wait, Me-Me."

The call ended. Sloan stared at his cell. Letting out a deep breath, he came to a realization that it was time for him to come to grips with his real feelings for her. No way could he continue to deny them or explain them away as if he were a scientist trying to figure out something he didn't understand. It wasn't hard to grasp. It was very apparent that he was in love with Natasha Jacobs, and it was as plain as the bloody nose on his face.

G STREET CHRONICLES
A LITERARY POWERHOUSE
WWW.GSTREETCHRONICLES.COM

GRETTA & DERRICK

Derrick ran his chocolate fingers over Gretta's naked flesh as they lay upon the black satin sheets on his king-size bed. He slipped inside of her with ease, and their passion grew like a heated volcano. Only sounds of pleasure filled the room as he made love to her. As they reached the threshold of their lovemaking, Gretta let out a piercing scream, and her nails dug deeply into the blackness of his skin, leaving her imprints. Gretta's eyes fluttered from their audacious activity, because Derrick brought her to newer heights each time they made love. But with the joy of her newfound love, she also held the feelings of a traitor. While her cousin was away on her trip, Gretta had pounced on the opportunity to screw around with her man. The guilt was beginning to weigh heavily on her shoulders. She untangled herself from her lover and sat up in bed.

Derrick peered up at her. "What's wrong, babe?" he asked, reaching for her hand. "Please don't leave tonight."

Gretta looked down into Derrick's dark eyes. "No, Derrick. I'm not leaving, but I know I should." Gretta folded her arms across her D-cup-sized breasts and sighed. "Derrick, what are we going to do when Natasha comes back?" she asked solemnly.

Derrick had been asking himself that same question since he'd had that horrific scene with Essence. He had made a decision, and he knew he would have to make his move real soon. But right now, he was at a crossroad. He didn't want to break things off with Natasha just yet, because she was the key to his plan to get back at Essence. But, on the other hand, he found himself falling in love with Gretta, which was the last thing he had expected to happen. But, somehow, she had managed to break the ice that shielded his heart. And he knew that losing her was definitely a possibility. She was now his joy. Maybe Essence was right after all. Maybe they could find tranquility after the storm.

"Derrick, will you answer me?" Gretta said as she pulled her sweaty hair away from her face. Pulling Gretta back down on the bed, he cuddled her in his arms.

"I'm going to tell her about us," he muttered. "You just keep calm about everything, okay. Give me a chance to break it down my way."

Gretta's heart did a flip. She hoped that meant what she thought it did. Derrick Perkins had never told her that he loved her, but after what he had just mentioned, he must have some feelings for her. She decided that at that moment, she wasn't going to analyze anything, all she knew was that she loved Derrick Perkins and that she wanted him for herself.

ESSENCE

Essence felt as if she had been playing dodge ball with Sloan all week. She thought he was avoiding her on purpose. Even at work, he managed to steer clear of her. Since Natasha was out of the picture for a while, she had thought it would be a perfect time to get closer to him., but Natasha's absence seemed to be having the opposite effect. Finally, the weekend had arrived, and she was determined to spend it exclusively with Sloan. As she shut off her computer, she grabbed her briefcase and hurried to his office. Her heels clicked loudly on the surface of the freshly-waxed tile floor. Arriving at his office door, she saw that he was on the phone; however, he motioned for her to come in. As she sat directly across from Sloan, she crossed her legs, and her skirt's side slit exposed her firm thighs. The fragrance of her Halle Berry perfume filled the air as she waited for him to end his call. She noticed the slight stare of Sloan's eyes as they grazed her shapely legs. He paused and then quickly looked away, as if he had just been caught with his hand in the cookie jar.

Essence glanced at her designer watch, and saw that it was after six o'clock. Most of the employees were already gone. While Sloan continued with his call, she stood up and closed the office door. She turned the lock and switched off the lights. She began to do a striptease for him. Sloan ended the call and peered up at her.

"Essence this is not the place—"

Essence's sweet lips touched his, silencing his protest as she kissed him deeply. Sloan fought for control as she groped for his belt buckle and eased off his trousers. She released his manhood, and a low moan escaped from his throat. Within minutes, Sloan had entered her. Papers and pens fell to the floor as their bodies centered on the desk. Moans and groans filled the room as they satisfied the desire that had ignited between them.

When it was over, Sloan stood silently as he pulled himself together. Essence forced herself to breath normally as she peered into his face. Even though their lovemaking was awesome, she felt some distance between them.

"Sloan, I get the feeling you've been avoiding me, and I want to know why," Essence came at him straightforward.

"Um…I think we should go home and discuss this," Sloan said as he picked up her briefcase and handed it to her.

"No, now is as good a time as any," she said, placing the briefcase back on the floor.

Sloan hadn't had much experience in breaking up with a woman, especially one he had deep feelings for. It was going to be harder than he had thought. And to make it even more difficult, he had finally found a woman that wanted the same things he did. But, looking at her now, he realized that she wasn't the one he really wanted. It had been Natasha all along that had his heart. And he was truly sorry he hadn't come to terms with his feelings long before now. He hated to hurt Essence, but he had no other choice. Sloan sighed deeply. He shouldn't have slept with her just now. *But…she came on so strong…* he thought. He knew he was screwing up, big time. Sloan walked over to her and stroked her smooth face.

Peering into her slanted eyes, he uttered, "I'm sorry, Essence, but we need to end this."

Essence backed away from him with a puzzled look. She began to breathe as if her air supply had shortened.

"What…what did you say?" she asked as tears filled her eyes.

Maintaining his stare, he said the words again. "We need to end this thing between us."

"No…we're not ending anything," she said as her voice rose.

"Essence, please don't do this. Let's not make it harder than it should be." Sloan placed his hand on his goatee and stroked it a couple of times, because he was feeling a little unsteady. He wondered how far Essence would take this. He considered a different route. Her eyes stared back at him like a wolf sizing up its prey. "Essence, I just need a little space. Just give us some time apart."

"But, sugar, I don't understand. We are so good together. We don't need any time apart. I love you, Sloan." Essence was taken aback as the words I love you rolled off her tongue. She couldn't be sure that she had meant what she had just said. After all the hideous games she had played with men, tearing their lives apart and stringing them along for her own satisfaction, she stood here now, begging for redemption.

"I…know we have been together for some time now, but I have some unresolved issues that I must take care of before I can be completely committed to anyone."

"No, I won't accept that!" she almost screamed as she said it. "You are committed to me. You've said you wanted to settle down and have a family with me. You told me those words, Sloan, and now you want to walk away from me?"

Tears began to fall down her cheeks, and her shoulders began to tremble. Sloan had never seen a woman, other than his mother sob this way, and it was tearing him apart inside. Was he doing the right thing by ending their relationship? Could she be the woman for him? What about his feelings for Natasha? They were real, and he knew after all these years that they weren't going away. Essence ran into his arms and held onto him for dear life.

"Please, Sloan, don't do this to me. I love you, and I know we can make this work," she uttered through her tears.

Sloan let out a long sigh, and he pondered which direction to take as he approached the crossroad of his heart.

*****

This was the last day of Natasha's cruise. She lay upon the lounge chair on the deck of the ship and gazed out into the blue waters of the ocean. Taking in the sun's rays and the ocean breeze as it caressed her complexion—which was now a shade darker—she closed her eyes and inhaled. Getting away alone had been the best decision she had ever made. Her mind was clearer now. She had finally sorted out the complex feelings that had held her bound, and now she felt free. Loving Sloan had been so easy, because she had loved him for years. He was her sunshine on a cloudy day. He was the wind beneath her wings and her rock when she needed him. Sloan knew the secret places of her heart.

They shared so many emotions known to man, except the most important one. The intimate one she had dreamt about through the years. The intimate one she couldn't wait to feel. She replayed their last conversation. He had spoken of their special night together. A night he said she would never forget. Natasha picked up her margarita, took a long sip, and closed her eyes. Sloan's face appeared before her as she entered dreamland. But then, another face appeared. Derrick Perkins stood beside Sloan, and she was startled from her dream.

A few days later, Derrick stood on the porch of Natasha's home with his finger pressed against the doorbell. Thanks to Gretta, he knew she was back. Things had been kind of strained between him and Natasha before she had left for the trip. He knew she wasn't putting her all into their relationship,

But, then again, neither was he. Their relationship hung by a thread, but tonight he was going to revitalize it, contrary to what he had Gretta believing.

Natasha finally opened the door. A warm smile creased her lips as she greeted him.

"Derrick, what are you doing here?" she asked timidly.

Derrick pulled a bouquet of flowers from behind his back and gave it to her. Her eyes twinkled as she looked at the pink and red roses.

"These are lovely," she said as he waited outside the door. "Well, aren't you going to let me in?"

Natasha responded, "I'm sorry, of course you can come in." She stood aside as he entered her home. "How did you know I was back?" she asked as she placed the vase of roses on the mantle above her fireplace.

"That's not important, Natasha," he said as he approached her. "The important question is why you didn't tell me you were leaving?" he said, staring into her eyes.

"Uhh…I'm sorry, Derrick. I should have told you, and it was so inconsiderate of me, but I needed some time alone," Natasha said, turning away from him.

He walked up behind her and placed his hands upon her shoulders. "What was bothering you so much that you couldn't confide in me?" Derrick asked as he turned her around to face him.

Peering up at him, Natasha mumbled, "It's complicated, Derrick."

"Don't you think I deserve an explanation? I'm sure if the table was turned, and I had pulled a stunt like that, you would probably have given me my walking papers," he tossed.

Natasha arched an eyebrow. Derrick was right. She would have been all up in his Kool-Aid if he had been the one doing what she had done. Natasha took in a slow breath and folded her arms.

"You're absolutely right," she murmured. Turning to face the sofa, she gestured for him to have a seat. Derrick sat, his eyes never leaving her face. "Derrick, I did a lot of soul-searching while I was away. I wasn't being honest with the people I love, and I wasn't being honest with you," she said with one hand to her chin. "I needed to separate fact from fiction."

Derrick's face was in a cloud of confusion. Natasha managed a small smile.

"I know you think I lost a couple of my marbles, but I assure you, I am sane." Natasha took Derrick's hand as she continued, "When my ex walked out on me, I hit rock-bottom. My hopes and dreams scattered like broken glass in my world." Tears tried to form in her eyes, but she forced them away. "For a long time, I blamed Darin for everything that went wrong between us. I couldn't, or just wouldn't, see what he was trying to show me. The very thing he wanted me to see was the thing that really wrecked our relationship." Derrick shifted in his seat as he stared into Natasha's emotional face. "My relationship with my best friend is what broke us up."

"Sloan?" Derrick questioned.

Natasha nodded her head. Taking in a deep breath, she continued. "Darin felt like an outsider, and I admit I may have spent a lot of time with Sloan, but…he was my friend and I loved him… But…I loved Darin too. As hard as I tried to limit my time with Sloan, the more irritated I became. I thought Darin was just jealous of us being so close, but then he started accusing me of sleeping with him." Now, Natasha was really getting emotional. Tears found their way to her cheeks. With one hand, she wiped them away.

"Well…did you?" Derrick asked.

Widening her eyes, Natasha blinked. "No!" she almost screamed as she stood. Derrick stood, as well.

"I'm sorry…I just had to asked," he mumbled. At a glance, he saw the anger in her eyes.

"Sloan and I have never crossed that line in our friendship," she said solemnly.

"I believe you, Natasha," Derrick responded.

"But Darin, in his altered state of mind, thought otherwise, and, after that, things weren't the same between us."

"Why are you telling me all of this now?" Derrick asked with a solemn look.

Natasha gazed into his dark eyes. "Derrick, I can't have a relationship with you or any other man until…" her voice faltered. "Not until I confront my true feelings concerning Sloan." With uplifted eyes, she relented, "And I have. I love him, Derrick."

Derrick didn't want to believe what he was hearing. *No, this can't happen now. My plans will be ruined,* he thought frantically.

"Of course you love him, Natasha. How can you not? He's been a very important part of your life for many years, and I don't have a problem with that. I understand where you're coming from, and, believe me…I am not like your ex. I'm secure in my thoughts," Derrick said firmly.

"No…no, Derrick, you don't understand," Natasha cried uncontrollably. "I really love him, like I…should be loving you," she sniffled as tears welled up in her eyes. They stood in silence as their eyes met. Derrick knew this would be the perfect time for him to confess his love for Gretta, but he just couldn't do it—not just yet.

"Does Sloan know how you really feel?"

"No, but I'm going to tell him tonight," she said, barely audible.

"And what if his feelings are not the same? Will things ever be right between you two again? Just think about what you're doing. The closeness you both have shared over the years will be lost forever."

"I can't let that stop me, Derrick. I must tell him," she bellowed.

Derrick took a step closer to her. He lifted her bowed head with his finger. "Natasha, when friends become lovers, it's not always for the best. Are you willing to take the risk?"

Natasha's heart was thumping loudly in her chest. She felt as if she were having an anxiety attack. She'd thought she had it all together, and now it was falling apart at the seams.

"Sloan is happy, Natasha. You should have seen him and Essence while you were away. They acted like lovebirds, and the last I heard, they may be setting a wedding date pretty soon," he lied intentionally.

"I don't believe you. Sloan would have told me," she sputtered.

"It is true, Natasha. In fact, I shouldn't be telling you this, but Essence told me herself that she and Sloan looked at engagement rings a few days ago."

Natasha stared at him as if he had two heads.

"Now tell me, are you sure you want to throw away your best friend—a man you claim to love—and all your happiness for some confused feelings you think you might have for him?"

The dam had burst. Rivers of tears flooded from her eyes as Derrick reached for her and held her tightly in his arms. Derrick began kissing her tears away. His kisses moved to the nape of her neck and then to her full, moist lips.

After kissing her deeply, he moaned, "Let me help you get over him, Natasha."

His hands slid underneath her skirt and Natasha found herself responding to his touch. Lost in emotions, she tried to reason with herself...Sloan was in a solid relationship—hadn't he told her he was tired of playing games? Hadn't he said that hopping from one woman's bed to another had become meaningless to him? Didn't he say he wanted to settle down and have a family? And in the middle of saying all that, never had he once said that he wanted all of that with her. Maybe the cruise had confused her and filled her with a sense of nostalgia that made her feel things that weren't mutual between her and Sloan. After all, it was a romantic setting, so romantic thoughts would follow. There were happy couples all around her. She told herself that somehow she had been caught up amidst a fairy tale that she wanted to come true. She imagined Sloan on a white horse, reaching down for her before they rode off into the sunset. Now, she had to come to terms with reality. She was like a man in the desert, seeking a mirage that vanished when he reached out to touch it. Reality came sweeping in when Derrick carried her to her bedroom. What was real was right here and right now, as Derrick made mad love to her. Natasha concluded that the fairy tale of a young girl in love was gone. The reality of a woman with a heart to heal had come.

SLOAN, ESSENCE, DERRICK & NATASHA

A truce formed between the foursome as they struggled for normalcy among their fellow coworkers at Emerson & Stuckey. Derrick and Sloan spoke only when it was necessary, and the same applied to Natasha and Essence. Lisa Ray observed them all and couldn't wait to get to the bottom of it all. It freaked her out to watch the four of them walking around each other as if they were stepping on eggshells. She wanted to know what had transpired between the two couples, because, whatever it was, it had to be very deep. Lisa Ray stared at Natasha who was seated in her office across the way from her. Her face looked pleasant enough, but she seemed to be wearing a mask. Something was hidden underneath, and Lisa Ray was determined to find out just what it was. Natasha got up from her desk and headed to the ladies room. She leaned over the counter in the ladies' restroom to freshen her makeup. The new Fashion Fair mulberry lipstick that she applied glazed evenly over her lips. She heard the sound of a flushing toilet just a few stalls down. She saw the woman's reflection in the mirror as she walked out of the stall. Essence looked beautiful as always, and not just for a woman of her age, but just beautiful in general. Her silky black hair draped over her shoulders like a horse's mane and her body held on to the curves of youth. Jealousy sprang forth like heat on a hot summer day as Natasha stared into her eyes. She wondered silently whether Essence really loved Sloan or if he was just a boy toy she flaunted to her friends. Natasha chastised herself for being so evil when it came to Essence. After all, she wasn't Sloan's first serious girlfriend. Monica Jenkins crossed her mind. *What if he was engaged to Monica? Would I be feeling this way? So, why now?* she asked herself. *What is so different about it? What makes me want to snatch this woman's eyes right out of her head like a cat gone wild?*

Essence parted her raisin-colored lips and murmured, "Hello, Natasha," her words were light and smug.

"Good morning, Essence," Natasha replied with as little emotion as possible as she washed her hands.

Essence reached into her black Chanel purse and pulled out her makeup bag. She took out the mascara brush and proceeded to brush her eyelashes. Natasha reached for the paper towels and quickly dried her hands. She wanted to get out of Essence's presence as quickly as possible. Natasha discarded the paper towels in the trash and was on her way out when she heard Essence's soft voice.

"Natasha, wait! I need to talk to you," she said.

Natasha turned around and met her gaze. "Yes," she replied with arched eyebrows.

Essence took a step closer to her. "This wall between us has to come down," she responded. Natasha held her gaze. "Come on, now. We're good friends here, and we should behave like it," Essence said with a trace of concern.

Natasha's lips grew into a thin line. "Essence, let's set the record straight. I am not your good friend. I consider you as a coworker and the girlfriend of my best friend. We were never chummy-chummy, and we never will be."

"And it's all because of Sloan?" Essence chimed in.

Natasha's expression was blank.

"You want him for yourself now, don't you? That's the real reason you hate me so much. You feel as if I snatched him away from you." Essence chuckled sarcastically. "Forgive me, Natasha, for laughing, but I've seen this before. Puppy love turns into real love, or should I say infatuation. But it doesn't work, you know. Infatuation isn't love, dearie. Sloan is a grown man now. Not some kid you ran around playing hide-and-go-seek with. And he is in love with me, and we are getting married." Essence held out her hand, displaying a three-carat diamond ring that sparkled before Natasha's eyes. Seeing the surprised look on Natasha's face, Essence gave her a triumphant smile.

"Yes, Sloan proposed to me a few days ago. And what I really intended to talk to you about was being in our wedding. But seeing that I'm not your friend, I guess there isn't a need for me to ask." Essence threw her a fake frown. "Poor Sloan is going to be so disappointed, though. He was looking forward to having you participate in our glorious event," she said with a smirk on her face.

"Listen to me, you old bird," Natasha said as she grabbed Essence by the shoulders and pushed her against the wall. "Stay the hell away from me!"

Fortunately, Lisa Ray walked in and quickly took control of the situation. She pulled Natasha away from Essence.

"What are you two doing?" she almost shouted. "Are you're trying to get escorted out of here in handcuffs?" she huffed. "And, Natasha, you, of all people, should know better. Mr. Emerson will not tolerate behavior like this."

Natasha took a deep breath as she straightened her clothing. Essence did the same as she glared at Natasha.

"You're right, Lisa Ray. I let this witch push my buttons. It won't happen again. I promise." Natasha said as she gained her composure.

Lisa Ray turned to Essence. "And you, Miss Kirkland, have been warned as well. According to company policy, I am supposed to report the both of you, but this time, I will overlook what I walked into. I certainly hope this doesn't happen again," Lisa Ray said as her eyes darted between the two women.

"It won't. Not here, anyway." Essence grimaced as she picked up her Chanel bag and headed out the door.

"Was that a threat I just heard?" Natasha flared as her arms went up in the air.

"Girl, what were you thinking? I could have been a supervisor or one of the directors and both of y'all asses would have been outta here," Lisa Ray chimed. "Now, tell me right now what that was about."

"Okay, but not in here. Let's go to lunch," Natasha said as they walked out.

Once the two women were away from the office and seated in The Silver Bullet, a luncheon café a few blocks from their office, Natasha sipped on her mocha latté as Lisa Ray watched her closely.

"Girl, I don't know what came over me. It's like, all at once, I just snapped."

"If I hadn't walked in when I did, God only knows what may have happened," Lisa Ray sighed.

"I would have been arrested for murder," Natasha quipped.

"Girl, bite your tongue. You know you could never do anything like that," Lisa Ray said, taking a sip of her café mocha.

"Maybe not, but I sure wanted to. The woman gets under my skin."

"You've got to get some self-control, Natasha. What's the reasoning behind all of this?" Lisa Ray asked as she scrutinized Natasha's face. Natasha looked away and stared out of the restaurant window. Her stomach was in knots and what little mind she had left was cluttered with questions.

"Natasha, does this have anything to do with Sloan? And don't give me no la-de-da answer," Lisa Ray warned. Natasha's bottom lip quivered as she turned back to face her. "Never mind, I already have my answer," Lisa Ray said as she watched a single tear fall down Natasha's cheek. "Natasha, you're obviously in love with the man. Why don't you go after him? It's not too late," Lisa Ray said as she leaned closer to her.

Natasha shamefully bowed her head. "I don't think I can do that now," she uttered.

"And why the heck not?" Lisa Ray quizzed.

"Derrick thinks that I'm just infatuated with Sloan. He says I've mistaken my feelings of friendship for love. In fact, Essence told me the same thing in the ladies' room. I think that's what made me go off on her." Lisa Ray rolled her eyes as Natasha continued. "Derrick also said that if I reveal my true feelings to Sloan, and he doesn't feel the same, our relationship could be ruined forever." Natasha pulled a napkin from its dispenser and wiped her nose.

"Tell me, what kind of degree does Derrick Perkins have in relationship management?" Lisa Ray asked firmly. Staring into Natasha's eyes, Lisa Ray continued, "Don't you see that this may be an elaborate scheme to keep you two apart?" Natasha's eyes narrowed. "Yes, think about it, Natasha. What if Sloan returns your feelings? Where would that leave Derrick?" she asked with raised brows. "He knows you will drop him like a hot potato."

"I don't know, Lisa Ray. Things haven't been quite the same between me and Sloan. We don't talk the way we used to before…she…came along," Natasha stammered. Cupping the coffee in her hand, she continued, "Before I came back from my cruise, Sloan and I talked. We came to an agreement about our relationship. It had been rocky for a while, but we decided to put it all behind us and start anew. He even told me that when

I got back, we would have a special dinner together, just the two of us. He also told me it would be a night I would never forget."

"And what happened, girl?" Lisa Ray asked with wide eyes. Natasha smirked with a wave of her hands. "Nothing happened. The dinner and that special night never transpired. We've only spoken a few times since. But it was all platonic. 'How are you?' Hellos and goodbyes at the end of the day, but that's about it," she relented with sadness in her voice and eyes. "Maybe it's all for the best," she said with another wave of her hand.

"Naw, naw. It's not all for the best," Lisa Ray said sternly. "You two need that special dinner to clarify things between you, whether you get together as a real couple or not. You need that, Natasha, so that you both can have closure and move ahead. Do you hear me?" Lisa Ray said as she shook Natasha's arm. "Call him up. Tell him you both need to talk and, girl…spill your heart out to the man that you truly love. Whatever you need to hear has to come out of Sloan's mouth and no one else's. He is the only one you should listen to." Glancing down at her watch, Lisa Ray realized they both had stayed long past their lunch time. "Girl, we better get back before Mr. Emerson has our heads, for real." Natasha gave Lisa Ray a hug before they left the restaurant.

"Thanks for everything. You have given me something to think about," Natasha uttered.

Walking to Lisa Ray's black Camry, Essence's words came to Natasha's mind. As she dipped her head to get in the car, she asked, "Do you think Essence meant what she said in the ladies' room?"

Lisa Ray slid inside and buckled her seat belt. "What was that?" she asked as she started the car.

"The part about it wouldn't be a next time, not at the office anyway."

Lisa Ray frowned as she pulled the car into traffic. "I think she was just blowing off some steam, girl. You probably scared the daylights out of her." Lisa Ray chuckled.

"Yeah right," Natasha joined in. "If she did mean it. I'm not afraid of her old ass, anyway. She can just name the place and the time, and I will be there," Natasha spewed with a roll of her head.

"Girl, just be careful. She has a look about her that I don't trust. I think we both need to keep an eye on that chick," Lisa Ray said as they headed back to the office.

The work day at Emerson & Stuckey had finally come to an end and neither woman had been approached by Mr. Emerson concerning how long they had taken for lunch. To Natasha's surprise, Mr. Emerson had left a note on her desk, congratulating her on finalizing the Morrison account. A wide smile creased her lips as she read it. If only he knew how hard she had worked on those figures. Maybe this was a sign that things were going to get better.

With a feeling of accomplishment, Natasha waltzed to her car. She was pleasantly surprised to see her best friend perched on the hood of her car. Sloan's eyes traveled over Natasha's curvaceous figure. She was neatly dressed in a gray, pinstriped Donna Karan suit with matching three-inch pumps. Her long, auburn hair hung loosely around her shoulders.

"My, aren't we looking as good as an ice cream sundae with cherries on top," he flirted. Natasha let out a soft giggle. It was another one of Sloan's audacious attempts to get back into her good graces.

"Oh yeah, you think? I thought you were too busy to notice these days," she said as she eased around him and opened her car door. Sloan wanted to refute her, but he decided against it. It had been weeks since they had really talked, and he wasn't about to blow it now.

"Me-Me, have dinner with me tonight?" he asked as he gazed into her light-brown eyes.

"Mmmm, aren't you a little late on the invite. If I'm not mistaken, I thought we were supposed to have that special dinner a few weeks ago."

Sloan lowered his eyes. "Yeah, I know, and I'm sorry about that. Things have been kind of…hectic," he uttered as he groped for words.

"I can imagine, with the upcoming wedding and all," Natasha babbled as she slid her briefcase onto the front seat.

"What?" he asked as his eyes squinted.

"It's okay, Sloan. If you're marrying the woman you love, who am I to stand in your way? I just can't be at the wedding, though," she said, trying to keep her emotions in check.

"Me-Me, what on earth are you talking about? I'm not marrying anybody," he replied as he stood before her. "Where did you get an idea like that?" he quizzed.

"Well, I saw the rock on your bride-to-be's finger just before lunch. And she kindly filled me in."

"No, no, no," Sloan said, shaking his head from side to side. "I don't know what game Essence is playing, but she's in it alone. I never asked her to marry me, and I certainly didn't place a ring on any finger of hers," Sloan bellowed as he let out an angry sigh.

"So, you're saying she's lying?"

"You're damn right she is. Me-Me, if I was going to ask anyone woman to marry me, you should know by now that you would be the first person to know."

Natasha gazed into Sloan's hazel eyes. She knew instantly that he was telling her the truth. There wasn't much about this man she didn't know. Sloan cupped her chin and kissed her lightly on the lips.

"Meet me tonight at our secret spot," he whispered.

Natasha felt as if she was melting. She could only nod her head yes, because she was speechless. Sloan stepped away from her and headed to his SUV. She knew the place he was referring to, and she would be there no matter what.

ESSENCE

"Sloan, honey…wait!" Essence called out breathlessly as she made her way over to him in the parking lot. She was late meeting him because she had been held up in a meeting. Catching her breath, she uttered, "Why didn't you wait for me inside? I went by your office, thinking you were there," she said in an agitated tone.

"Sorry about that, but I needed to take care of something," he said, looking away from her.

He stuck his hand into the pocket of his black trousers and pulled out his keys. Essence's face took on a whole new look. Her eyes narrowed, and her voice deepened.

"What did you have to take care of, Sloan, or should I say…whom?"

Sloan remained silent as he pressed the remote and unlocked his SUV door.

"Don't think I'm stupid, Sloan. You couldn't wait to talk to that dubious friend of yours," she fumed as she approached him.

"Yes, damn it, yes. I needed to talk to Natasha, and I don't need to feel guilty about it. And if you have a problem with it, then all I can say is deal with it."

Essence's eyes narrowed as she leaned into him. "I sure as hell have a problem when you have to sneak around on me. Are you trying to play me like you've played those teeny boppers you've dated? I told you from the beginning that I'm not the one."

Sloan gave her a perturbed look. "And I'm not the one to explain my every move to you. I didn't do it in my previous relationships, and I'm not doing it with you."

Sloan turned his back and proceeded to get into his SUV. Essence was livid with him, but she knew she had to calm down. Sloan wasn't the type of man who would allow anyone to control him.

"Honey, wait!" she yelled as she grabbed the passenger door handle.

"I'm sorry, alright! Today has been a hectic one for me," her voice was now soft and smooth. "I didn't mean to act that way," she said as she fluttered her long, flirtatious eyelashes. "But, honey, we do need to talk." Sloan gave her a sidelong glance and exhaled.

Essence leaned in to give him a warm kiss. Sloan held up his hand. "Look, you said talk, and talking is what we need to do, nothing more." Essence backed away slowly as she held his gaze.

"Well, if that's what you want," she relented. "Mmmm, how about spending the weekend with me? We could rent some movies and order in. You know, like we used to do when we first got together," Essence chimed as her eyes lit up.

"No, that won't work," Sloan said with a nod of his head. "Ricky got some tickets to the game on Saturday; and Sunday I'm having dinner with my folks."

Essence smiled broadly as she clasped her hands together. "That's perfect, Sloan. I can come along and meet your parents."

"And tell them what, Essence? That I've asked you to marry me, and then show them the ring I didn't purchase. You were way out of line with that."

Sloan watched her squirm like a fish out of water. Essence's mouth opened then shut. Her eyes squinted while waves of anger rushed through her. The stunt she had pulled in the ladies' room with Natasha had been necessary. She had to let her know that Sloan belonged to her now, and there was no better way to get her message across.

Stifling her anger, she said in a controlling tone, "Honey…I can explain—"

"I gotta go. Save it for our talk later," Sloan said dismissively as he started up his engine.

"Sloan," Essence called out his name. It held a sweet, but hurtful sound.

He paused as he turned to look into her eyes. Just like her voice, her eyes revealed love and hurt, simultaneously. *What am I doing?"* he asked himself. *Why am I playing her like a yo-yo?* He knew it wasn't right, but now he understood the depths that she would go to in order to keep him. Sloan ran his hand across his face and let out a low breath. "Look, Essence, you're right. It has been a long day for the both of us; and standing out here, dispelling our relationship is not something I had in mind." Sloan held her gaze. "I think this will be a perfect weekend for us both to take a break from each other. Clear our heads," he said consolingly. "You know I'm going to be hanging out with Ricky, and you can call up a couple of girlfriends. Go let your hair down. Get a manicure and take in a spa," Sloan said with a smile.

Essence remained solemn. "I don't want to let my hair down or go to some damn spa, Sloan. I want to be with you. Kissing you, hugging you, and making love to you," she whined.

"Nothing I've said has gotten into that head of yours, has it? It seems to be all about Essence and what she wants. What about what I want?" he said defiantly. "Do you ever think about anybody else but yourself?" Sloan asked as he tried to keep his temper in check.

Essence curled her lips. "This isn't about me. I know what you're up to, Sloan. You just want me out of your hair, so you can go play with your friend, Natasha. When are you two ever going to grow up? You're not children anymore, damn it!" Essence spat.

"I see we're not getting anywhere with this," Sloan said, slamming his door shut. "I've told you my plans." Without another word, Sloan backed out of the parking space and sped away, leaving Essence steaming.

NATASHA & SLOAN

Natasha sat quietly as she surveyed the elegant interior of the restaurant where she and Sloan were meeting. The atmosphere was like an aromatherapy bath: soft, sensual, and soothing. The sound of jazz played gently, easing the patrons into a relaxing and mellow mood. Natasha scanned the room; she noticed several couples holding hands or snuggling close together as they chatted. There were others who danced to the slow, rhythmic music. Contrary to what was going on around her, her hormones had gone ballistic. Several emotions filled her soul as the candlelight flickered before her. Natasha wasn't sure if this was the right place for her to meet Sloan. Strangely enough, she and Sloan had been at this restaurant twice before, and the romantic setting hadn't bothered her then. "So why now?" she asked herself. "What is so different now?" her inner voice whispered softly.

Her emotions were like a newly-born butterfly begging to spread its wings. She wanted nothing more than to finally acknowledge the feelings she had carried for so many years. But she wondered if her feelings surfaced, would they bring her the joy she had dreamt of so many times? Or would her heart be torn to threads? Most importantly, would she still have Sloan in her life?

Natasha continued to scan the room. She glanced down at her designer watch, and it read 7:30 P.M. She was beginning to get a little nervous. *Maybe he changed his mind. Maybe he realized that all of this was just foolishness*, she worried inwardly. They were adults now, with responsibilities and separate lives to lead. Natasha stood up and grabbed her Prada purse. She was leaving behind not only the restaurant, but the romantic feelings she held for Sloan. As she headed to the door, she ran smack-dab into Sloan. He looked as fine as wine in his office attire. Giving her a sexy smile, he asked, "Are you going somewhere?"

Natasha managed a nervous chuckle as she mumbled, "The ladies' room."

Sloan looked in the opposite direction. "I think the restrooms are over there." He pointed.

"Uh…yeah. The lighting is so dim in here…I guess I got mixed up," she stammered.

"Well, I'll be waiting for you at our table," he said as he cupped her elbow before walking away.

Natasha entered the ladies' room and made her way to the mirror, where she noticed huge beads of sweat on top of her perfectly-colored lips. This always happened to her when she was nervous. She pulled a Kleenex tissue from her purse and gently blotted the perspiration.

She took a deep breath and exhaled. No man had ever had this effect on her, not even Sloan—the old Sloan, that is. The Sloan that was waiting for her out there tonight seemed to be a totally different person. The look he had given her was purposeful. A chill ran down her spine. Just thinking about him as a man made her mad crazy. After tossing the tissue in the trash, Natasha arched her back and strutted out of the ladies' room. Her persona was one of strength, but deep inside, she was laden with nervousness, as well as hidden desires.

ESSENCE

Pacing restlessly in her living room, Essence called Sloan several times, and each time, she got his voice mail. Essence slammed down her phone. She blew at a strand of hair that fell in her face. *Why is he doing this to me? Surely he knows how much I love him*, she thought. After all these years of mistakes, she had finally found someone who could make her happy, someone she was certain would never bore her. Sloan Stevens had her wrapped up like a Christmas present. His sex was amazing, and he treated her like the queen she knew she was—until lately. Now, she felt like a discarded mistress, which was a role she never played.

Essence sat down on the plush chaise in her bedroom. Her vanilla-colored satin robe fell away from her thigh as she crossed her long legs. She gloated, because not a hint of cellulite could be found on her body; she kept her body in mint condition, and men—young and old—took notice. She remembered that first day Sloan had laid eyes on her. The man had practically drooled. And when she had let him into her sacred cave, he nearly went mad. The sex between them was heaven sent. He had stolen her body, as well as her love, and now he had the audacity to tell her that they both needed some space. Did he not know who he was messing with? She knew how men thought. Lord knows, she'd had her share of duds. Their pathetic, little minds sought to be deceiving, but it never worked; she knew the game too well. In fact, she was the master of games. And for Sloan to think that she would believe the skimpy little lie he'd told her about hanging with his boy, Ricky, was utterly demeaning to her character.

Surely he knew by now that he was dealing with a real woman, not some bimbo with boobs and no brain. Men can be so dense, she mused.

Essence's eyes darkened as she stared out her bay window. She knew exactly where Sloan was—and with whom. *Why couldn't Natasha Jacobs accept the place she held in Sloan's life?* Essence wondered. *But no…she wants to keep my man tangled in her childhood web of a so-called best-*

friends-forever relationship.

It was a game Natasha was spooning. She wanted Sloan like a woman wanted a man, but she wasn't going to have him. Sloan was hers now and hers alone. Essence's mind drifted to Derrick, who she had known as Brandon in a previous life. She had gone through hell and high water to break up his marriage to that dingy broad he called a wife. And he would have been with her right now if she hadn't walked out on him. Now, here he was in Atlanta, licking his wounds like some sick little puppy. She wouldn't be intimidated by him or Natasha. They both were going to pay if she didn't get what she wanted. And what she wanted was Sloan Stevens.

SLOAN & NATASHA

As they dined, the couple stayed on safe topics such as the weather, politics, and the happenings in their families. After a sip of his nonalcoholic drink, Sloan asked, "And how's your cousin Gretta doing these days?"

Natasha's eyebrows lifted. "To tell you the truth, Sloan, your guess is as good as mine," she said as she picked up a forkful of steamed rice. "The girl has been staying away from me as if I have a plague or something," she chuckled as she placed the food into her mouth.

"Mmmm, that certainly is strange," Sloan said with a frown. "I thought you two were as close as we were…are," he fumbled.

Natasha picked up a forkful of veggies and chewed silently. She needed a minute to get her thoughts together. Sloan noticed her distress. Sidestepping his comment, he uttered, "So what do you think she's up to?"

"I don't know for sure, but I think it has to do with a man," she chuckled as she sat down her fork.

"Oh, so you think Stella has finally found her groove," Sloan teased with a wide grin.

She and Sloan had always joked about Gretta finding a man. The girl had some terrible taste when it came to the opposite sex. Gretta's lists consisted of thugs, scrubs, and momma's boys. Natasha hoped her cousin would find a man with a career and a positive future to latch onto one day.

"Well, if it is a man, I hope it's one that is worthy of her love. Gretta is a sweet person who deserves the best," he said. Natasha held Sloan's gaze. She wondered if he was referring exclusively to Gretta or if there was a hidden message lurking inside his remark.

Damn, Sloan swore silently, *another slip of the tongue.* This walking on eggshells wasn't working for him. The sole purpose of this dinner was to get to the bottom of what they were feeling.

"Natasha."

"Sloan." They each said the other's name in unison. They both stared at each other and smiled nervously.

"Look, Me-Me," Sloan began. "We've got to stop this feather-walking ritual. How long has it been since we behaved like ourselves?"

Natasha tilted her head and asked, "When was the last time we were alone like this?"

A song that they both loved began to play. Robin Thicke's "Lost Without You"

filled the room.

"Let's dance," Sloan said, standing. Natasha followed suit, and they made their way to the dance floor. Sloan held her close. Her scent was intoxicating. His thoughts floated to her senior prom. He had ended up being her prom date because the boy she was seeing at the time had broken his leg a few days before. Natasha was devastated; she and her mom had gone all out finding the special gown for that special night. Looking back, he wondered if that was the night that his feelings for her began to change—the moment when he fell in love with his best friend. He saw the sadness in her eyes when she talked about not going to her prom. Sure, she could have gone alone, but that wasn't an option she cared to entertain. So, unbeknownst to her, he went out and rented a tux. He filled Momma Florene in on his little plan, and she convinced Natasha that it would be a total waste to let such a pretty gown hang in the closet on prom night. So, Natasha relented. She agreed to attend the prom for only one hour.

Natasha nearly fainted when he rang her doorbell that night. And he nearly passed out from her beauty. Feelings began to stir within him that made him tremble as if it was the Second Coming. He wanted to kiss her so badly it hurt. As they danced and mingled with friends, he couldn't keep his eyes off her. And when they did return home that evening, he did what he had wanted to do all night. He kissed her softly. And then the porch light came on, which ended the special night. That night was truly special, because that was the night that changed him forever. He had never, in all these years, told Natasha about his true feelings, but now the time had arrived. And this time, no porch light would interrupt them. They swayed like swans to the music. Sloan held her even closer as the lyrics danced in his head. He knew he would be lost without Natasha. She was the woman he had been searching for.

Breaking his reverie, Sloan muttered, "Natasha, are you in love with me?" he felt her stiffen in his arms. The time had come for her to break away from the cocoon and let the butterfly spread its wings. She only hoped that her little butterfly would roam freely as it thrived and lived.

Natasha's voice was barely audible when she whispered, "Yes, Sloan, I am."

Sloan exhaled as if a weight had just been lifted from his shoulders. He felt light, free, and very happy.

"Me-Me, I'm in love with you too," he murmured back.

Tears graced her eyes as Sloan kissed her long and deep. Oblivious to their surroundings, they felt as if they were the only people in the room that night as time stood still for them. It was tomorrow they had no control of.

SLOAN

Sloan woke up on Saturday morning feeling as if he had won the lottery. He just had to share his good fortune with someone, so he dialed his homeboy Ricky's digits.

"Hey, man. What's up?" Sloan sang into the receiver.

Ricky grumbled into the phone. His voice sounded as though his mouth was filled with rocks. "Dude, do you know what time it is?"

"No, I don't, and I could really care less to be honest." Sloan grinned. "All I know, man, is that I am in love, dog!" "Dude, are you drunk?" Ricky's voice had cleared and so had his head as he waited for Sloan's replay. His friend must have tied one on last night.

"Come on, man. You know I don't drink."

"Well, did someone slip you something?" Ricky quizzed.

"Ricky, man, what's wrong with you?" Sloan retorted. "I'm trying to tell you something."

"Yeah, I got the 'I'm in love' part. And you didn't have to wake me up at seven o'clock in the morning to tell me some crap like that."

"This is no crap, man. This is real. I'm in love. I'm in love, Ricky. For the first time, I really know what it feels like. And, dog, it feels good, man." Sloan fell back on his bed and spread his legs. He felt like a kid.

"Dude, whatcha calling me for anyway? Wake up Essence and tell her your great news. I'm sure she would appreciate it more than I do," Ricky quipped.

Sloan sat up straight. "Man, you got this all wrong. Essence is the last person I want to talk to at the moment."

Ricky was suddenly wide awake. "Dude, are you sure you not recovering from a hangover, or did somebody go upside that head of yours?"

"Neither," Sloan popped.

"Well, stop talking in sprints and tell me the facts."

"You want some facts, man. I'll give you the facts," Sloan said, swinging his legs off the bed. "Natasha and I are in love!" he shouted.

Ricky began to chuckle. "Yo, dude. I think I've been telling you for quite some time that the lady had the hots for you. But you never told me you felt the same way. When did all this happen?"

Sloan let out a whiff of air and took a seat on the edge of the bed. "Ricky, we had dinner together last night. We had a long talk and I…don't know. It all just came out. I asked her straight out if she in love with me, and she said yes. I couldn't believe what was happening, man."

"Dude, this is huge," Ricky asserted. "I mean, you and Natasha as lovers…that's a ball out of nowhere, man."

"I know, Ricky, I know. But I have loved her for years. I guess my feelings for Natasha in *that* way were buried deep within me, you know."

"So, when did you know you were in love with her? I mean, I know you love her, but you're talking something totally different than that."

"Ricky, it's deep, man. And I know it's a lot to comprehend at the moment, but our love for each other has been with us all these years," Sloan exclaimed. "And to answer your question when did I know?" Sloan paused as he ran his fingers through his shortly-cropped hair. "I think I knew that night I took her to the prom; but we were only friends…best friends at that. Back then, I was young and didn't know anything about love. I thought it was just a fleeting feeling that would pass. The girl was stunning that night, Ricky. Natasha looked like an angel sent straight from God, man, and last night brought it all back to me." Sloan released a slow breath of air. "The woman I've been searching for so long has been with me all the time." Sloan felt tears well up in his eyes. His love for Natasha washed through him like a flowing river.

No woman had ever touched him so deeply. Natasha's love was embedded in his heart. Things were so clear now. His life was going to be grand. Ricky broke the silence that seemed to settle between them as Sloan was caught up in his thoughts.

"Yo, dude. What about Essence? Does she know about this sudden revelation of yours?"

"No," Sloan said quickly.

"Well, dude, according to what you've been telling me these last few months, I would hate to be in your shoes right about now."

"It shouldn't come as a total surprise. Essence knows our relationship had been cooling off for quite a while now. At first, I thought things were going in the right direction, but I soon realized that I wasn't really in love with her. I guess I was so caught up in the idea of being in love and taking it to the next level that I fell for the first thing smoking. Man, I got tangled," Sloan confessed.

"Naw, dude, the word is chained. Like on the chain gang…root, root," Ricky sang into the phone.

Sloan ignored his friend's observation. "It's all good, man. I will make Essence understand," Sloan uttered.

"I don't know, dude. That woman is stuck on you like Elmer's Glue," Ricky said, grabbing a cup of coffee.

Sloan furrowed his brow. He felt like a man with a heavy weight on his shoulders, again. "Maybe…but I have to leave her, man. My heart is with Natasha."

NATASHA

The best friends had decided to keep their true feelings for each other hidden for a while. They both had relationships that needed resolving before they were able to begin enjoying their lives together. Natasha lay in bed with a wide smile imprinted on her face as she reflected back to the night before. It had touched her in a way that she couldn't explain. She and Sloan had bared their very souls, peeling away layers of time they could have shared. As the warmth of the sun touched her face, a feeling of despair came over her. What if this was all a mistake? What if she and Sloan were about to ruin the very thing they both cherished so much? She was letting negative thoughts ruin her day.

Her eyes darted to the silver-framed clock on her nightstand. It was nine o'clock in the morning. She mused over her options for this beautiful Saturday morning. Shopping popped into her head. Natasha never liked to shop alone, so she reached for her phone and proceeded to dial Gretta's number. Natasha placed the phone in the crook of her neck as she waited for Gretta to pick up. There was one ring, then two, and then three. Natasha was about to hang up after the fifth ring, when Gretta finally picked up.

"Hello," Gretta uttered.

"Girl, what took you so long to answer your phone? And why haven't I heard from you lately? Who have you been hiding from? The police?" Natasha asked playfully. She chuckled. A short pause formed.

Then, Gretta muttered, "I ain't hiding from nobody. I've just been busy."

"Mmmm ummm, if you say so," Natasha said, curling the phone cord around her finger. "Well, Miss Busy, let's take in a day of shopping. We can hit a few stores and then have lunch." Another pause came between them. "Gretta, are you there? Maybe I need to come over there and see what's going on with you, girl," Natasha huffed.

"Why are you coming down on me, cousin?" Gretta responded.

"Because you're acting like you're hiding something from me. Do you have a man stashed in that apartment of yours?" Natasha chuckled.

"And whose business is it if I do?" Gretta said curtly.

"Mmmm, you don't have be so nasty, Gretta. Are you on your period? You always get nasty when your friend is in town," Natasha said with a quick breath.

"What time are we leaving?" Gretta asked, skipping Natasha's observation of her malady.

"Say, in about an hour. I'll pick you up—"

"No, cousin, I'll pick you up," Gretta said just before Natasha heard the dial tone from the phone.

Now, she knew for certain that something was up with Gretta. And by the end of the day, she would know exactly what it was.

DERRICK & GRETTA

Gretta untangled herself from Derrick's sleeping body. He'd come over the night before and never left. As much as she wanted to put a stop to their secret love affair, she just couldn't do it. She was in love with the man. Derrick had promised her weeks ago that he was going to confront Natasha about ending their relationship, but, as of today, she was still waiting for him to do so. His excuse was always that he needed more time.

Well, how much more time? she wondered. She didn't know how long she could keep up this façade. Her nerves were already frail, and with Natasha playing detective, she was sure it wouldn't be long before the cat was out of the bag. Gretta went into her bathroom and looked in the mirror. Lines were starting to form across her forehead, and she didn't like it one bit. This relationship with Derrick was becoming very stressful. She let out a long breath as she applied her facial-cleansing crème. Never in her life had she been in a situation such as this. Sure, she had dated men who had women on the side, even dated a man who was married, but she didn't find that out until the heifer cornered her in Wal-Mart, of all places. The woman had nearly attacked her in the vegetable aisle; hurling obscenities at her as if she wasn't anything but a skank. Talk about embarrassing. That incident had happened nearly a year ago, and she hadn't set foot in that Wal-Mart, which was only about ten minutes from her apartment, since then. She'd shopped at the one on the other side of town for almost a year. The women of the men she'd dated were just faces in a crowd. She didn't have an emotional connection with any of them. She wished with all her heart that this situation was just like the others in her past. However, it wasn't. Among the faces in the crowd was a face she had known all her life. And if that wasn't bad enough, they shared the same bloodline.

Gretta rinsed her face with warm water and then patted it dry with the soft, white washcloth on the rack nearby.

"Gretta, where are you, babe?"

She was standing at the sink, washing her hands. Derrick stuck his head inside the bathroom. Looking at him, she said, "Derrick, you gots to go. I'm meeting Natasha in less than an hour." Derrick's serene gaze met Gretta's perturbed one. Gretta stepped into the shower and turned the water on full blast.

Competing with the noise of the water, Derrick yelled out, "Gretta, I'm going to tell her, alright."

As the water poured over Gretta's body, she shouted, "And the beat goes on!"

Derrick stood next to the glass shower door and sighed. "Come on, babe. You got to believe me."

Gretta poured on more of her Bath-N-Body body wash and continued to lather herself. Standing directly under the water, the soap ran down into the shower and made a circular motion as it entered the drain. Derrick felt his manhood growing as he took in her glistening body. He slid open the shower door and attempted to join her. Gretta put up her hands and gave him a threatening look. Turning off the water, she stepped out of the shower and reached around Derrick, who looked like a man who had just lost his dog. She pulled her pink and white towel from the rack and wrapped it around her wet body as she made her way back into the bedroom, with Derrick following close behind her.

"Gretta, I know you think I'm playing you, babe. But I'm for real. I'm just waiting for the right moment."

Gretta turned so sharply that Derrick almost ran her over. "And when is that right moment, Derrick? When she catches us in bed together?"

Regaining his composure, Derrick gave her a bewildered look. "Naw, babe, that's not going to happen," he said, shaking his head from side to side. "Just trust me, Gretta. Can you do that?" Gretta rolled her eyes as she proceeded to get dressed.

"So, what are you two doing, anyway?" Derrick asked cautiously. He watched Gretta slip on a baby-blue summer sheath dress and pull it down over her wide hips.

"She wants me to go shopping with her and then have a bite to eat. Lord only knows how I'm going to get through this. I've been avoiding her for weeks now, and she's going to ridicule me with questions."

Derrick approached her. He placed his arms around her waist and kissed her gently. "Just be cool, babe, and tell her the truth."

Gretta gave him a stabbing look. "Oh, I get it now," she said as she removed his hands from her waist. "You want me to the do the dirty work here. Uhhh… I should have known this is what you were holding out for!" she shouted.

"No, no, Gretta, that's not what I'm saying, exactly," Derrick muttered as he pulled her into him. Gretta stared blankly at him. "Just tell her that you do have a new man, which is the truth," he rattled. With uplifted eyes, he mumbled, "Just don't tell her it's me." Gretta pushed Derrick so hard he almost fell backward. "Damn it, Gretta, what's wrong with you!" he shouted.

"I've had it with men like you, Derrick, always using us women as if we were just pawns. You don't care about me or my cousin. You've just wanted to burn the candle at both ends. Well, guess what, Derrick? The candle is out and so are you!" she screamed.

"Is this what you want, Gretta?" he asked as he picked up his jeans from the arm of the wooden chair and pulled them on.

"Yes, this is exactly what I want," she said firmly. Derrick grabbed his white tee shirt and slid it over his head. He put his feet into his leather sandals, walked over to the walnut dresser, and picked up his keys and wallet. Gretta watched in silence.

Placing his designer shades on his face, he hollered, "I'm outta here!" He never looked in her direction as he made his way out the door.

Hearing the slamming of her apartment door, Gretta fell upon her bed in a mountain of tears. She was caught between the cousin she adored and the man she loved.

NATASHA & GRETTA

"Girl, what took you so long? You must have fallen back to sleep," Natasha said as Gretta drove down I-85. Her eyes stayed planted on the freeway as her Avalon cruised along with ease. Traffic wasn't bad, and she was able to maneuver her car around the slower-moving vehicles.

"Gretta, I think you got a case of the hearing impaired," Natasha popped loudly, turning her head and looking at the side of Gretta's face.

Gretta's lips flattened. "I heard you, Natasha, and yes, I fell back to sleep. Is that a crime?"

"Mmmm, in your case it may very well be," Natasha said with a wiggle of her head. "You might have a body of a man in your closet for all I know." She chuckled lightly. Gretta failed to laugh. She just stared ahead. Natasha folded her arms.

"Gretta, I don't understand. We have always talked about everything, and now you treat me as if I'm a total stranger to you."

Gretta felt even worse after hearing the hurt in her cousin's voice. How do you tell your first cousin that you're screwing her man? Not only that, but you're planning a future with that man. Gretta's brow furrowed as she gripped the steering wheel a little tighter. She should never have agreed to go shopping. This was going to be a hell of a day.

"So, you're not going to explain yourself, Gretta?" Natasha smirked.

Gretta thought about Derrick's suggestion. *Like I should really be taking advice from him,* she said to herself. *Girl, you can do this*. Exhaling, Gretta began her lie—sort of.

"Alright, cousin, I guess it's time for me to spill the beans," she muttered, giving Natasha a sidelong glance. "I. . .have been seeing someone."

Natasha's face held a triumphant expression. "I knew it!" she beamed. "Tell me all about him, Gretta. Is it the same guy from the pool party or someone you met at your job?" she asked as she wiggled in her seat.

"Dang, Natasha! Slow your roll, will you?"

"Well, tell me how you met him," Natasha squealed. With a solemn expression, Gretta responded, "He was a blind date…that turned out well," she stammered. "He is a nephew of a girl on my team at work. He just moved here a few months ago," she continued as she pieced together her lie.

Natasha turned in her seat. "Well, is he good looking and what's his name?" she asked in a single breath. Gretta was glad she was the one driving, because if she had to look into her cousin's eyes, she would have been through. There was no way Natasha would have believed her.

"Well, Gretta what's the man's name?" Natasha insisted.

"Dustin," she said, "Dustin Cole."

"Dustin Cole." Natasha repeated his name like a teacher in front of her class. "My, that does have a ring to it. Now, what is his occupation?"

Gretta could feel Natasha's eyes boring into the side of her face. She knew her cousin was waiting on a negative reply. She remembered all the conversations she and Natasha had had about her dating guys that were going nowhere.

"I know where you're going with this line of questioning, Natasha. You can rest assured, Dustin is gainfully employed. The brotha has a degree in marketing."

"Mmmm," Natasha said with a nod. "I see you have moved up in your selection process."

Gretta managed to roll her eyes before changing lanes and heading to the exit that would take them to the mall.

"Now, tell me how fine he is," Natasha said, smiling.

Now, that is an area I feel comfortable talking about, Gretta mused as a smile creased her lips. "He is a cross between Denzel Washington and Idris Elba. He has a deep voice like Barry White, and the man is drenched with chocolate skin that is as smooth as a baby's bottom."

"Are you sure you're not describing Derrick Perkins?" Natasha laughed out loud. Gretta nearly ran into the car in front of her as it slowed down. She hit the brakes, and they both pitched forward.

"Gretta, what's wrong with you!? Don't tell me you didn't see the car in front of us," Natasha screamed as beads of sweat covered her forehead. Catching her breath, she uttered, "You almost made me piss in my panties."

"Blame it on Moms Mabley, here!" Gretta screamed as she honked the horn. "Old people need to be taken off the freeway." Gretta sneered as she gave the old woman an evil eye.

"I think we should stop talking about men now and focus on the freeway. I'd like to get to the mall with all my limbs in tow, if you don't mind," Natasha muttered as she sat back in her seat. Gretta breathed a sigh of relief, at least for the moment.

ESSENCE

It was seven o'clock in the evening when Sloan pulled into the driveway of Essence's townhouse. He had phoned her earlier that day and made dinner plans. He wanted to end their relationship in a dignified manner, and he was hoping a nice, quiet setting would ease things along. Sloan thought about how he had changed in a matter of months. The old Sloan wouldn't have cared how a woman felt when he wanted out. At that point in his life, his relationships with women were like a line at the checkout counter. When one customer was finished, the cashier shouted out "next" and kept the line moving.

Sitting in his SUV, Sloan's mind retreated back in time to a conversation he'd had with Uncle Leroy. Even though he'd married Sloan's mother, it was still hard for him to think of Uncle Leroy as a stepfather. However, the advice he had given him over the years, including the tips about being a man, had never faltered. They were seated in the backyard of his mother's home on a Saturday afternoon. Uncle Leroy was never a drinker, which was something they both had in common. They were just talking about the men in the neighborhood where he had grown up. Some pursued their dreams, while others missed the mark. Some had a slew of baby mammas, while others were residents of the local prison wards. Before their conversation ended that day, Uncle Leroy left these words with Sloan.

He said, "Son, loving a whole lot of women doesn't make you a man. Loving only one and making her happy makes you a real man."

At the time, Sloan thought his uncle was talking a bunch of gibberish, but now he understood all too well. Being a real man meant being responsible for one's actions. Sloan thought about his career at Emerson & Stuckey and how he had fought to maintain a high level of integrity so his clients would trust and believe in him. Too bad he didn't carry that same ideology into his personal life. *At least I've been lucky*, he thought. He had only two regrets thus far. Mostly, he regretted not realizing the love that he had sought for years was right there by his side.

"Hello, sugar," Essence greeted Sloan as he got out of his SUV, walked over to the passenger side door, and opened it for her. Essence looked beautiful in her satin two-piece, olive-colored pantsuit with matching earrings and sandals. Her sexy fragrance filled the vehicle as Sloan slid inside and started the engine. Essence leaned over and gave him a warm kiss.

"Why didn't you wait for me to meet you at the door?" Sloan asked.

"Sugar, I saw you when you pulled up. I guess I'm just anxious to begin our evening together," she said slyly.

Sloan's stomach felt as if he had swallowed a bowl of rocks. He knew from the look on her face that breaking up was going to be hard to do.

LISA RAY & NATASHA

"Thanks, girl, for coming over today," Natasha said as she sat a silver platter of wings and buttered rolls on the patio table, where the women were dining by the pool.

"Anytime, girl, I think I needed a break from Jerry, anyhow," Lisa Ray sighed.

"Oh, you got to be kidding me. As hard as you tried to land that plane and now you need a break," Natasha stated as she poured Pepsi into their tall glasses. Lisa Ray couldn't help but laugh.

"Girl, you are too comical. Have you ever thought about becoming a comedian?"

"Naw, girlfriend. I'm not that funny," Natasha quipped with a wave of her hand.

"Mmmm, I must admit you hit the nail on the head. I used every trick in the book to get that man of mine."

Natasha noticed the faraway look in her friend's eyes. "Is something wrong, Lisa Ray?" she asked, taking a seat next to her.

Lisa Ray reached for the tall glass of soda and took a sip. "Girl, I don't know. I mean, Jerry is perfect. He treats me like a queen, but I'm afraid..." her voice faded.

"Afraid of what?" Natasha asked with arched brows.

"I never had a real good man in my life. The ones I've encountered started off as princes and then turned into frogs. I'm afraid the same will happen to Jerry. So you see, it's not that I need a break from him. I just don't want him to get tired of me."

"Lisa Ray, girl, get a grip. Just because those other clowns turned out wrong for you doesn't mean Jerry will. You two have been together for a while now, and the man treats you as if you two just met."

Lisa Ray picked up a wing and bit into it. After swallowing, she uttered, "Jerry has been wonderful to me, Natasha. No one could ask for a better man."

"I think you should just relax and stay positive. Stop comparing him to the duds of yesterday," Natasha quipped. Natasha picked up her buttered roll and held it.

"It's easy for you to say, you lucky thing you," Lisa Ray chimed. Natasha gave her a puzzled look. "You've got me snowed, Lisa Ray."

"Yeah, I bet I do," Lisa Ray said skeptically. "How does it feel to have two men in love with you, Natasha?"

Natasha sat her roll back onto her plate. She knew it was no use trying to hide the obvious from Lisa Ray. She looked into her eyes and muttered, "Scary."

The wide grin on Lisa Ray's face vanished. "I wasn't expecting that kind of answer. I thought having two fine hunks of men fawning over you would make you feel like a princess."

"Now, Lisa Ray, you know loving one man is hard enough. What do you think about two?"

Lisa Ray leaned forward in her seat. "Girl, you're not telling me that you have feelings for Derrick, as well." She squinted in amazement. "I thought you were only in love with Sloan."

"I am in love with Sloan," Natasha retorted. Lisa Ray slumped back in her seat and looked at Natasha, dumbfounded. "Don't even look at me like that," Natasha said as she tilted her head. "I know in my heart that Sloan is the right man for me. There's no doubt about that now. But Derrick and I had some good times together, and if…" She leaned in as her eyes met Lisa Ray's eyes. "If Sloan was not in here," Natasha said as she pointed at her heart. "Derrick and I could have been the hottest couple in the ATL," Natasha chuckled.

Lisa Ray picked up another hot wing. "Girl, and I thought my boat may have been rocking in the wind. But looks like yours might be heading for a storm."

They enjoyed the rest of the evening, chitchatting and dining on hot wings. Later that night, when all was said and done, Natasha lay quietly in her bed. The room was dark, except for the angel night-light that glowed softly, sending a pathway of light out the doorway. Natasha's mind took flight as she thought about her life, which had been a good one thus far. There had been a few bumps in the road, but that's how life goes; and no one lives without experiencing them. Darin floated through her mind, which made her frown. Sloan made his way through and she smiled. A warm feeling engulfed her, leaving butterflies in her stomach. Why hadn't she told her cousin Gretta about the newfound love she had with Sloan? She felt like such a hypocrite for making Gretta come clean with her about her love life when she was hiding something herself. If only Gretta hadn't been behaving so strangely, maybe she would have told her about Sloan. There was something else Gretta was hiding, she could feel it in her bones. She wondered why Gretta didn't feel like she could share it with her.

What was so secretive about this new man in her life? Was he married? Surely Gretta had better sense than to go down that road again.

Natasha turned over onto her side and exhaled as she thought to herself. Closing her eyes brought Derrick Perkins's face into view. Sloan had warned her so diligently about Derrick. Finally, she had to admit that he was a mysterious man—mystery that went beyond his "playa" ways. From listening to Derrick, she picked up on some past hurt that he held deep down inside. She cared for Derrick, but not enough to let go of Sloan. She was hoping to end things with Derrick tonight, but when she called him, he said he couldn't talk. He was in the middle of an important meeting and said he would get back with her later. She was alone on a Saturday night, so she picked up the phone to call Gretta, thinking that maybe a movie would do both of them some good. But Gretta also declined her invite after feigning exhaustion.

Gretta tired on a Saturday night? she thought, *That's one for the books.*

So she lay in her bed, just her and the soft glow from her angel night-light.

SLOAN & ESSENCE

Surprisingly, dinner was going so well. *Just like old times,* Sloan thought, staring up at Essence as the candlelit hue glowed on her face. Essence was updating him on the account she had helped to land that day. A hefty bonus was coming her way and Sloan was proud that he had trained her so well. Truth be told, the lady hadn't needed much training. Essence was as smart as a whip and quick on her feet; and she could make quality decisions in the blink of an eye. Anyone coming close to her would fall under her charming spell, and that included him as well.

"Excuse me for taking over the conversation, Sloan. How rude of me," she said as she stared into his eyes.

"That's quite alright, Essence. I was enjoying listening to you. I can tell that you are loving your career."

"That's true, sugar, but I would rather be loving you tonight," she said alluringly.

Sloan knew Essence always spoke her mind. She'd been doing exactly that from the very first day they'd met.

The waitress brought their food, and Sloan was glad for the reprieve. He didn't want to spoil the dinner. At least she deserved to have a nice meal.

After dinner, they took a stroll on the sandy, white beach. The sounds of the crashing waves danced around in their ears. Essence insisted on holding hands, so Sloan obliged.

"Essence, we need to talk seriously," he finished before he paused for a moment and peered down into her eyes. Essence stood still.

"Sloan, marry me," she whispered as the wind blew through her black, silky hair.

Sloan let out a soft chuckle while saying, "I thought the man was supposed to do the proposing," he tried to joke.

"Sugar, its 2013 and we women have come a long, long way." Essence smiled. Sloan saw that this was definitely going to be hard, and his mind raced.

"So, what do you think about early September?" she said as she continued to gaze into his eyes.

Sloan began to walk again. They were still holding hands. "Mmmm, I don't know, Essence. That's only a couple of months away. You couldn't plan a wedding in such a short period of time."

"Okay, what about October, around the end of the month? And not Halloween," she spouted excitedly.

"No," Sloan stated clearly.

Essence stopped abruptly. "Okay, you pick the date," she said as she looked into his eyes.

"I said no, because…we're not getting married… ever."

Essence's face held a glow of light, even on this very dark night. But it began to fade. Sloan's face grew serious as he stared at her while holding both of her hands. He said, "Essence, I don't love you enough to marry you. You are a beautiful, wonderful woman, and you deserve a man that can give you all of him. To marry you would be doing you a great disservice, and you deserve much better than that."

Essence quickly snatched her hands away. "Are you giving me a verbal strawberry letter? If so, I want no part of it!" she yelled. Her face was distorted in anger.

"Look, Essence, I'm keeping it real with you. I know I should have told you long before now—"

"How long have you been feeling this way, Sloan?" Essence interrupted.

Sloan bowed his head. "About two months after I moved in with you."

"You screwed my brains out all this time, and you're just now realizing how you feel about me?" she asked as she glared at him.

"Essence, I do have feelings for you, but it's not enough to spend my whole life with you. I've searched deep down in my soul; and that kind of love is not there for you. It's not happening for me, Essence, and I'm sorry," Sloan said honestly.

"Well, I'm sorry, too," she yelled as her face hardened. "And I'm sorry you're going to cause that little bitch of yours to get hurt," she shouted. "I'm not one of your brainless chicks, Sloan. I've been in this game a long time, and I know how it's played. It's been that selfish little bitch of a best friend that's been between us all the time. You two probably been screwing behind my back and just waiting for the moment to plunge this knife in me."

"Stop it, Essence!" Sloan yelled. "You don't know what you're talking about."

"Damn it, Sloan, you tell me what I'm talking about. Fill me in on your revelation!" Essence screamed.

There were several other couples now on the boardwalk. They stopped and stared at them. Sloan grabbed Essence by the hand and proceeded to walk farther away from the crowd. After a few feet had separated them from the other couples, Sloan stopped. He stared at Essence, who practically had steam coming out of her ears.

"Essence, look, I never meant for this to happen. When we first met, I honestly thought that you were the one for me. But as time went by, I realized that I wasn't in love with you."

Essence folded her arms. She was getting cold, and she wasn't sure if the chill was from the breeze off the water or the coldness of Sloan's heart.

Sloan took in several breaths before continuing. "I am in love with Natasha. We have been in love for quite some time, but we both fought it. It wasn't like we planned for this to happen. Our feelings were buried inside of us for several years, until we both stopped denying them."

Sloan pulled her into his arms. She was trembling. He rubbed her arms and then held her close. "Essence, I never ever meant to hurt you. You've got to believe that," Sloan said, kissing the top of her head.

Essence cried softly in his arms as he held her. Sloan's heart was also breaking. He truly meant what he had said.

"Essence, I'm sorry things had to end this way. But I will always be your friend," he whispered.

"End? Oh, Sloan, this is not the end of anything," Essence spewed as she pulled away from him. "You both are going to be very sorry, and you both are going to pay!" she yelled as she ran down the beach.

"Essence, wait!" Sloan yelled out.

Essence never looked back as Sloan stood still, watching as she disappeared into the darkness of the night.

G STREET CHRONICLES
A LITERARY POWERHOUSE
WWW.GSTREETCHRONICLES.COM

NATASHA & DERRICK

Natasha watched silently as Derrick and Mr. Erickson concluded their business meeting. The deal had gone through without a hitch. The men shook hands as Mr. Erickson looked her way. He turned to face her.

"And thank you, Miss Jacobs. It was such a pleasure meeting you," he said as his dark eyes roamed over her body. She should have been used to it by now. She couldn't count how many men she had encountered since she had been with the company that looked at women as if they were pretty ornaments just waiting to be played with.

"Mr. Erickson, I'm sure you will be pleased with our services. And please don't hesitate to call if you have any more questions," she uttered as she gave Derrick a quick glance. Once Mr. Erickson was aware of Derrick's stare, he quickly nodded.

"Thank you, Miss Jacobs and Mr. Perkins," he uttered as he headed out the door. Derrick closed the door, and Natasha took a seat in the plush chair adjacent to his desk.

"Yes, yes!" Derrick spun around as he waved both hands. "Another one bites the dust!" he exclaimed. Natasha smiled.

"I knew we had him by his shoelaces. Are you done for today?" Derrick asked with excitement still lingering in his voice.

Natasha stared at his handsome features. "Yes, I am," she muttered as she crossed her legs. "What did you have in mind?" she asked, peering up at him.

"A night out on the town, babe, what else!" Derrick beamed.

He pulled Natasha out of her seat and danced around the office. Then he pulled her in and gave her a passionate kiss. He felt Natasha stiffen in his arms.

"What's wrong, babe?"

"Uh…we need to talk, Derrick. But not here."

His brow furrowed. "Sure. Meet me downstairs in say…" Derrick said as he glanced down at his watch, "fifteen minutes."

"Fine. See you then," Natasha uttered as she walked out the door.

Derrick stared out of his high-rise window. He knew a choice had to be made, and he hoped like hell he would choose the right one. Derrick cruised down the avenue with Natasha seated beside him. Both were silent choosing to wait until they reached their destination before revealing what was really on their minds.

The live band, Just for You, played a soft melody as Derrick and Natasha sipped on their glasses of wine. Each seemed to be lost in their own little worlds as they listened to the music. Natasha had rehearsed her speech to Derrick a million times in her head, but now that the moment had arrived, the words eluded her. Sloan had called her late last night and filled her in on how his evening with Essence had transpired, and it had ended ugly. She prayed it wouldn't be the same way for her and Derrick.

"So, babe, you said you wanted to talk," he said, leaning into her.

Natasha stared into his dark eyes. "Derrick, I really don't know how to begin," she stated.

"At the very beginning always worked for me," Derrick said matter-of-factly.

Natasha exhaled. "Derrick, where do you see our relationship going? I mean you've told me more than once that since your divorce, you weren't really interested in a long-term commitment."

"Yeah, I did say that, now didn't I?" Derrick took a sip of his drink.

"So, are you saying your feelings have changed?" Natasha asked with a confused expression.

Derrick took in her beauty. He wanted to be straight up with her. "Natasha, since I met you a whole lot has changed—some good, some bad," he said with a nod. Derrick lowered his eyes from her gaze. He couldn't look her in the eyes and tell her that he was sleeping with her cousin, even though the words were on the tip of his tongue. He had to bring it to her in another way.

"Natasha, I'm going to let it all out on the table," he said, looking back at her. "I've done something I'm not proud of, and I don't want to hurt you." Derrick scratched the tip of his nose.

"And neither do I, Derrick," she said.

He gave her an intense look. "What?" he quizzed.

"I don't want to hurt you either, Derrick."

"What are you trying to say, Natasha?" he asked.

Natasha let out a sigh. "Look, Derrick, I weighed everything you've been telling me about Sloan and my relationship, and I…no, *we* have come to the conclusion that we *are* in love. Sloan and I are really in love and have been for quite some time."

Natasha held her breath as she waited for Derrick's response. His mouth opened and then closed again. A rush of relief ran through his veins. Talk about perfect timing. Now he wouldn't have to say a thing about the other woman in his life.

"So this is the end of the road for us, huh?" he said, trying to sound as disappointed as he could.

Natasha nodded. "Yeah, I assume it is, Derrick."

Derrick reached for her hand and held it. "Please say that we can still be friends," he said with a small smile.

"I would like nothing more," Natasha uttered as she returned his smile.

This was too easy, they both thought to themselves, *maybe breaking up between friends isn't so hard after all.*

ESSENCE & DERRICK

"Derrick, you are unbelievable. Surely you could have put up a fight. How could you let her go so easily?" Essence fumed.

"So, what do you think I should have done? Killed her for being in love with someone else?" he asked with raised brows. Essence had phoned him, ranting hysterically and begging him to come over to her place.

"You know, that's not a bad idea," she boasted with a twisted look.

Derrick froze. *She couldn't be serious*, he wondered silently, *Or could she?* "Get a grip on yourself, Essence. No one is killing anybody," he said as he peered over at her. He had prepared himself a drink from her wet bar.

"Look, I've been doing some thinking," he said as he took a sip of his wine. Essence stared in his direction. "That vendetta I had against you… well, I've decided to let it go. You were right, Essence. What happened in the past can't be erased, but it can be forgotten. We are here in a new city, with wonderful careers going for us." Derrick opened his arms and motioned for her to come to him. She went freely, and he held her close. "We've both made mistakes.

I can't blame you for everything that happened in my life. I didn't have to cheat on my wife. That was a choice I made, so I'm not blaming you anymore, Essence." He moved her away from him and stared into her eyes. "I'm sure you will find a new love soon. For a woman as beautiful as you are, it will only be a matter of time." Derrick chuckled.

Essence's expression darkened. Her eyes were ablaze. "Don't you see that I've already found the man that I want? I finally found one that is single. There is no wife for me to push aside, and I'm not letting him walk out of my life!" she shouted.

"Essence, the man isn't in love with you. Now, let it go! Take your own advice and start anew."

"Oh, now it's so easy for you to say," Essence said as her eyes narrowed. "You got the woman you want now, don't you Derrick. Too bad my man got away," she huffed.

"Essence, you're free now, babe. I'm not out to hurt you anymore. Spread your wings and fly to a higher ground. There are more Sloan Stevens out there. Trust me," he said as he picked up his keys and headed toward the door.

After hearing it slam, Essence walked over to Derrick's empty wine glass and slammed it against the wall. She watched it shatter into tiny, little pieces. She was going to have Sloan Stevens one way or another, and no one was telling her anything different.

GATHERING OF FRIENDS

As Ricky flipped the hamburgers, he shouted, "Ladies and gents, the food is almost ready. Can I get some plates, please?"

"Here's one coming right up," Sloan said while getting a paper plate from the stack on the picnic table. Natasha, Lisa Ray, and Gretta chatted with Asia, Ricky's latest love interest. They had been talking nonstop as the men prepared the food. Earlier, Natasha had asked Gretta why her man was missing in action. But, as usual, she had given her a lame explanation. He just happened to be out of town on a beautiful Saturday afternoon.

Yeah right, Natasha thought to herself. She had concluded that the man was definitely married. They had all gathered for a special reason; Natasha and Sloan were going to announce their engagement. They had shared their true feelings with the gang, but no one knew they had decided to get married. Natasha smiled inwardly as she remembered the night Sloan had proposed. Sloan had taken her to an elegant restaurant and when they had just finished dining, the waiter brought over a beautifully-decorated cupcake, which made her laugh out loud. She and Sloan had loved cupcakes as children. They couldn't get enough of the homemade cupcakes her mother always prepared for them on special occasions.

"This is a special occasion," Sloan announced as he gazed into her eyes. He placed one of the cupcakes in his hand and instructed her to position her finger in the middle of it.

"Sloan, what is this?" she protested.

"Just do as I ask," he responded with a mischievous grin. Natasha stuck her finger inside and pulled out an eight-carat solitaire covered with icing. Tears swelled in her eyes as he took the ring out of her hand and licked off the remaining icing. Peering into her misty eyes, he said eloquently, "Natasha Jacobs, you have been my best friend for half of my life. Now, I'm asking you to spend the rest of it as my wife."

Natasha could no longer hold back the tears. She let out a sob and mumbled, "Yes…Yes." The restaurant patrons began to clap and cheer as he slid the ring onto her finger.

"Honey!" Sloan called out to her, breaking her out of her daydream. When she glanced up at him, he asked, "Are we ready?"

Natasha nodded as she stood from her seat.

Sloan instructed everyone to gather around. The friends looked at each other with puzzled looks on their faces as they followed his gesture.

"What's up, dude?" Ricky chuckled and gave Sloan a questioning stare. Sloan took Natasha by the hand and kissed her gently on the lips. Then he pulled out the diamond solitaire. The women gasped at the sparkling diamond.

"We have a confession to make," Sloan uttered, "I've already asked Natasha to be my wife."

"And I've accepted." Natasha smiled broadly.

"And because we love you all so much, we wanted you to be a part of our happiness."

"Hear, Hear!" Ricky said, holding up the spatula he was using to flip the burgers. The friends exchanged hugs and kisses. Natasha's and Gretta's eyes met.

"I'm so happy for you, my dear cousin," Gretta uttered with a satisfied smile.

"Thanks, Gretta," Natasha responded. Gretta turned toward the picnic table and picked up a paper plate.

"Gretta," Natasha called out. Gretta turned to face her again. "Are you okay?"

"Sure. Why wouldn't I be?" she asked with a slight grin. "I'm happy for you and Sloan, Natasha…truly happy," she said as she gave her cousin a big hug.

GRETTA & DERRICK

Derrick whirled around the room with Gretta in his arms. "Babe, we are home free!" he shouted. Gretta beamed with happiness, as well. She was so happy that Sloan and Natasha had finally realized their true love for each other and that they were about to be married. Talk about great timing. Now she and Derrick could look forward to their own future. After kissing each other for several minutes, the bright light in Gretta's eyes began to dim. The smile she held had gotten smaller. In fact, it had shrunk to a thin line on her lips. Derrick stared into her eyes.

"Babe, what's up with that grim look you're giving me?"

With an exasperated sigh, Gretta said, "Do you even have to ask, Derrick?" She folded her arms across her chest and stared into his dark eyes. "Tell me, how are we going to explain our relationship? Has it even crossed your mind at all?" she asked with a roll of her eyes.

Derrick's expression grew solemn, and then he said, "Babe, of course it has, and you know what? I have a plan."

Gretta unfolded her arms and gave him a skeptical look. After their heated fight a couple of weeks ago, she had sworn never to see him again. But here she was, in his presence. The man had a part of her now. She found herself deeply in love with him, and no matter how hard she tried to deny those feelings, they were there as clear as the blue sky. She wondered how Natasha would feel about her after their relationship was revealed. Would she hate her guts? Would she ever forgive her for sleeping with Derrick? Those questions rattled around in her brain like misplaced marbles. Coming out of her trance, she quickly remembered that Derrick said he had a plan.

With a tight expression, she asked, "What is your ingenious plan this time?"

Derrick took her by the arms and stared straight into her face. "Babe, think about it, now. No one knows that we are seeing each other, right?" Gretta wondered where he was going with this, but she nodded her head yes. “So we just tell everyone that we just happened to run into each other at a club, had a few drinks and started talking,” he said with a twinkle in his eyes. “Natasha is engaged now, and I’m a free agent, babe!” he exclaimed as he waited for her response.

A broad smile creased her lips. She pointed her finger to the middle of his chest.

“Oh no, you’re not, my handsome boo,” she said, shaking her head from side to side. “You belong to me now, Derrick Perkins.”

Derrick let out a loud chuckle as he pulled her into his arms and kissed her passionately.

*****

Essence stood in the damp parking lot of the restaurant and watched the smiling couple enter the establishment. They were so engrossed in their own little world that they failed to notice her standing there. The tall frame of a man lowered his head and kissed the lips of a beautiful woman with cinnamon-colored hair. Essence pulled on the belt of the black trench coat she was wearing. It tightened around her waist as she trembled in the dark, damp weather. Cars passed by, sending blinding lights into her direction. Her eyes squinted in the dark. Peeking inside the restaurant, she saw the happy couple seated at a table near the window. She leaned against the cold brick wall as visions of her plan danced before her. Like a sniper on a rooftop, she would aim at her target. With a pull of the trigger, she would take them out, one by one. It tore her apart to have things end this way.

*****

Florene’s head was buried in a bridal magazine when the doorbell chimed. Placing the magazine on the glass coffee table, she walked slowly to the door. She opened it to find the smiling face of her daughter.

“Good morning, Momma,” Natasha uttered as they embraced.

“My, aren’t we a little early?” Florene chirped as they made their way into the living room.

“I know, Momma, but I’m too excited to sleep. There is so much to be done in so little time,” she said in one breath. A line formed across Florene’s forehead.

"I know, baby, and that's why I don't understand why you and Sloan won't extend the date for a least a couple of months."

Natasha turned to face her mom. "Momma, we have wasted too much time as it is. We should have been married years ago. If only we would have…"

"…come to terms with your feelings for each other," Florene finished as she sat down on the couch.

"Yes," Natasha uttered as she joined her.

"I know, honey, but three months to plan an extravagant wedding? Mmmm, baby, I don't know if we can pull this off," Florene said.

"Oh, Momma, we can do it," Natasha said with a wave of her hand. "I already secured our church. I've spoken with the people at the print shop. My invitations should be ready in about two weeks. Sloan has asked Ricky to be his best man. Gretta is my matron of honor, and the bridesmaids and groomsmen have already been contacted." Natasha let out a whiff of air as she continued. "And, mother, you are the best caterer in the city." Natasha chuckled.

Florene laughed at her daughter's enthusiasm. Natasha had everything lined up like bands in a parade. "Baby, you are something," Florene said as she smiled.

"Well, it's the truth. Florene Catering Service is well known throughout the city."

Natasha remembered when she was a child helping her mother prepare foods for the white folks after they had hired her to cater their special events. Her mother had been in business for more than seventeen years now. It had paid the mortgage and put Natasha and her brother through school.

"Well, I guess we're set," Florene said, reaching over and giving her daughter another hug. When she released her, she saw remnants of tears in her daughter's eyes.

"Now, now, baby, there is no need for tears until that wedding day," Florene said as she cupped Natasha's face. With her small fingers, she wiped the tears away.

"Momma, I can't help but shed some tears," Natasha spoke as the happiness within her rose to the surface. "When I think of all the years I've spent looking for that special man to share my life with, and he was right here with me all this time." Staring into her mother's eyes she said, "I should have listened to you, Momma."

"Baby, God has His own way of making things happen in due season. This is you and Sloan's season," Florene smiled happily.

SLOAN

Sloan woke up to find Essence perched at the foot of his bed. Startled out of his wits, he jumped out of bed.

"How in the hell did you get in here?!" he shouted. Essence gave him a twisted look, and then her face broke into a knowing smile. She dangled a silver key before his eyes. Sloan reared back his head. He had forgotten they had exchanged keys and he'd failed to get his back.

"I…uh forgot you still had my key," he managed to mumble.

"I think you've forgotten a lot of things, Sloan," she said, barely above a whisper. Her eyes focused on the navy cotton sheets on the bed. She had purchased them only weeks ago. With a smile forming on her lips, she looked up at Sloan and said, "I remember the heat we made between these sheets, Sloan." Her hand glided across the bed as if she were smoothing wrinkles from the sheet. Then she pulled the top sheet up, looking underneath and giving him a sexy stare.

"This is an open invitation for you to join me," she said. Sloan stared back. For the first time, he noticed the white, sheer lace negligee she was wearing. He must admit that she looked sexy as hell. Her full breasts stood out like a light to a lost ship in the night. Clearing his throat and taking his eyes off her chest, he uttered, "No, Essence. We've been there, and we're not going back."

Essence popped straight up with her hands situated on her full, smooth, cocoa-colored hips.

"Well, I'm not accepting that. If I can't have you, neither will she," Essence spewed. Sloan rubbed his forehead as he peered into her distorted face.

"Essence, I think you need some help." Sloan remembered that one of his clients whose wife was a psychiatrist had given him a card once. He walked over to the nightstand and picked up his wallet. Going through the folds, he found the beige card. "Dr. Tammy Daniels," he read out loud as he gave the card to her.

With a wave of her hand, she swiped the card from Sloan's fingertips. The card floated to the floor. "I don't need a damn psychiatrist. What I need is you!" she nearly screamed. She ran into his arms and planted kisses all over his face. She ran her hand over his white briefs, feeling the firmness of his manhood. Sloan sucked in a deep breath as her soft hands caressed him. Fighting the temptation to succumb to his sexual urges, he grabbed her hand and pushed her away. The impact caused her to fall backward upon the bed.

"Get out of here, now!" he said sternly.

Essence's eyes filled with tears. "You don't mean that, sugar. You're just confused. The feelings you have for her is only friendship, Sloan. You don't love her. You can't love her. You love me," Essence rambled.

"How many times do I have to say it, Essence? It is over between us. Over! Do you hear me?" Sloan emphasized. "Now, accept it and get on with your life," Sloan said as he pulled her up from the bed. He bent down and picked up the card from the floor. He shoved it into the palm of her hand. "Where are the rest of your clothes?" he asked as he scanned the room.

"I have no other clothes," she said with a wicked look on her face. Sloan pivoted to his closet and grabbed a black sweatshirt.

He pulled the sweatshirt over Essence's head. It was so large that it looked like a mini-dress on her body. He then took her by the shoulders and led her to the front door of his townhouse. Sloan opened the door, and with a gentle push, she was standing on the opposite side.

"Take care of yourself, Essence, and please call the number on the card," he uttered, trying not to yell. With a look of concern etched into his face, he also said, "I'm really sorry about all this."

Essence returned his gaze with her twisted look and said, "Not half as sorry as you will be."

SLOAN

"The chick was in my apartment, man, while I was sleeping. She had this wicked look on her face," Sloan muttered as he rubbed his hand over his head. "She could have killed me, man." Just the thought of it sent cold chills down his spine.

Ricky was seated on the barstool next to him. They were at Dobby's, an after-hours bar and grill. The place was filling up by the minute as people made their way inside. Ricky finished off the last of his wings and took a swig of beer to wash it down.

"If I were you, dude, I would get me a gun," Ricky said.

Sloan's eyes popped out of his head. "A gun? What am I going to do with a freakin' gun?"

"Shoot the crazy-ass chick, dude," Ricky answered sternly.

Sloan bowed his head and let out a deep breath. "Naw, man. Now you're trippin'," he said to Ricky. "Essence is not a psycho, man. She's just confused right now. I think some dude in her past did a real number on her, man."

"Uh huh," Ricky said with a nod of his head. "And if you don't do something, she's going to do a real number on you," he warned. Ricky's eyes narrowed. "Sloan, dude, listen to me. I got this gut feeling this chick is disturbed. I would hate to see anything happen to you or Natasha."

Sloan's mind wandered as Ricky's statement soaked in. *Was Essence really capable of hurting someone?* he asked himself. During the months they had been together, she had showed no inclination of violence. The only thing he had experienced was a hefty dose of her possessiveness.

"Hey, dude." Ricky's voice brought him back to reality. "I'm not saying she is off her rocker, but I'm sure you've heard of a woman scorned. Chicks like that have been known to do some stupid shit. You know, like slashing tires, breaking windows, and cutting up clothes."

"Yeah, I know," Sloan responded. He picked up a celery stick and stuck it in his ranch dressing. "So far, I've received several nasty messages on my answering machine, but nothing physical," he murmured.

With a stern look, Ricky uttered, "All I'm saying, dude, is watch your back…and Natasha's. If the twisted chick hurt either of you, let's just say I won't be responsible."

Sloan reached out and patted Ricky on the back. "Thanks, man. It's good to know we're like that."

Ricky smiled as he picked up his bottle of Heineken. He held it up as Sloan grabbed his bottle of ginger ale. With the sound of the glasses touching, Ricky uttered, "You're the only good dude I got."

FRIENDS OR ENEMIES

Things were awkward for the group of what used to be friends at Emerson & Stuckey. Each day was like walking a tight rope as they put on their business faces, along with their suits, each day as they came through the door. It was even more daunting for Natasha and Essence. If looks could kill, both women would have been dead and buried. Natasha tried her best to maintain her distance from her rival. Sloan also managed to keep his distance from Essence, but he kept abreast of her whereabouts thanks to Lisa Ray, whom he privately confided in. It was equally disturbing for Natasha to see Derrick every day, especially since he appeared to be so happy and carefree. She was certain he had a special woman in his life. Deep down inside, it bruised her ego to see that he had gotten over her so quickly. And as far as Derrick was concerned, he, too, was feeling the effects of their broken relationship. He felt as if he were swimming among a sea of sharks, waiting for one to strike. Icy stares and dark eyes existed among the once so-called circle of friends.

SLOAN & NATASHA

The couple was seated at The Vistro, a small but elegant restaurant downtown. It was a beautiful day in August. The weather was pleasant as they dined outside on the restaurant's deck. Natasha talked nonstop about their upcoming nuptials and, of course, their honeymoon. The couple had decided to remain celibate until that special night planned for the Cayman Islands. The reservation had been made, and everything was in place. Sloan gazed into his fiancée's eyes as he traced her soft lips with the tip of his finger.

"Baby, I can't wait for us to become man and wife," he uttered with solid emotion.

"I know, Sloan, I can hardly wait either. I have dreamt about this moment so many times…and I wanted to tell you, but…"

"No buts, Me-Me, we're here now," he said as their fingers intertwined. "Words can't express the feelings that are going through me right now," Sloan said as he kissed Natasha's hand.

"I'm marrying my best friend," Natasha exclaimed as a single tear fell from her eye and slowly rolled down her cheek.

"And what do we have here?" a sassy and familiar voice asked.

The couple looked up simultaneously and gasped. Essence Kirkland was staring down at both of them.

"What in heaven's name are you doing here?" Natasha shrieked.

"Are you following us?" Sloan demanded.

Essence gave them a wicked smile. "Now, why on earth would I be following the both of you?" Essence asked as she feigned sincerity. "I was just leaving when I saw you two sitting on the deck." She held a white bag in her hand. "I ordered take-out," she said as the couple's eyes fell on the bag. "Anyway, I decided to come over and say hello and, of course, to congratulate you two again on your upcoming wedding," she said innocently.

Natasha gave her the benefit of the doubt and muttered, "Well, thank you, Essence."

Sloan gave her a *you're-full-of-it* look.

Essence placed her finger to her cheek.

"By the way, I didn't get an invite in the mail. I'm hoping that was an oversight." Essence smiled as she stared at Natasha and Sloan gave her a cold gaze.

"You didn't get one, Essence, because you're not invited," he replied.

"With our past history, surely you didn't expect one," Natasha added as she tried to resist the urge to hit her right between the eyes. Essence's eyes grew dark as she pursed her lips.

"Sloan, sugar, are you certain you're marrying the right woman? Her attitude is one to be reckoned with. It seems as if her mother has done a poor job of raising her correctly," Essence taunted.

Natasha stood angrily. "Why, you old bitch," she said as she took a swing at Essence.

Sloan was able to block the blow. "Essence, will you please just leave us alone?" he asked sternly as he held on to Natasha.

"That old broad is going to make me kill her," Natasha reeled..

"Not if I kill you first," Essence said with a wicked smile. "Have a good day," she said as she strutted away from the couple.

Sloan and Natasha breathed a sigh of relief, but Sloan knew Essence wasn't going away that easily.

GRETTA

"The woman sounds as if she's missing a few screws," Gretta said, holding the phone in the crook of her neck as she polished her toenails.

"I'm telling you, Gretta, if it wasn't for Sloan, I would have had a case this morning. It would have been assault and battery with every intention of killing," Natasha huffed.

Switching to her other foot, Gretta said, "Don't let her get under your skin, cousin. So what if she has a chip on her shoulder? You're marrying the man of your dreams, and there's not a damn thing she can do about it."

"Except work my last nerve," Natasha said as she let out a low breath. "But you're right, Gretta. I'm not going to let her get to me. I have other things that need my attention…like your new man, for instance." Natasha chuckled. Gretta gulped.

"Uhhh…my man, what does he have to do with anything?" she asked as she stared at her freshly-painted toes.

"I want him in my wedding, Gretta, as one of the groomsman," Natasha said.

"I thought you had everyone chosen already," Gretta replied as she arched her brows.

"I do, except I was saving a spot for him."

Gretta sucked her teeth. "Why don't you ask Ham? He's dependable."

"I don't want Ham. I want Dustin," Natasha chided.

"Forget it, cousin. You better dial Ham's digits," Gretta responded.

Natasha sighed. "Well, alright, but you better be bringing him to the wedding. I want to meet him before then, but it seems as if you're keeping him under wraps. Are you afraid someone's going to steal him away from you?" Natasha said, letting out a belly laugh. Gretta remained silent as her cousin's laughter subsided. "Tell me, Gretta, why all the secrecy?"

"There is no secrecy. Things have been going extremely well for us, and I don't want to jinx things by bringing him around my family too soon. You know I don't have a great track record with men. I'm just taking it slow on this one. So, please cut me some slack."

"Mmmm, okay, Gretta, but I want to see him at my wedding. No excuses," Natasha scoffed.

"We'll see. Now, let me go. He's picking me up in an hour."

"Alright, Gretta, and you be sure to tell Mystery Man that your cousin can't wait to meet him." Natasha chuckled as she hung up the phone. Gretta placed the receiver into its cradle.

"Natasha, you already know who he is, because you used to date him," Gretta mumbled to herself.

NATASHA

Natasha stared at her phone. Something felt weird. She couldn't seem to get Gretta's mystery man out of her mind.

"Why was she being so tight-lipped about him? Just like I thought before…that man has got to be married. Or maybe she's doing one of Monica Jenkins's numbers and dating her boss. Naw, that couldn't be it," Natasha said as she shook her head. Gretta's boss was a woman. Not unless…no, her cousin was a straight-up female who loved men. Natasha ran her fingers through her auburn curls. She looked over at her kitchen clock. Gretta said he was picking her up in an hour. A light bulb went off in her head. Natasha ran into her master bedroom and retrieved her keys, purse, and cell phone. Then she headed out the door. *Mystery Man isn't going to be a mystery anymore,* she thought as she jumped into her Lexus and sped out of the driveway. Gretta's apartment was only twenty minutes away, and Natasha swore she'd made it there in ten minutes as she pulled up. The apartment complex was a nice, quiet development with well-maintained parking lots and attractive greenery. Natasha decided to park a few apartments down from Gretta's. She was wearing her dark, designer sunglasses. Her momma had left a pink silk scarf in the car a few days ago. She wore it draped over her head. She felt like one of those female detectives on TV. She couldn't help but let out a soft giggle at her tactics. Stepping out of her car, she headed toward the apartment. She stopped at the black iron gate that led to Gretta's second-level apartment.

Trying not to look suspicious, Natasha reached into the pocket of her shorts and pulled out her cell, pretending to make a call. A young, white couple descended from the stairs and opened the black iron gate. They headed down the walkway and didn't bother even to look her way. Several minutes passed without a sign of the mystery man. She figured she might have missed him already as she glanced at her watch for the third time. Natasha exhaled and placed her cell phone back into her pocket.

Just my luck, she thought as she began her walk back to her car. The iron gate opened again, and this time, Gretta's laughter rang out as they came down the stairs.

Natasha darted behind a large bush on the side of the building and lowered her head. Her heart was racing with anticipation of finally seeing her cousin's mystery man. The tall, chocolate-colored man, who was handsomely dressed to the nines in his a beige designer linen suit, had his arm draped around her cousin's shoulder. Gretta was wearing a long, flowing yellow frock that danced around her shapely legs with each step. She could only see their backs as they headed across the street. The remote alarm sounded as the black Infinity's lights flashed. He opened the passenger-side door and Gretta slipped inside. Then, he walked around to the driver's side. With a pleasant grin on his face. Derrick Perkins slid in and they sped away, leaving Natasha with a

look of shock on her face.

SLOAN

"Me-Me, are you sure you're okay? You seem a little distant tonight," Sloan said as he stared into her eyes.

Natasha lowered her eyes from his intense stare. How could she tell her fiancé that she was fanning the flames of seeing her ex-boyfriend with her cousin? So many emotions had tugged at her heart as she'd stood outside Gretta's apartment. First, she was in shock, and then, she was angry, which left her with feelings of hurt and betrayal.

Sloan grabbed the *Ebony* magazine out of her hands and placed it on the coffee table. He scooted closer to her. They were spending a relaxing evening together.

"Come on, Me-Me, tell me what's on that mind of yours," he said as he gave her a peck on the lips.

Letting out a soft sigh, she uttered, "A lot of things, Sloan, the wedding is only a few weeks away and—"

"And everything is going to be fine," Sloan said, "so, don't think for a second that I believe your aloofness is all about our wedding," his expression turned serious.

Natasha knew there wasn't any use trying to hide it. She and Sloan could practically read each other's minds. "Is this how our marriage is going to be, with you looking through the window of my soul?" she smiled.

"Yes, my darling Me-Me, because you're my soul mate, and I want to share my all with no one but you," he said as he touched her nose with his. "I want to know what's going on with you, baby. Please tell me," he said as his gaze met hers.

Natasha knew that Sloan wasn't going to rest until she had spilled the contents of her mind. She decided to tell him everything, except the part where she still held some feelings for Derrick Perkins. After filling him in, Natasha waited for Sloan's response. She had curled up in Sloan's lap like a kitten. Sloan ran his fingers through her hair as he exhaled, "Me-Me, that doesn't surprise me at all. I told you from day one what kind of man Derrick Perkins was. Thank God we found each other before he had you entangled in his web of women. I'm just sorry Gretta is caught up in his game, though." Sloan motioned for Natasha to sit up. He wanted to look into her eyes. "Since we are having a heart-to-heart conversation, I want to ask you a very important question."

Natasha swallowed hard as she returned Sloan's gaze. "After tonight, Me-Me, I promise I will never bring this up again," he said as he cupped her chin. "I know you and Derrick had been together for a while, so…do you have any leftover feelings for him?"

Natasha felt the battle between truth and lie squabbling within her. Should she tell him no and live with the lie, or should she be straight with the man she'd never held anything from except her true feelings for him? Natasha licked her dry lips.

"Sloan…I wasn't deeply in love with him. I mean… maybe if we never came to realize our true feelings for each other, as time went on I probably would have fallen in love." Sloan let out a low breath. "But, Sloan, I did care about him," she said. Sloan stiffened. "To be fair, let me offer you the same question. Are you harboring any leftover feelings for Essence? I mean, you two did live together, and I, on the other hand, only dated Derrick."

Sloan wished now that he had never opened Pandora's Box. Natasha had a good point. He had lived with Essence, and for a while, he'd thought he was in love with her. Sloan took her hand.

"Me-Me, to be honest, I did think at one time that I was in love with Essence. But I came to realize that I was in love with the idea of being in love. I wanted so desperately to have a family. And when Monica cheated on me…I guess I rebounded. Essence came along, and I fell for her charm. Now, I can honestly tell you that there is only one woman I am in love with, baby, and that is you."

The couple melted in each other's arms as they kissed long and lovingly. After pulling apart, Natasha offered Sloan a cold can of ginger ale.

Sloan chuckled. "Baby, as much as I love my ginger ale. It's not what I want at the moment," he said, pulling her back into his arms. Sloan kissed her passionately as his hands roamed over the white cotton blouse she was wearing. Natasha broke the kiss and pulled out of his arms.

"Just two more weeks," she whispered breathlessly as she headed into the kitchen.

NATASHA & GRETTA

Natasha was hesitant to open her front door. She heard the doorbell chime several times, but she moved like a turtle. She spotted Gretta's black Avalon turning down her street when she was outside putting her garbage in the dumpster. Natasha hated this moment, but she knew it would come eventually. There wasn't any way to avoid the inevitable. She felt sick in the pit of her stomach even though she tried to put her ill feelings away. Finally, she reached her front door and opened it. Gretta came floating in like a dove bringing good news.

"Cousin, what took you so long to come to the door? For a minute I thought you weren't home, but I saw your car in the garage." Gretta greeted her. Natasha stood silently in her lemon-colored robe with matching slippers while Gretta looked as if she'd just had a makeover from head to toe.

Her hair was done in spiral curls. Her deep-set eyes were framed with long lashes and her dark, satin skin glowed with smoothness. Natasha had never seen her look more beautiful.

"Don't we look beautiful today?" she managed to say in a dry tone.

Gretta's eyebrows furrowed as she peered into Natasha's dim face. She placed one hand on her hip and asked, "What's with the cold expression? Don't tell me you're still holding a grudge about Dustin being in your wedding."

Right then, Natasha wanted to knock her off her feet for lying to her face. There was no Dustin. *The man's name is Derrick,* she fumed inside. Natasha pursed her lips and folded her arms. She would play her little game for now.

"Oh yeah, Dustin is it?" she mused aloud as she sank into the sofa.

Gretta eyed her suspiciously as she took a seat in the wingback chair adjacent to the sofa. Gretta decided to change the subject quickly. She had an eerie feeling growing inside of her. "Natasha, Momma spoke with Aunt Carol last night, and she will be able to attend the wedding after all," she spouted. "You know, Aunt Carol hadn't been home in almost four years. Can you believe it has been four years since she moved to California?" Gretta chimed.

Natasha responded with a weak smile as she sat on the sofa like a frog on a bench. Gretta crossed her legs after catching her breath from her rambling. "Did you and Sloan have a fight or something?"

"No, but you and I might be throwing down any minute now." Natasha sneered as she leaned forward in her seat.

"Girl, what are you talking about?" Gretta laughed uneasily as she pulled a spiral curl away from her eye.

Natasha squinted. "What is going on between you and Dustin, or should I say *Derrick*?" she uttered with a tight voice. "And, Gretta, don't even try to play me," she fumed with a pointed finger.

Natasha was surprised at herself for keeping such a cool demeanor. Usually by now, her temper would have been rolling like thunder. Gretta's mouth opened, but no words came out as Natasha stared her down.

"Girl, don't play with me," Natasha scolded as she stood up.

Gretta's heart did a flip; she knew her cousin was about to get ugly. "Uh…Natasha…we been meaning to tell you…" Gretta stammered.

"We…what in the hell do you mean by 'we'?" Natasha asked as her eyes widened.

"Derrick and I," Gretta mumbled.

Natasha flapped her arms as she spun around in a circle.

"Natasha, listen to me," Gretta said, standing. "It's not what you're thinking."

Natasha faced her with a contorted stare. "Now, Gretta, you know that's the raggediest line in the books. I know you can do better than that," Natasha huffed.

"I'm telling you the truth. Derrick and I hooked up recently."

"How recently, Gretta?" Natasha asked with a tilt of her head. "From the way you two looked the other day, it seemed to me this hookup has been going on for a while."

Gretta's face was a jigsaw puzzle of confusion.

"That's right, the other day," Natasha quipped. "I saw you two lovebirds in front of your apartment. I could have walked over and slapped you both to hell if I wanted to. How could you, Gretta? Do you know how it felt to see my own cousin messing around with my man? How am I supposed to take that?" Natasha felt the sting of tears in her eyes. She paced the floor as the anger she fought so hard to control rose to the surface. "Of all the times I tried to help you find a man. But you didn't need any help, now did you? Why go out and find a man when you could help yourself to mine?" Natasha sneered.

Gretta felt tears slipping down her cheeks. She didn't want to hurt her cousin this way. "Natasha, I'm sorry, alright. This wasn't something we planned."

"Gretta, who do you think you're talking to? I know your skanky-ass ways. It doesn't bother you one bit to share your men. But it bothers the hell out of me."

Now that was a low blow, Gretta thought to herself. Why did she have to bring up her past? Being angry with her was one thing, but to attack her character was completely uncalled for. Gretta shook her head to clear it. "Wait a damn minute, Natasha. Derrick is not even your man. Or have you forgotten that fact? You are marrying Sloan in a few days, and you should be beside yourself with happiness."

"I haven't forgotten that at all, and don't try to cover up what you did, Gretta."

"I don't see the problem here, Natasha," Gretta said lightly.

Natasha's lips curled into a frown. "You're making it sound as if you just started dating Derrick a few days ago. You know you were seeing him when he was my man. All those times I called you and you acted as if a sock was stuck in your throat. Weeks went by before we saw each other. You were fooling around with him, now, weren't you?"

Gretta grew quiet.

"Oh my God!" Natasha exclaimed as she put both hands to her face. Closing the gap between them, she stared into her cousin's eyes. "When I went away, were you two together? And, Gretta, don't you dare lie to me."

Gretta buried her face into her hands and sobbed. "Natasha, I never meant for this to happen. Derrick and I just connected. He was going to tell you," she choked.

"What about you, Gretta? Why didn't you come to me? I'm your blood, for heaven's sake. How could you do this to me?"

Gretta let out a deep sigh as the pain registered in her chest. Her heart felt as if it were breaking apart. She knew she had hurt her cousin deeply and she was sorry.

"Natasha, you don't know how much I wanted to. But I...just couldn't do it," she stammered.

Natasha dropped her head. "How long were you sleeping with him?" she almost whispered.

"It doesn't matter now, Natasha," Gretta uttered.

"It does matter...to me. So tell me, Gretta!" Natasha shouted.

"We knew we had a connection when we met at the pool party. But I swear nothing happened then. I knew you were digging him, so I backed off. A few weeks later, he came to my work and wanted to have dinner with me and—"

"And you ended up sleeping with him," Natasha said in a cold tone of voice. Natasha held her hand to her forehead. She felt a headache coming on. She looked long and hard at her cousin. Then, she uttered coldly, "Get out of my house."

"But, Natasha...Derrick and I love each other. You shouldn't be so upset about this. We both are getting what we wanted. I finally found a man who loves me, and you have Sloan. Isn't that what you wanted all along? Now, why can't we both be happy?"

Natasha sailed to her front door and opened it. She pointed outward, and Gretta ran out without saying another word.

DERRICK

Derrick answered his phone. He never bothered to look at the number, because he just assumed it was Gretta. But you know what they say about assuming; and he definitely made an ass out of himself.

"Gretta, baby, I was just thinking about my doll," he crooned into his cell.

Natasha fought for control as her lips parted. "Derrick Perkins, you won't believe how much I've been thinking about you. How dare you use me as if I was some low-budget hoe of yours? Not only have you been cheating on me, but with my own cousin. How low can you be, Derrick?"

Derrick took in a deep breath as questions ran rampant through his mind. How had she found out? How was he going to explain it all? Natasha continued with her wrath as he held his cell phone. "Sloan warned me about you. He said you were a playa from the start, but I thought you had the decency to be straight with me. You tried to convince me that I would get hurt if I made my feelings known to Sloan, and you turned around and hurt me even more," she expressed painfully.

Derrick could tell from her voice that she had been crying. Lord knows, he hadn't meant to hurt her this way.

"You've said many times that you wanted to help me get over Sloan. Were you helping my cousin, as well? You're nothing but a scumbag, Derrick. You are a lowlife and a poor excuse for a man," Natasha heaved.

Derrick allowed her to vent. He knew that he had hurt her deeply and that he deserved her wrath. But the name-calling had to stop. He needed to say his piece, as well.

"Now, Natasha, that's enough," he insisted. "Look, I am sorry you had to find out about me and your cousin this way. I wanted to tell you several times, but—"

"Everybody wanted to tell poor little ol' Natasha. But guess what, Derrick? Nobody did," Natasha interjected. Both of you make me so sick," she huffed as her tears flowed. "I know all about you and Gretta's love affair. I'm certain she told you how I found out about you two."

"Natasha, you've got to believe we never meant to hurt you. When I saw your cousin at the pool party, we just hit it off." Derrick paused a moment.

"Go on," Natasha urged.

"You don't need to hear the details," Derrick relented.

"I want to hear them, Derrick!" she practically yelled. "We just talked, laughed, and had a little fun," Derrick explained as the memories flowed through his mind.

"Yes, I saw your fun in the pool. I watched you two for a while, you know." Natasha's voice cracked. "It was then you had an attraction for her, wasn't it?"

"Natasha, nothing serious happened that night. We ended up exchanging numbers as friends. That's it, I swear. As time went on…I don't know…I just felt the urge to see her again. And from there…well, you know the rest," Derrick expressed.

"Why, in God's name, didn't you both come to me with this?"

"Natasha, you were going through your own emotional times. You were trying to figure out your feelings for Sloan. Here you are giving me the third degree when you yourself were torn between me and him. I should be angry at you, but I'm not," Derrick responded. "Natasha, I need to see you and Sloan. There are some more things I need to get off my chest."

Natasha couldn't believe what she was hearing. "You want to have a meeting with me and Sloan?" This was totally weird to her.

"Yes, I need to talk to the both of you. Will you meet me tonight at Sam's in, say, about an hour? We all need to find some common ground here. I don't want the both of you to end up hating me, and I certainly don't want to be responsible for a rift between you and your cousin," he uttered sincerely. Natasha agreed to meet him at Sam's Bar.

ESSENCE

Derrick dialed Essence's digits after hanging up with Natasha. She answered on the second ring.

"Our game is up," he mumbled as she held the phone.

"Derrick, what are you talking about?"

"I'm talking about…I've had it with all the lies, the hurt, the guilt, everything about this, Essence. I'm coming clean with it all. I'm meeting with Natasha in an hour, and I'm going to tell her the truth. The whole truth and nothing but."

"Derrick, have you gone ballistic? You can't do this. My plan is working. Sloan will be mine. I'm sure of it," Essence scoffed.

"Essence, give it up. Sloan is marrying Natasha in less than a week. You've got to let the chips fall, babe. It's over."

"No, I won't accept that. Natasha will soon be out of the picture, and Sloan and I can finally have the kind of life…"

"Essence, look, get a grip, okay. This all will be over soon. I'm moving back to Texas, and Gretta is coming with me. We're going to make a new life for ourselves together. Now, I suggest you do the same."

"Well, well, well. Things are working out perfectly for you. What about me, Derrick? Don't I deserve a piece of happiness?" Essence stormed.

"Yes, and you will have it if you let the notion of you and Sloan go. The reason why I fell in love with Gretta is because she helped me see that taking people for granted and using them was very wrong. I would only end up hurting myself. And, Essence, she is right. I wanted to hurt you so badly for destroying my life. But I realize it was me who allowed that to happen. And it was me who allowed that anger to fester in me while I went on my vendetta of using women. I'm sure you can let go as well. There are other men out there who would *die* to have you in their lives."

Funny, Essence was thinking along the same lines. *Someone will die, and soon,* she thought silently.

"Don't do this to me, Derrick," she shrieked into the phone.

"Think of it like this, Essence. I'm doing it *for* you," he said as he ended the call.

DERRICK, NATASHA & SLOAN

After their meeting with Derrick, Sloan and Natasha sat in disbelief. They'd listened attentively as Derrick led them down the spiral of events that had transpired between him and Essence Kirkland. He ended his confession with the plan they had to keep Natasha and Sloan apart. Sloan wanted to strangle Derrick with his bare hands, but, surprisingly, it was Natasha who calmed him down.

"He's not worth it and neither is she," Natasha said as her eyes held Derrick's gaze. Turning to Sloan, she said, "We're getting married next weekend. I don't think either one of us need a rap sheet to start our new life with."

On the drive home, the couple rode in silence. They were lost in their own thoughts as they traveled back in time, all the while, trying to process what they had been told. How could they have become pawns in such a sick scheme? Their lives were nearly torn apart at someone else's hands—for the sake of their own twisted pleasure. Even though Natasha despised Derrick and Essence for what they had done to her and Sloan, she also owed them her gratitude. If they had

not come into their lives, she and Sloan may not have ever revealed their true feelings for each other.

Sloan startled her as he reached over and took her hand. "I love you, Me-Me, and no one will ever come between us again. I promise you that," Sloan uttered sternly.

Natasha gripped his hand tightly as a single tear fell from her cheek.

As they pulled into her driveway, Sloan shut off the engine of his SUV and turned to face her. "Are you still going to have Gretta as your matron of honor?"

A lump formed in Natasha's throat. Gretta was more than a cousin to her. She was the sister she'd never had and a best female friend all rolled into one. Forgiveness is hard at times, but it's not impossible. Natasha kissed her future husband deeply as she wiped the tears that fell silently.

"We're not going to let anyone or anything come between our love and happiness, ever," she whispered softly as they embraced.

A WEDDING BETWEEN FRIENDS

The cathedral was filled to its capacity with family, friends, and acquaintances on Sloan and Natasha's wedding day. You would have thought a celebrity couple was tying the knot as photographers snapped pictures of the happy couple. Natasha appeared to be a living doll in her pearl-white Donna Karan wedding gown trimmed with pearls and Sloan was dressed handsomely in his white tux. He took her by the hand as they headed down the aisle, anticipating the start of their new life together. Well-wishers met them outside as rice was thrown.

A satin-white stretch limo waited patiently on the curb for the glorious newlyweds to come out of the church. There were so many people gathered around to catch a glimpse of the happy couple that no one noticed the lady in black. A frilly black hat adorned her head, and dark designer shades covered her eyes. She weaved through the crowd with the gentleness of a butterfly as she clutched the small black purse she was carrying. As the couple approached the limo, the driver opened the limo door, and Natasha turned to face the crowd. She took one long look at the cheering crowd and smiled at their happy faces.

Natasha's heart swelled with joy; she had married the love of her life. She found her mother's tearful face in the crowd, throwing kisses at her and Sloan. She waved her hand and blew a kiss back to her mother. Just then, a shot rang out and Natasha felt a stinging sensation in her chest. Slowly, darkness fell upon her as her legs collapsed. The cheering sounds of joy turned into screams and sounds of panic. Natasha slumped over in Sloan's arms. He held his bride in utter shock. The once-beautiful wedding gown was now stained with the dampness of Natasha's blood as it seeped through the satin fabric. Florene pushed through the thick crowd as she frantically made her way to her daughter. Her tear-stained face held a look of horror.

"Stop that woman!" Ricky shouted as the noises from the crowd grew louder. Gretta's face was frozen in fear as she saw Derrick and Ricky running after a woman dressed in black.

Who was that woman, and why, in God's name, did she hurt Natasha? Gretta thought as she peered down at her cousin, who looked as if she were only sleeping in her husband's arms. Sloan's chest heaved with great sobs as he repeated, "Hang in there, baby, help is on the way."

Sirens grew louder and louder as they made their way to the church. What was once a beautiful event had now turned dark and ugly.

EPILOGUE

One year has passed since Sloan and Natasha's wedding day. It's a day most couples can look back on with fond memories, but theirs is tinted bittersweet. However, the newlyweds are grateful that things have turned out as well as they have. Natasha survived the shooting with minimal damage. After six months of therapy, she is almost back to her old self again. She and Sloan are looking forward to their first little bundle of joy.

Derrick and Gretta were married a few months after Sloan and Natasha, and then they left Atlanta. But before his departure, Derrick helped place Essence Kirkland behind bars. After she shot Natasha, he and Ricky captured her before she made her getaway. He also gave the authorities a rundown of her erratic behavior and the threats she had made to him previously about her plan to hurt Natasha. Now, Essence is doing twenty years in the state prison. Natasha has forgiven her cousin Gretta and Derrick for sleeping with each other behind her back. There was one lesson Natasha learned after being shot—life is too short to carry grudges, even if the one who did you wrong was supposed to be the one who loved you the most.

Whoever said there was a thin line between love and hate knew exactly what they were talking about. The line can be crossed so easily, but the repercussions of doing so can last for a life time.

We'd like to thank you for supporting G Street Chronicles and invite you to join our social networks. Please be sure to post a review when you're finished reading.

Facebook
G Street Chronicles Fan Page
G Street Chronicles CEO Exclusive Readers Group

Twitter